Critical Praise for the D Hunter Mystery Series

for *The Lost Treasures of R&B*

• Nominated for the Brooklyn Public Library's
Brooklyn Eagles Literary Prize for Fiction

"This is a fine mystery and [protagonist] D Hunter is as world weary, yet steadfast, as Philip Marlowe, Spenser, Dave Robicheaux, or Easy Rawlins. A definite yes to purchase for both mystery and African American collections."
—***Library Journal*** (Starred Review, Pick of the Month)

"George covers a lot of ground with style: the rhythm-and-blues music scene past and present, the sometimes startling evolution of Brooklyn and its environs, and the multitude of hangers-on, wannabes, and grifters who want a piece of the action."
—***Publishers Weekly***

"Real relationships and real talk frame the mashup of mysteries in George's street-framed series."
—***Kirkus Reviews***

"The wonderful singsong street slang dialogue and esoteric industry knowledge make *The Lost Treasures of R&B* a richly entertaining addition to George's evolving series."
—***Shelf Awareness***

"George uses *The Lost Treasures of R&B* to tackle the hot-button issue of the gentrification of Brooklyn (and elsewhere) as protagonist D struggles to come to terms with the ghosts of his childhood in 'old Brooklyn.'"
—***Philadelphia Tribune***

"Written in the spirit of authors such as Walter Mosley and Donald Goines . . . The book blends music from the past with thug appeal of the present to appeal to young and old alike."
—***Baltimore Times***

"George is a historian of his culture."
—***The Stranger***

for *The Plot Against Hip Hop*

• Finalist for the 2012 NAACP Image Award in Literature

"George is an ace at interlacing the real dramas of the world . . . the book's slim length and flyweight depth could make it an artifact of this particular zeitgeist in American history. Playas and haters and celebrity cameos fuel a novel that is wickedly entertaining while being frozen in time." **—Kirkus Reviews**

"This hard-boiled tale is jazzed up with authentic street slang and name-dropping (Biggie, Mary J. Blige, Lil Wayne, and Chuck D) . . . George's tightly packaged mystery pivots on a believable conspiracy . . . and his street cred shines in his descriptions of Harlem and Brownsville's mean streets." **—Library Journal**

"George is a well-known, respected hip-hop chronicler . . . Now he adds crime fiction to his resume with a carefully plotted crime novel peopled by believable characters and real-life hip-hop personalities." **—Booklist**

"George's prose sparkles with an effortless humanity, bringing his characters to life in a way that seems true and beautiful. The story—and the conspiracy behind it—is one we all need to hear as consumers and creators in the post-hardcore hip-hop world." **—Shelf Awareness**

"Part procedural murder mystery, part conspiracy-theory manifesto, Nelson George's *The Plot Against Hip Hop* reads like the PTSD fever dream of a renegade who's done several tours of duty in the trenches . . . *Plot*'s combination of record-biz knowledge and ghetto fabulosity could have been written only by venerable music journalist Nelson George, who knows his hip-hop history . . . The writing is as New York as 'Empire State of Mind,' and D is a detective compelling enough to anchor a series." **—Time Out New York**

"A breakbeat detective story . . . George invents as much as he curates, as outlandish conspiracy theories clash with real-life figures. But what makes the book such a fascinating read is its simultaneous strict adherence to hip-hop's archetypes and tropes while candidly acknowledging the absurdity of the music's current big-business era." **—Time Out Chicago**

Nelson George is an author, filmmaker, and lifelong resident of Brooklyn. His books include the first three novels in his D Hunter mystery series, *The Accidental Hunter, The Plot Against Hip Hop*, and *The Lost Treasures of R&B*. Among his many nonfiction works are *The Death of Rhythm & Blues, Hip Hop America*, and *The Hippest Trip in America: Soul Train and the Evolution of Culture & Style*. As a filmmaker he has directed the documentaries *Brooklyn Boheme, Finding the Funk*, and *A Ballerina's Tale*. He is also a writer/producer on the Netflix series *The Get Down*.

TO FUNK AND DIE IN LA

TO FUNK
AND DIE
IN LA

A D Hunter Mystery

BY

NELSON GEORGE

BROOKLYN, NEW YORK, USA
BALLYDEHOB, CO. CORK, IRELAND

Published by Akashic Books
©2017 Nelson George

Hardcover ISBN-13: 978-1-61775-585-9
Trade Paperback ISBN-13: 978-1-61775-586-6
Library of Congress Control Number: 2017936116

Akashic Books
Brooklyn, New York, USA
Ballydehob, Co. Cork, Ireland
Twitter: @AkashicBooks
Facebook: AkashicBooks
E-mail: info@akashicbooks.com
Website: www.akashicbooks.com

ALSO AVAILABLE IN THE D HUNTER MYSTERY SERIES

The Lost Treasures of R&B

The Plot Against Hip Hop

The Accidental Hunter

For Sly Stone,
Rick James,
Maurice White,
and the many funk gods of Los Angeles

Thanks to my editors at Record World *and* Billboard *back in the 1980s who allowed me to cover the dark soul of a sunlit city.*

CHAPTER ONE
TO FUNK IN SANTA MONICA

At first no one really paid attention. He was just another gray-bearded, raggedy-looking old black man pushing a metal laundry cart across the Santa Monica promenade. The homeless had made this liberal city by the ocean their residence of choice for decades and, annoying as they were, the locals had become expert at ignoring them.

Even when the old man stopped near the AMC multiplex and pulled a beat-up mini Moog synthesizer, a small Marshall amp, and a tiny generator from his cart, the shoppers heading to Pottery Barn and Steve Madden kept their distance and, wisely, held their noses. It was only after he squatted on two milk crates and pressed his long brown fingers onto the yellowed keys that a couple of curious souls slowed down, hearing the magic in those wrinkled fingers.

When he opened his mouth to sing, a magnificent sound emerged: it was the choir in a Southern backwoods church; working people drinking in a Midwestern bar; the rustle of sequined shirts and star-spangled pants; the chemical stink of Jheri-curl juice; the wind in Africa; and the prayers of those kind beings who left us the pyramids.

Each passerby heard him differently. For one woman it was the sound of her grandmother's favorite song. For an aging hip hop head it was a sample used by Biggie or Tupac or Raekwon. To a bunch of folks on the Santa Monica promenade it was a new sound that made the latest hits seem tiny, like Mozart heard through earbuds. He was lean and he was old, but his voice was a mountain.

Smartphones appeared and images were recorded. Tints were applied and snappy captions concocted. Selfie nation took over the Santa Monica promenade. People angled to include themselves in pics near, next to, and almost on top of this gray-bearded revelation.

On his keyboard was a small plastic cup, which began filling with quarters and dollars, and one welcome twenty-dollar bill. It was all good until a man close to the keyboard said, "I think that's Dr. Funk."

And then it was over. The old man shut his mouth, his fingers left the keyboard, and he glanced around at the crowd like a turtle outside its shell. He stood up—or, rather, half stood, half bent—and swiftly slid his gear back into his laundry cart. Several people tried to engage him but his replies were a low mumble or a distant stare.

From the old man's pocket appeared a shiny new Samsung, seemingly his only possession from this century. He tapped his Uber app, confirmed a pickup point, and pushed his cart toward Santa Monica Boulevard. A white woman claimed she saw him at the Hollywood Palladium in 1982 (though he had shown up two hours late). A man walked next to him saying he had a vinyl copy of Dr. Funk and the Love Patrol's classic *Chaos: Phase I* that he'd love to get signed. To their consternation the old man pressed on, determined to meet his Uber and ignore their conversation.

Then an imposing man with salt-and-pepper hair, a serious tan, and an expensive suit appeared by his side. "I saw a video of you on Instagram," he said quickly. "I'm Teddy Tapscott, a movie producer. I was associate producer on *Straight Outta Compton*. My partner and I are anxious to set up a meeting with you."

"So you associate with producers?" Dr. Funk said drily. "I used to do that too. Now I'm too busy."

"You deserve a film biopic," Tapscott said quickly, trying to slow the old man down. No dice.

"See that guy over there?" The musician gestured toward a sleeping homeless man. "He deserves a meal. What do *you* deserve?"

Tapscott held out his business card. The old man ignored him and kept moving, so the producer dropped his card into the laundry cart.

"You saw me sing, right?" the old man said.

"Yes," Tapscott replied excitedly. "Yes. On Instagram."

The old man turned to look at this well-dressed fan. "You're welcome," he said, then waved down the waiting Uber.

After dumping his gear in the trunk and avoiding eye contact with the disappointed producer, the man known as Dr. Funk, who was the soundtrack for millions, a sage for thousands, and a bandleader for a select few, negotiated his lean, bony frame into the backseat of a white Hyundai. The car headed east, in the direction of wherever he was living these days. And, like the melodies he'd just played, Dr. Funk evaporated into the moist Santa Monica night.

CHAPTER TWO

TO FUNK AND DIE IN LA

L ike so many mornings since 1992, Daniel Hunter, known to friends and neighbors as Big Danny, stopped his beautifully maintained green 1970 Buick Electra 225 convertible in the parking lot behind the minimall at Crenshaw and Vernon. Happy Pizza was the anchor tenant, located diagonally across from Leimert Park, but Big Danny didn't fuck with that place. It was the kind of fast-food joint that killed black folks with fried crap. Anyway, his attention was focused on his ride. He worried that dust from the unending Metro light rail construction had tainted its shiny coat.

Between his dutiful, loving care and the forgiving Southern California weather, Big Danny's ride had been rolling through the LA streets for decades. His rims didn't spin (too old for that mess) but they glistened like medals on a five-star general. Big Danny was a tall man who, at seventy-two, still stood up straight, though his trademark bop had become a shuffle after two hip replacements. From a distance, Big Danny, in a blue Dodgers cap and jacket, beige shorts, white tube socks, and white Stan Smiths, looked more like a retired athlete than a semiretired shop owner.

Also exiting the car was his grandson Walli Hunter, a lanky teen with his woolly hair cut into a black peak, wearing a black T-shirt with A *Tribe Called Quest* across the front in white letters, skinny orange jeans, and black-and-white Vans. The MacBook he had under his arm was adorned with a Kendrick Lamar sticker.

Next to Happy Pizza was Classic Crenshaw Coffee, a relatively new café operated by two twentyish white men who wore long beards, black horn-rimmed glasses, and matching white-and-red-checked button-down shirts. A few of the young white couples who'd purchased homes in nearby Leimert Park were inside tapping away on laptops, nibbling on gluten-free baked goods, and drinking free-trade coffee. Leashed outside was a feisty brown-and-gray Yorkie, who yapped as he walked up. Big Danny looked down, barked back, muttered, "Little dishrag dog," and laughed.

"You gonna sit in there and e-mail and shit?" he asked Walli.

"Yeah. They make a great chai latte, Grandpa. You should try it."

Big Danny smiled. "Chai latte? If that excites you, please enjoy it. I'm gonna get a paper and a coffee and then go handle some business. I can swing by and pick you up on the way back."

"Why you buy coffee and the paper there, Grandpa? You have your own store," Walli asked.

"You gotta support your people."

Walli shrugged and said, "Sounds good," then entered the coffee shop.

His grandfather looked inside with a slight shake of the head. *Chai latte,* he thought. *Used to be a good cup of joe was enough. Now every morning drink has to be fake Italian.*

Next door to Classic Crenshaw was K-Pak Groceries, a mom-and-pop minimart that had been in biz since the eighties, back when the first Korean immigrants started retailing in black hoods. It had survived two generations and a lot of LA history. Behind the cash register was Lawrence Pak, the son of the original owner. He greeted Big Danny with a tight nod and then reached under the counter for a very specific copy of the *Los Angeles Times.*

"*Annyeong haseyo*," Big Danny greeted with a decent Korean accent.

Lawrence smiled and said, "Good morning, sir," before handing the newspaper to Big Danny, who then walked over to the coffee machine and poured himself a cup of the thick black brew.

"Feels like a pamphlet these days," he said of the newspaper.

"I read it mostly online," Lawrence replied. "So my father says this is it," he added, quickly changing the subject. He looked intently at Big Danny.

"Yes it is," Big Danny said evenly. "It's been a long time coming. But then, me and your father move at a different rhythm."

There was an awkward pause until Lawrence asked, "So have they raised your rent on your store too?"

"Not yet," Big Danny said, "but it's coming. Once that new Metro line is really pumping, everybody's rent is going up as high as hell. But I ain't leaving."

"We may move," Lawrence said. "Not sure yet. Maybe nearer Koreatown. It keeps growing."

"I'm sure your mother and father have a plan."

"They always do," Lawrence said without a smile.

Big Danny reached over and shook the young man's hand before exiting. He glanced through the coffee shop's window as his grandson sat amongst the new people, chai latte steaming, laptop glowing. Big Danny watched Walli live in the present and future, then wondered how much longer he'd linger in the now and then.

This time the Yorkie just glared at Big Danny, saving his voice for the next tall black stranger who strolled by. Back inside the Electra 225, Big Danny leaned the *LA Times* against the steering wheel and flipped through it. Stuck inside the sports section were a medley of hundreds, fifties, and twenties—nearly $8,500 in total. He picked up the eight-track cassette from the passenger seat and slipped Dr. Funk and the Love Patrol's *Chaos: Phase I* into the player under his dashboard. He did have Sirius Radio and liked to listen to the Dodgers on KLAC, but Big Danny was never one to ditch technology that still worked.

He sat back in his seat and sighed. Well, that was done. He took another swig of coffee, then frowned at the bitter taste, thinking that maybe the fancy new coffee shop was worth a try. Scanning through the Dodgers' box score to see how Yasiel Puig had done last night, Big Danny didn't notice the shadow pass his side of the car or look up when the little dog started yapping again.

Puig went one-for-four last night. Just a single. He loved that damn Cuban for the way his baserunning drove white folks crazy. Big Danny put down the paper, checked his watch, and started the car. He turned onto Crenshaw and headed north, thinking about Kershaw and young Thompson in left field.

He rolled his big green vintage machine up past Maverick's Flat, a music club he'd been competing with since the eighties. Big Danny had done his best with his club Heaven's Gate, but it had never quite matched the vibe of the Flat, which was where Richard Pryor, the Commodores, the Soul Train dancers, among many, had made their first LA impression. But the great Dr. Funk had always favored Heaven's Gate, which was something Big Danny remained proud of.

He glanced over at the construction where the Metro line extension was to open in 2019. Change was coming to the area fast and, despite his age, Big Danny wanted to benefit from it. A group called Capri Partners was adding two million square feet of new hotel and retail space near the Baldwin Hills Crenshaw Plaza. The artist Mark Bradford (thankfully black, Big Danny thought) had opened an art space called Art+Practice in Leimert Park that hosted exhibitions and sponsored workshops for kids.

He'd spent his life in the hood and, one way or another, Big Danny wanted to cash in. (But how?)

A driver in a blue Mustang honked and nodded in respect at Big Danny's Electra as he crossed West Adams. His big Buick, with its 370 horsepower V8 engine and glittering chrome rims, always got love on these Cali streets. By the time he passed Pico he'd changed up from Dr. Funk to an old CD of Dr. Dre's KDAY mix, smiling as Prince's "17 Days" flowed into Roger's "So Ruff, So Tuff," with 808s booming out of the ride's recently revamped speakers.

Though it was early in the day Big Danny thought about rolling over to the Beverly Hot Springs, a Koreatown spot just a few blocks east of Western and the stately homes of Hancock Park. A sauna, a dip in the natural hot spring, and a deep-tissue massage from one of those big-shouldered Korean women would be dope. He should celebrate. After all, it had taken years, and lots of cajoling, but he'd gotten his money back with interest. It was like the end of a chapter in the long, drawn-out book of his life.

Big Danny was at the light on Crenshaw and Wilshire, contemplating whether to make the right toward Koreatown or head to his bank to the left, down near LACMA and the Petersen Auto Museum. He was having this internal debate when a Chevrolet Impala SS pulled up on his passenger side. The driver rolled down his window and aimed his Glock at the older man's head.

Big Danny felt a presence and turned.

In his last moments on earth Big Danny saw his life, his town, and his soul. Mayor Tom Bradley. Roscoe's House of Chicken & Waffles. Rick James. The Motown building on Sunset. Dorsey High. Locke High. Don Cornelius. Marcus Allen. The Coliseum. Kids rocking Raiders gear. O.J.'s #32 at USC. O.J. as public enemy #1. Fuckin' Daryl

Gates. Magic. "Showtime!" The Great Western Forum. The Slauson Swap Meet. The Crenshaw mall. Cruising on Crenshaw. Maverick's Flat. The Baldwin Hills theater. Rodney King. *Black-owned* signs on Manchester. Koreans on a rooftop with twelve-gauge shotguns. A bundle of twenties. A naked breast and a brown nipple. Bongos. Electric bass. His home. His wife. His tears. Her eyes.

And then—*bang!*—Big Danny was gone.

CHAPTER THREE

DEAD MAN'S MIXTAPE

The funk mix Dwayne Robinson had made for him years ago still made D Hunter head-nod, foot-pat, and, when he thought no one was looking, play some mean air drums. The first twenty-five songs were from the 1970s with grooves driven by trumpets, trombones, congas, Fender bass, and chanted vocals, with lyrics that referenced spaceships, Egyptology, and hot pants. The last twenty-five songs were from the 1980s and were created by LinnDrums, Roland 808 bass lines, Fairlight computers, keyboard horn stabs, and lyrics about dancing, freakin', Jheri-curls, and Spandex.

The late music historian had made several mixtapes for D and he treasured them all, finding particular comfort listening to them on long flights. As D floated across America he listened to funk's evolution from Kool & the Gang, the Ohio Players, Betty Davis, Graham Central Station, Rufus featuring Chaka Khan, and, of course, Sly & the Family Stone. The J.B.'s and Maceo & the Macks got him from JFK to Missouri, while the Time, Prince Charles, Kleeer, Cameo, the Gap Band, Midnight Star, the Dazz Band, and Prince took him to Nevada.

D's funk focus was an attempt to forget his last meeting before leaving New York. First Zena Hunter forgot a name or place here or there. D used to joke that she was just saving her memory for the neighborhood poker games. Then one day it all went south. She couldn't remember names. She couldn't remember *him*.

Yesterday he'd sat across from her and she'd called him Rashid, Jah, and Matty. Being mistaken for one of his dead brothers? Okay. That he could stand. But then she called him Fred, his father's name, which he hated. But what could D say? You can't scold a woman battling Alzheimer's and think that's gonna do any good.

His mother had cried thick, deep tears when D told her Danny Hunter, her father-in-law, had been killed. It was only after he'd hugged her and listened to her whispers that he realized she was crying, once again, about the shooting of his big brother Matty.

D himself teared up, kissed his mother's brow, and then left her, wondering which of his three dead brothers she thought he was. This absence from his mother's memories made him feel truly like he was her only dead son.

D had saved the Dr. Funk tracks for the end of the flight because the man's sound transcended eras—sweet doo-wop harmonies bumped up against chugging Latin percussion, Fender Rhodes against 808s, Hendrix leads against James Brown chicken scratch, Bootsy Collins plucks and Larry Dunn keyboards supporting a lead vocal that mated Larry Blackmon cartoon pronouncements by way of Maurice White huskiness. These sounds clashed like swords in battle, yet it was this loud, shimmering, insistent, driving, conquering contrast that made his songs anthems.

D saved Dr. Funk because these songs reminded him of Grandpa Big Danny cruising down Crenshaw Boulevard on one of those crazy car-show days when the street pulsated with lowrider engines and the sound of Dr. Funk anthems like "California Sun" and "Hard and Fast." D would gaze up at his granddad smoking a Tiparillo and wearing a cream-colored wide-brimmed hat and know this man was the coolest motherfucker on the planet.

D was about to dip into Dr. Funk's crazy catalog, starting with the classic *Chaos: Phase I*, when the seat-belt sign flashed and the pilot announced that the plane was starting its LA descent.

He had lost an hour in memories of his grandfather. He put down his earphones and switched off his iPod Mini. He'd wandered through the deep percussive rhythms of funk for almost five hours, but now he had to acknowledge that this trip west was not going to be funky like an old bag of collard greens. It was going to be funky in the classic sense of nasty, foul, and maybe a little mean. Big Danny was dead. No, Big Danny had been *murdered*, which meant the funeral wouldn't be the end of this story.

D closed his eyes. He hadn't seen or heard from his father in years. Not since the funeral of Jah, his last surviving brother, where Fred Hunter had fallen into a drunken stupor at the wake. Right after that service he'd hopped aboard a Greyhound bus headed south. Like a broken bottle in a ghetto playground, his father's soul was shattered. Fred Hunter finally got off the bus in New Orleans, his clothes a stinking mess of alcohol and regret. A week later he was on a merchant marine steamer, though no one in Brooklyn was sure if he could swim.

D wasn't certain how much his father knew about his ex-wife's current illness. Aunt Sheryl said she'd told him. Truth was that the time Fred Hunter could have been helpful to her or to D had long since passed. As the youngest of Zena and Fred Hunter's four sons, D had had the least contact with his father. For him, Fred Hunter had been more a collection of images than a fully developed character. It was like he'd glimpsed his father's close-up in a trailer though his scenes hadn't made the final cut.

But his grandfather? That had been a true leading man. D had spent parts of several summers out in LA with Big Danny, Grandma

Shirley, his Aunt Sheryl, and little cousin Walli. It was the first time D had slept in a house—a Craftsman with wooden beams, a fireplace, and a wide porch where on many evenings he and Big Danny would play chess. He'd hang out at Granddad's grocery store, helping lift boxes, check inventory, and listen in on rambling conversations with the customers. When D first visited LA at ten, all the customers were black, many with roots in Texas and Louisiana. The twang in their voices was strange music to D.

Gangs were rampant in South Central but Big Danny never feared them—perhaps due to the foreboding presence of Red Dawg, a.k.a. Rodrigo Brown. The connection between Big Danny and Red Dawg was as mysterious to him as Cali accents were to his East Coast ears. All he knew for sure was that the redheaded half-black/half-Mexican kid had a fearsome rep and undying loyalty to his law-abiding granddad.

Which was crucial, since when D revisited LA in the early 2000s, the area was experiencing an influx of Mexicans and Central Americans, and gangs were shifting from Bloods and Crips to a jigsaw puzzle of Bloods, Crips, Mexican Mafia, and Mara Salvatrucha, battling the city's most enduring gang—the Los Angeles Police Department.

That Big Danny maintained his store despite these demographic changes seemed in retrospect a bit of a miracle. Only years later did D wonder if Granddad had more than one business going on in South Central, and what role Red Dawg had in it. The way his granddad was murdered suggested there was a subterranean aspect to his life, a level that D was sadly about to be introduced to, which caused his curiosity to burn with sadness.

As the plane continued its descent, D gazed down at Los Angeles, a series of disparate villages and small towns tenuously linked by boulevards, freeways, and beaches. Maintaining close friends in LA was largely dependent on how short the drive was between their house and yours. A half hour was way too long except for true love or overwhelming lust. Otherwise, people didn't seem to become close friends. They were just people you knew—perhaps even cared about—but rarely saw. Traffic and distance determined the intensity of your friendships like daybreak defined working lives. D always felt isolated out here. This city, wide and long, was a thousand worlds where people listened to the Eagles or NWA or the Beach Boys or Black Flag or Shalamar or Charles Mingus or X or Tyler the Creator or Dr. Funk and thought they were in sync with this landscape when, in fact, they only had a piece of it. D didn't really know LA or even if he liked it. But here he was.

CHAPTER FOUR

BIG DANNY'S HOUSE

D stood at the curb outside the American Airlines baggage claim for thirty minutes, looking for, texting, and calling his cousin Walli before giving up and hopping into a taxi. The driver was Russian, very earnest and new to the job. D gave him his grandfather's address and the driver asked, "Is that in South LA?"

"South LA? It's in South Central," D corrected.

The driver plugged the address into his GPS and said, "South Central? I know no South Central. South LA I know."

As the taxi pulled out D recalled that the Los Angeles City Council had voted for a name change a few years back, apparently trying to erase a lot of unwelcome history. While they worked their way through traffic from LAX, D mused on the way the twenty-first-century real estate business was so committed to the renaming game. Got an old-school twentieth-century ghetto you want to change? Rebrand it. Build a slick website, post pictures of rehabbed homes, talk vaguely about the area's *rich history* and the housing stock's tradition, promote the glitz of condos with gyms and in-house cleaners (no need to walk outside, folks), and spotlight its closeness to downtown (which was a reason the previous generation had split for the suburbs in the first place). It had worked in New York and D was sure that, in some form, this hustle was going down in Cali. The geography was different but the rename game was relentless.

When they reached Adams Boulevard, D steeled himself against the sadness and rage he expected to feel for the next few days. The cars on the block were different but the homes, mostly Craftsman houses in a variety of shades, looked as sturdy as he remembered. Back when he visited as a teen, the block had been almost entirely black, save for a white woman and her black husband two doors down. Now he saw Mexican and American flags dangling from one porch. In front of another house two brown kids sporting soccer jerseys did tricks with a ball. Next to his grandfather's house was an empty home with a *For Sale* sign on the lawn.

D gathered his suitcase from the trunk and rolled it slowly up the walkway, noticing all the lawns on the block turning brown from a water shortage. At the front door D found his key fit but the door wouldn't open. He knocked.

"Who is it?" a timid voice called out.

"Walli, it's D. My key isn't working."

The door opened, revealing seventeen-year-old Walli Hunter, a lumpy, bushy-haired kid with hood experiences but boho tendencies, who was the product of a hyperprotective mother, an intermittently present father, and doting grandparents. This resulted in an earnest, romantic young man who had been both smothered and abandoned. Which is to say, you were never quite sure which Walli you were about to meet.

Like all the Hunter men, Walli had big shoulders and a solid frame. But he hadn't done a thing with those genetic gifts, having spent more time online than outside. He had his mother's reddish-yellow complexion (sans freckles) and sour expression, but was also open to joy and the fantastic. Out of loyalty to his granddad, Walli paid lip service to liking the Dodgers, but his real passion was history. He'd inherited D's spot at

Big Danny's store, sitting there on long afternoons after school while his mother worked, listening to stories about black LA ("before these damn gangs fucked shit up") being spun back and forth across the countertop. As a result, Walli had become a good listener and collector of stories in a way that reminded D of his late friend and mentor Dwayne Robinson, which he thought was a great thing. To D, getting to spend more time with Walli was the only obvious benefit of this trip west.

But instead of projecting warmth, Walli looked at D and, by way of greeting, said, "Ma had the locks changed awhile ago."

"Well, someone should have told me."

Walli shrugged.

D gave him a hug, which was returned with a stiff embrace. "How you doing?"

"I'm good," Walli mumbled.

D followed him into the house and dropped his suitcase in the living room. As if being pulled on a string, D walked over to a framed picture of a man he revered (Big Danny) with a man he missed (Fred Hunter) sitting on the steps of this house, sporting Dodgers' caps and holding baseball bats.

"Damn," he said under his breath. "Walli?" No answer. He turned to find his cousin wasn't in the living room; he was now at the kitchen table playing a game on his phone.

"Is that why you didn't pick me up at the airport?"

"I went out there, D," Walli said, "but the phone service is so bad. Lots of dead spots, even texting is hard out there. I didn't get your messages until I got back over the hill."

"Over the hill? Were you at Burbank Airport?"

"Yeah. I waited outside JetBlue for an hour."

"JetBlue? American doesn't land there."

"That's what I found out. You know Ma." Walli shrugged again and turned back to his phone.

"I know. Details have never been her thing. Hey, I saw the house next door is for sale. How long?"

"A while."

"Damn. The Jacksons used to live there. They were so country they had the nerve to name their kids Tito and Marlon." D smiled, expecting a laugh at this, but Walli didn't get the reference. "Tito and Marlon," D continued. "The Jacksons. You know, like Michael and Janet?"

Walli said, "Oh," and took a bite of his sandwich.

Realizing it would take time to establish chemistry with his young cousin, D headed upstairs. While the living room was filled with natural light, the hallway and staircase felt as old as yellowed newspaper. The stairs creaked like an old man's joints and had cracks like a wrinkled brow.

On his left was his father's old bedroom, where D used to stay and Walli now bunked in. D peeked in and spotted copies of *Wired* magazine, web-design manuals, and a MacBook on the bed. Across the hall was Aunt Sheryl's room, which she'd moved back into three years ago after her mother died. The room was an odd mixture of her adult life (magazines on hair care, samples of various products) and youth (Prince posters, colorful sneakers).

D walked down the hall to the master bedroom and opened the door slowly. On his grandfather's wooden dresser was a hairbrush, a bottle of Old Spice cologne, an empty money clip, and two bottles of blood-pressure medication. D picked each of them up, rubbing his fingers across them as if their surfaces carried some kind of magic.

He stepped over to the bed; Aunt Sheryl had freshly made it up. There was a taut, military feel to how the sheets fit the mattress. D brought a pillow to his nose, sniffing for a familiar scent. Frustrated by the minty detergent smell, he tossed the pillow on the bed and then climbed on after it. His big black-clad body curled up like a child's. He gazed up at the ceiling, where two large beams connected over the middle of the room, and thought of his grandparents staring up at it night after night for thirty-five years, the two of them connected like those beams.

It wasn't until Walli walked in and looked embarrassed that D realized he'd been crying.

CHAPTER FIVE

NIGHT IN THE VALLEY

D was gazing up at the ceiling again, but this time in the living room as he laid on the sofa. He didn't want to share a room with Walli and sleeping in his grandfather's bedroom was out of the question. He was looking at the photo of his father and grandfather when his phone rang out the opening notes to Night's hit "Black Sex," meaning it was Al Brown, an old friend and Night's longtime comanager/support system.

"I heard about your grandfather passing," Al said softly. "My condolences. How you holding up?"

"I'm okay," D answered, lying. "Crazy how it happened. If he'd just died of old age, we would all have been okay, you know. But to die this way—"

"You thinking about playing detective again, D?" Al sounded anxious.

"No," he said, lying again. "It's too personal. I can't even think about any of that. Just want to help my family get through this."

"Night and I would like to come by the services. Maybe the wake since it would be a little more private."

"Thanks for offering," D said. "Be good to see you guys. I'll text you the address and time. Is Night loving Cali?"

Al sighed. "In my opinion LA is not the best place for him to spend time. But Amos Pilgrim wanted him close, and the label feels they can keep an eye on him out here too." His tone was changing, but even on the phone with a friend he remained cautious with his words. "Honestly, I'd prefer he was back on the East Coast. The temptation to go to pool parties in secluded homes is not the best thing for a guy with too many babies and a drug problem."

"I agree," D replied softly, realizing that Al was telling more than he was saying. "I was planning to come out for some of the sessions a little later. After the services I'll definitely stop by."

"The offer to be a comanager still stands, D. Pilgrim and I are both good with it. Night mentions it all the time. He's still a little hurt you didn't come on board after the last tour."

"I know." Now it was D's turn to sigh. "The timing wasn't right. After all that stuff in Brownsville last year I had a lot of testifying to do. A couple of cops wanted to charge me for obstruction of justice. Lucky for me a black DA got elected and shut that shit down. If Hynes had still been the Brooklyn DA, I would surely be in Rikers."

Al laughed. "But all that's behind you now, D. I know you're dealing with your grandfather's death. Take some time for yourself and then come see us."

"Where're you cutting?"

"Some joint in the Valley," Al said sourly. "The idea was to get Night some sun during the day and then cut at night. Instead he cuts in the a.m. and hangs out all night."

"That doesn't sound like our man."

"Yup. That's why I'd love for you to come on board. I'm babysitting and I'm getting too old for this shit. I am really thinking about retiring to the R&B old peoples' home."

D chuckled. "Somewhere in Vegas, right?"

"Of course," Al said. Then he went quiet for a moment. "Between you, me, and the light pole, he's not cutting much worth hearing."

"Oh man, Al, I can feel you sucking me in. But I gotta deal with my fam right now. Can't get into Night's drama at the moment. I just can't."

"Understood," Al said. "Deeply understood."

After that D got off the call quickly, not wanting to leave any more space in his already cluttered mind for Night's musical problems. Tomorrow he was going to see his grandfather's body and talk to an LA detective. He didn't need any additional reasons to be sleepless.

CHAPTER SIX

BIG DANNY WAS A LOAN SHARK

Detective Israel Gonzales agreed to meet with D at the Starbucks at the Holiday Bowl, which back in the seventies had been a bowling alley and in another incarnation the Sakiba Lounge and sushi bar. It was one of the most prominent examples of an architectural style that had appeared futuristic in the 1960s, when images of atoms and flying saucers were cutting edge. Starbucks, always smart about putting a local spin on its franchise, had kept much of the original design flavor.

Gonzales was sipping a fruity red concoction at a window seat when D entered. The heavyset policeman waved him over to the empty chair across from him.

"Mr. Hunter, my condolences," Gonzales said, "A grandfather murdered like that is quite a shock." Gonzales took another sip of his drink and then shook his head.

"It is for me and all the family, detective. Who would gun down a seventy-year-old man at a stoplight?"

"A semiretired retailer in South LA at that. His wallet in his pocket. He had $8,500 cash in the glove compartment." The detective's voice betrayed a hint of mental rehearsal. "He paid for his coffee with small bills. It's a little strange that the owner of a grocery store would go to another place for coffee, but it seems like that was your grandfather's regular spot. I mean, he went there even though there's an excellent new coffee shop right next door." Gonzales let that sit with D a moment before continuing. "Were you close to your grandfather, Mr. Hunter?"

"I mean, we communicated. Whenever I came out here on business I always tried to see him." As D talked, the question of his grandfather's coffee habits and the cash nagged at him.

"Your grandfather did well for himself. Had that grocery store, the athlete shoe shop next door, and that club on Manchester."

"I believe he sold his interest in the club years ago."

"Apparently not. According to the club's manager, a Hank Cauldwell. He sold some shares in it but still controlled 51 percent."

This surprised D. "Oh. Like I said, I thought he'd sold it off a few years ago. I wasn't privy to all his moves."

"I didn't think you were, Mr. Hunter." Gonzales shifted in his seat and then clasped his hands together in the center of the wooden table. D leaned back; he could feel a punch coming but didn't know which way to duck. "I'm gonna be frank with you because your family apparently hasn't been. Your grandfather was a loan shark."

"C'mon," D said. "I mean, even if that was true, it would've had to have been some kind of mom-and-pop-type thing. Something for friends in the neighborhood."

"It was a small operation," Gonzales conceded. "Maybe it started as a little hobby, but he was known in the area for helping people with loans. Payday loans. Sometimes with gambling debts. If a wife needed money for rent because the father was high or drunk, I hear your granddad was helpful. Rodrigo Brown at the sneaker store was his collector and, if need be, enforcer."

"Wow, I have to think about this." D almost wanted to laugh at the absurdity of it all. "This makes the case a lot more complicated," he said, trying to regain his footing.

"Well, maybe not," the detective responded coolly. "Loan sharks tend to get killed by people who owe them money or friends of people who owe them money, especially since this was a very neighborhood thing. I mean, a desperate man would as soon kill you for two hundred dollars as twenty thousand. If he was picking up cash that day and someone knew he'd have it on him, then it becomes a hit. But they didn't get the cash. Maybe they missed their moment. I know your background is in security and that you've aided the NYPD in the past. If you want to help solve your granddad's murder, finding a list of his debtors would be a start."

"So I assume that Red Dawg wasn't helpful?"

"No, Mr. Brown hasn't helped us at all. In fact, I'm worried that he's going to take matters into his own hands. He's an ex-gangbanger and one violation away from going back in. Your grandfather gave him a break that he wouldn't have gotten otherwise. Him hurting someone on a hunch is not gonna bring your grandfather's killer to justice. If you can get Mr. Brown to cooperate, then maybe we have a chance at finding out who did it. Otherwise, this could become just another cold case. I know you don't want that, Mr. Hunter."

Gonzales's phone played a snippet of "O Tu, O Ninguna," a ballad by Luis Miguel, a.k.a. El Sol de Mexico, and the policeman quickly answered it. He spoke in Spanish with a coy smile on his face. "Listen, Mr. Hunter, I have to take this call. You have my number. If you speak to your grandfather's friend and get some info, please reach out."

With that, Gonzales returned to his call, still grinning as he exited the Starbucks, while D sat alone and his eyes fixed on a series of lights intended to resemble an atom. But he didn't see them. Not at all.

CHAPTER SEVEN
RED DAWG HAS A THEORY

Big Danny's Electra 225 sat in the garage and D approached it cautiously, like a feisty animal he wished to pet. He'd been around death a lot as a child, dealing with the murders of his three older brothers. Each had been a profound tragedy. If his granddad had simply died from natural causes it would have been sad and understandable. But that man was not supposed to get shot. D noticed a bullet hole in the passenger-side door, reminding him yet again that his grandfather had been cheated of the peaceful passing he deserved. D thirsted for vengeance. He didn't want to feel or think that or, in the back of his mind, plan it. But it was what it was.

"We had it cleaned up," Walli said over D's shoulder. Glancing inside the vehicle, you'd never even know a murder had occurred. "It's spooky, right?"

D rolled back the canvas top, opened the driver's door, and slid behind the wheel. "Is there gas in the tank?"

"I think so," Walli said. "You're not planning on driving it, are you?"

"Yes, I am. Get in."

"Really? You sure?" Walli stood a few feet away, unsure what to do. "My car is out front . . . we haven't driven the Electra since we brought it home."

"I'm gonna go see Red Dawg," D said. "You can stay here, you can drive in your car, or you can get in here with me." He turned the key in the vintage car's ignition. "You coming, or what?"

"Fuck it," Walli said, sliding reluctantly into the passenger seat.

D couldn't sleep in Big Danny's bed, but he felt okay riding in his beautiful car. He didn't own a car and rarely drove in New York. He really didn't even like driving. But he was going to drive Big Danny's 225 until the wheels fell off or his heart broke, whichever came first.

"So," D asked once they pulled out, "school's good?"

"It's okay, I guess."

"Okay? I hear them eses been beating up black kids at schools out here. I hear that between Dr. King's birthday and Caesar Chavez's birthday, it's on between the black and Chicanos out here. Is any of that right or is it just some Internet drama?"

"It depends or where you are and who you know."

This answer did not sit well with D. "Hey Walli, I'm your cousin. Don't talk to me like I'm LAPD."

"I'm sorry, D, but I don't like to focus on that shit," Walli began, his voice soft but insistent. "I want to go to college out of state, hopefully to University of Washington or someplace else up north. I do my work. I stay with my friends. I'm going to get out of LA. I felt that way even before what happened to Granddad. Now I really don't want to be here. If you want to talk about Mexicans and all that, go talk with Red."

That satisfied D. Not that he particularly liked Walli's reply or his tone, but it was a real answer and felt like the start of them communicating again, which was all D desired.

The green Electra 225 rolled into the strip mall on Washington Avenue, where D's eyes focused on the gated grocery and liquor store, Big Danny's Place, which looked forlorn like a down-home blues. In front of the adjoining store, Red Dawg's Athletic Assets, was an LAPD cruiser.

"What's he into now?" D mumbled to himself, but Walli answered.

"Nothing, D. The police always coming around to mess with him."

Patrolmen Hernandez and Diaz were talking casually with Red Dawg when D and Walli entered. Whatever tension had been in the air had already dissipated. There were some legal papers on the cash register by Red Dawg's hand. The cops were solidly built men with square heads and solid jaws who viewed everybody as a potential felon.

Red Dawg was burly with red hair on top and on his chin, and thick, tatted-up arms exposed by his black tank top. He wore a silver chain around his neck that held a small red skull and an old-school African medallion. There was a medley of shiny rings on his fingers. A fading bruise hung above his left eye and he had a reddish tan that made him look angry even when he was chill. Red Dawg was the kind of man you quickly noticed and then turned away from.

"I can't root for no damn Angels," Red Dawg said. "C'mon, Hernandez."

"The Angels are owned by one of us, you know," the cop replied.

"That man looks real white to me," Red Dawg said before spying D. "Oh shit, it's my dawg."

"How you doing?" D said in response.

Red Dawg emerged from behind the counter and gave D a deep hug. The patrolmen watched casually and acknowledged Walli with a nod.

"I'm okay, my man," Red Dawg said. "Makes me happy seeing you." Then he introduced the officers to D by name. After sharing obligatory handshakes, he explained the family connection.

Diaz said, "Your granddad was Big Danny? He was a nice guy. My condolences."

Hernandez added, "Yeah, a real solid citizen. Sorry for your loss." Then he turned back toward Red Dawg. "Okay, Red, we'll head out. Sorry about that. I think it's for your own good."

NELSON GEORGE 3 43

Red Dawg shrugged. "Maybe."

As the two patrolmen exited, Red Dawg followed them with his eyes.

"What was that about?" D asked.

"They wanted to talk baseball."

D gestured to the papers on the countertop. "So what's that—a box score?"

"You don't miss shit, do you?" Red Dawg picked up the papers and handed them to D. They were a court order that restricted Red Dawg from several areas, including a local park where the neighborhood branch of the Bloods traditionally congregated. Red Dawg would be in violation of his parole if he was seen at any of these locations.

"Told you they wanted to talk baseball," Red Dawg said, ignoring the paper's ominous warning. "Who am I supposed to talk baseball with? Niggas don't care about baseball, do they, Walli?"

"Nawn," Walli said.

"D, I tried to get your little cousin to play catch with me a few times, but this boy throws like a girl."

"Fuck you."

Red Dawg gently grabbed Walli around the neck and pretended to twist it, a sign of intimacy notably different from the vibe between the teenager and D.

"Shit, fool, you better be glad your tough New York cousin is here, or I'd squeeze your big head into one of these sneaker boxes."

Walli pushed his way out of Red Dawg's grip and tried to tackle him, but Red Dawg deftly deflected the attack. It was like a young pup trying to prove himself to a much bigger dog—in this case a red dog.

"Don't they have any black cops around here?" D asked.

"Why you need black cops in a Latino neighborhood?" Red Dawg said as he grabbed Walli's arms and pinned the teenager. "Unless you want to move out here to serve and protect."

D smiled at that. "Tomorrow. Tomorrow I'm gonna enroll in the academy and join a crash unit."

At the mention of the LAPD's antigang unit, Red Dawg turned serious and let Walli go. "Walli, why don't you take over the counter for a minute? D and I need to go in the back and have a sit-down."

"You had enough, huh, Red?" Walli said, way out of breath and a little sore.

"Yeah, I give up."

In the back room there were racks lined with boxes of sneakers, posters of athletes on the wall, and sports jerseys on hooks. There was a minifridge, from which Red Dawg pulled two Tecates, and a small safe half visible under a Kobe Bryant purple-and-gold home jersey. A cluttered old wooden desk sat in a corner. Red Dawg balanced on a gray ball behind the desk, while D squatted into an unsteady white plastic chair. Red Dawg didn't waste any time.

"I know who killed Big Danny," he said, then swigged a deep gulp of beer.

"I take it you didn't share this with the police?"

Red Dawg snorted and took another drag from his beer. "There's not a lot of support for Black Lives Matter in these parts."

"But you care enough to do something about it."

Dead serious, Red Dawg looked D in the eye. "I care enough about Big Danny to kill a whole gang of niggas. But I don't have to do that. I know who did it."

"You know, or you *think* you know?" D wasn't buying Red Dawg's gangsta attitude. He'd heard a lot of shit-talking over the years and wasn't convinced this rose above chest-pounding.

"I shoulda killed that motherfucker years ago. You know him. Teo Garcia."

D sat back in the plastic chair. "Oh," he said, surprised.

"Yeah, *oh*. That nigga. You don't feel so bad about it now, do you? He's been threatening Big Danny for years."

"So why now?" D asked.

"Big Danny was retiring."

"So why was Big Danny collecting debts? I thought that was your job."

Now it was Red Dawg who was surprised. "That detective told you Big Danny had a side business, huh? Well, some people Big Danny handled, some people I handled."

"Yeah. Wish I'd known before."

"At least that fat Chicano fuck could *deduce* that," Red Dawg said. "Otherwise he don't know shit."

"So you planning to murk a man on a hunch?" D asked pointedly. He knew Red Dawg wasn't a punk, but all this *Sicario* talk seemed out of character.

Teo Garcia. That bitch-ass. When D spent a summer in LA as a teenager, the sound of gangsta rap dominated the radio, but things were evolving. Tupac was dead. Snoop was working in New Orleans with Master P. Dre was in the lab working on *Aftermath*. The thuggish specter of Suge Knight hovered over the hip hop biz.

For the novice MCs of Los Angeles, gangsta rap was a music of opportunity and Red Dawg had the bug. When he wasn't delivering groceries to gang-fearing shut-ins for Big Danny, Red Dawg had formed a rap trio dubbed Trey Blaxicans, which featured himself MCing, a DJ named Ramon J, and MC Tee O, another half-black/half-Mexican kid. Red and Teo first met in grade school, where they bonded over their love of West Coast rap (from "We Want Eazy" on) and dual outsider status. The DJ was a light-skinned black kid, real name Romel Johnson, who went by a Spanish first name for promotional purposes.

Before Red Dawg turned it into a sneaker store, the space next to Big Danny's grocery had been used for storage. Trey Blaxicans moved some boxes around, then hooked up turntables, a sampler, a mixer, and a Mac to create a modest recording studio/rehearsal space. Teo was smooth on the mic with a flow similar to West Coast legend DJ Quik, and was capable of a slick rhyme. Though Red Dawg was okay (he could sound like NWA's MC Ren when inspired), Trey Blaxicans molded the group around Teo.

Red Dawg's problem with Teo was that for all his talent, he was impatient. The whole do-showcases, make-a-demo, and shop-it-to-labels dance didn't appeal to him. A few years later Trey Blaxicans could have uploaded tracks to YouTube, and maybe Teo would have become the rap star he already thought he was. But the band was just a bit too early to exploit that business model. So Teo's solution was to rob some gas stations to fund real studio sessions and to press a twelve-inch single.

His two bandmates, who'd gotten into music to avoid doing crime, turned down invitations to get involved in his capers. When confronted about it, Teo pointed out that Big Danny was a loan shark ("He should just give us money anyway") and that Red Dawg worked for him, so what was the big deal? But Big Danny knew just enough about hip hop not to want to be involved. His estimation of it as music and business was simple: "Too many guns. Not enough brains."

This dispute curtailed Trey Blaxicans' activities and angered Teo. So, one summer night he walked into Big Danny's at closing time, "hiding" behind a red bandanna and sporting a Mossberg 550 Tactical shotgun. Whether he meant to just rob, or to actually hurt Big Danny, would never be known. The official LAPD report said that the store owner had wounded the perpetrator with bullets in both legs. Big Danny got away with only a flesh wound in his left shoulder.

D, who visited the emergency room and saw how shook his grand-dad was, always suspected that Red Dawg had played a role in stopping the robbery. Red Dawg was at the hospital that night and D remem-bered seeing a proud, wary, amped look on his face—a look that D recognized from too many acts of violence back in Brooklyn.

Teo told the police that Red Dawg had shot him. Big Danny said he did the deed himself in self-defense. LAPD believed the wounded shopkeeper. At the hearings, Teo threatened retribution and violence as soon as he got out of jail. Unfortunately for Teo, his earlier revenue-generating robberies came back to haunt him and he went away for many years. So many that he'd gradually become an insignificant bad memory to D. But not so to Red Dawg. Was Big Danny really the victim of a wannabe MC?

"You gotta have more than that to go on. I mean, is Teo even out of jail?"

Red Dawg pulled out his iPhone, clicked on a file, and slid the de-vice in front of D. "He's been out quite awhile, D. Has a whole new life. He's big in *narcocorridos*."

"What's that?"

Red Dawg laughed. "I thought you knew something about music. Guess you only know East Coast shit. *Narcocorridos*. It's gangsta rap with accordions and tuba."

"What the fuck?"

"It's a Mexican thing. You wouldn't really understand, negro. Bot-tom line: it's songs about drug kingpins and what they did and who they did it to. Just listen to this."

The music emanating from the iPhone had a jaunty polka beat with a tuba providing the bottom and an accordion carrying the melody. A Spanish voice emoted on the track, which Red Dawg translated as he sang: *"Old shop owner tried to control me / I blasted out, he fell down / He no longer own me / I ride away with vengeance / My nine by my side / My spirit abides / Blessed by a dead man's blood."*

"When was this recorded?"

"A year ago," Red Dawg said, then clicked off the music. "I'd call that evidence."

"Red, all it proves is that Teo wrote a song about revenge. How do you know it's aimed at Big Danny? If it's about my grandfather, I don't like it. At all. But it doesn't mean he did it. You got any more *proof*."

Red Dawg wasn't bothered by D's reluctance to believe in his thesis. "I already went looking for him. That nigga's underground right now. Off the motherfuckin' grid. His phone is dead. Must be using a burner. He's got some bullshit production company with people making records for him but he's not around. So yeah, I think he shot Big Danny. I think he's holed up somewhere getting high or with some ho. I'll bury his ass right behind Chavez Ravine."

"So that's your plan? Bury the motherfucker at Dodger Stadium? A guy with his own business, who's making and producing music, just decides to murk a man for an old grudge? Wouldn't he hire someone to do it?"

Red Dawg did not want to hear any of D's logic—his mind was made up. "Look, don't you worry, you undertaker-dressing motherfucker. I got this. I was closer to Big Danny than you or your fucking father. I understand if you ain't got the heart for this, but I do."

Though Red Dawg spoke with certainty, D could tell he wanted his help or support, and was willing to insult D to get it.

He continued on: "That man was better to me than my own father. The only reason I'm telling you is that if I get got, you'll know why and you'll be prepared to deal with Sheryl and the kid. One thing I know about your ass is that you can keep a secret."

D didn't really like beer but he took a swig anyway, as he considered Red Dawg's words. Finally he asked, "You love my aunt?"

"Yeah."

"You love my little cousin?"

"What's your point?"

"You need to think this through," D said passionately. "You're the glue holding this family together right now. Going after Teo will end badly—it just will. It always fuckin' does. Believe me, I got some shit on my conscience that I thought was righteous at the time. I left a man in a room with another man. Only one of those men is still around. Now, that other man was a piece of shit. But I'm no better. Sometimes I wake up at night thinkin' about it. It wasn't right and it didn't make his wrongs right. I don't expect you to change your mind. But this ain't no macho shit. This is life and death. I will support you. I would love revenge too. But revenge ain't the end of anything and it won't change anything . . . Well, it will change something. It'll change *you*."

Red Dawg finished his Tecate and then belched. "Lecture time is over, D. I gotta go out and pick up a shipment of shoes. I'm a businessman." He stood up, reached over for D's beer, and finished it.

D stood up too and said, "Don't do anything without letting me know."

"We'll see." Red Dawg turned his back and walked toward the front of the store.

A few minutes later, D pushed open the door to Big Danny's grocery store and stood in the doorway as daylight illuminated a dusty newspaper rack with old copies of the *Los Angeles Times*.

"Lemme go turn off the alarm," Walli said and pushed past D, who stood there mesmerized.

After a moment the lights came on and Walli appeared behind the counter. D walked toward him, past racks of cosmetics, cereal boxes, and toothpaste.

"I threw out or gave away as many of the perishables as I could, but it's been a hot summer," Walli said. "There are probably a couple of critters in here by now."

"You want to throw away some more stuff now?" D asked.

"It would be great if you wanna help."

D took off his jacket and dropped it on the counter. Glancing behind the counter, he saw a small chair propped against the wall. "He kept that chair, huh?"

"Yeah," Walli said. "I used to sit there."

"So did I." D went down an aisle and opened a carton of trash bags and pulled out a big black one. He sighed, walked back around the room, and asked Walli, "Where do we start?"

CHAPTER EIGHT

DR. FUNK MAKES A GROOVE

Dr. Funk walked over to the TR-808 drum machine in the corner and flipped it on. He hadn't played it in a couple of months and was worried that it might not work. The rhythm device was damn near as old as he was, he thought. Well, maybe not quite that old. Still, you never knew when the insides would rust and the lights would stop flashing on.

But the TR-808 came to life, just as it had over countless sessions since 1983. Back then he'd been seduced by it when he heard it on Run-DMC's "Sucker MCs" and the Soulsonic Force's "Planet Rock." After those records, he had put his LinnDrum in a corner despite what Prince was doing with it. Dr. Funk had been messing with the Linn as the culture shifted—he'd even had a minor hit with it. But the Linn-Drum felt too cold and metallic to him. That little bastard from the frozen north had figured out how to get interesting flavors from it. Still, most tracks made with the Linn sounded like they'd been baked in a microwave. By comparison, the 808 tracks still felt as fresh as homemade biscuits, while all those Linn records from the eighties sounded as dated as blue contacts on black girls.

Dr. Funk pressed buttons and turned knobs, trying to figure out if he could imitate the movement of a big-hipped Mexican woman he'd spotted at a Ralphs. She'd pushed a shopping cart through the produce section with her right hand while balancing a small girl on her left hip.

The cart's forward motion—its rubber wheels against the floor—and the weight of the little girl created two syncopations in Mamasita's walk, generating counterrhythms in her hips that intrigued Dr. Funk (as did her body-hugging Lululemon aqua stretch pants).

In his mind Dr. Funk heard "Planet Rock" mixed with a maria- chi band. He wasn't even sure if that combination could be achieved. Which, of course, was the main reason to try. He rigged his Mac to interface with his 808, so he got the real 808 sound and not a second- hand version of it. He refused to make records designed to be heard on earbuds—all tinny and high end with bass that lacked personality and commitment.

Once he had a drum pattern he liked, Dr. Funk pulled out his Fender bass and listened for spaces where he could lock into the groove. Hip hop had been built on block-rocking beats, but Dr. Funk was a groove man, addicted to building layers of rhythm. Anything less than that and a song just felt naked.

Dr. Funk messed around with the Fender for about fifteen minutes, creating a placeholder bass line he could live with. He laid it down and then looped it. Next he hobbled over to where his keyboards were stacked—Yahama, Korg, Oberheim, all tools from his era of musicmak- ing. He'd had these instruments so long the keyboards had yellowed and a few keys stuck if pressed too hard. A couple of backstage passes from nineties tours were pasted here and there, the stickers frayed at the corners and the adhesive worn.

Though these symbols of long-ago tours were multicolored and damn near psychedelic in style, Dr. Funk barely noticed them anymore. Hadn't in years. The stickers had become invisible to him, totems from when he worshipped at his own temple. Now he had renounced that Satan and rebuked himself, and all that mattered these days was the music. *Just let it flow*, he thought. *Be the current and not the boat and you'll always travel well. You'll eventually reach shore, but the destination should remain a delicious mystery.*

Dr. Funk messed with a mariachi melody he'd heard once in a Mexican restaurant and then dropped in some flattened thirds that clashed with it but still sounded kind of cool. He told himself he was marrying something corny and traditional with some jazz shit, like Miles on *Sketches of Spain.*

That bastard Miles was always so free, Dr. Funk thought. Whenever they'd met, Miles would always make him feel like he was playing around in comparison, just making songs that fit between soda pop radio commercials. Sure, Miles messed around with funk—but at the end of the day, he kept a space between himself and anything too simpleminded. Even when they got high together, Miles never let Dr. Funk think that he was at his level.

Now this groove was starting to sound like something. It wasn't a song yet, but a serious groove could drive a song. At this point in the old days, Dr. Funk would have brought in some top sidemen, like Greg Phillinganes or Jeff Porcaro or Eddie "Bongo" Brown, and would have had them join in, using their fingers to extend his brain. *Try this. Try that. No, slower. In G. In E. No, F-sharp. Maybe D.*

Sometimes these session cats thought they were songwriting. They weren't; they were just better at their individual instruments than he was. They had extraordinary facility and great feel. But they had no more ownership of Dr. Funk's songs than his 808 or mini Moog. This reality led to some misunderstandings, especially with band members. *There are always serpents in the garden*, he thought. That bastard Scratch had some of his music. Original tracks too.

But Scratch couldn't do anything with those songs. He could play—

yeah, that fool could play the guitar. But he couldn't write a good song if it was Judgment Day and a solid melody would keep his ass out of hell.

Still, when Dr. Funk slumped back in his chair and listened to the drums, the bass, and the keys he'd laid down, he yearned for a fresh set of ears in his dungeon studio. It would have been good to play the track for Ollie Brown or Harvey Mason. Even when they made an I'm-not-feeling-it face, it was still helpful. Dr. Funk would read their expressions and know what to discard and what to save.

Shit, I wouldn't even need them if I had the right woman, he thought. Not for sex. It was about sensuality and how the music moved them. Not some fake-ass twerkin' that any silly chick could do. It was how their bodies moved naturally. Whether it was a hip roll or the way she held her hand when she spun around or how much she sweated or whether she was willing to sweat at all when the rhythm hit her. The greatest percussion player in the world was a woman entranced by a groove.

Dr. Funk hadn't had a woman like that in years. In a decade maybe. No, longer—much longer. At a certain point in his life he was having sex not for genuine pleasure but because it was expected. Women thought that's all he wanted. They performed for him and they expected—demanded—he do the same. He was just another notch on their bra straps, a wild story to tell girlfriends, and a cherished memory from the days of their girlish figures.

It made Dr. Funk angry to think back on it. He remembered nights he couldn't get it up. Yeah, he ate pussy like a champ, but that usually wasn't enough. They wanted Dr. Funk inside them and his tongue wouldn't do the job. It all just became too much work. Women wanted to brag that they'd fucked him or gossip later that he couldn't. Sometimes he'd lashed out, and these memories shamed him. He'd hit at least one woman. He'd waved a gun at another. Tossed a half-naked woman into a hotel hallway without her shoes.

He used to blame it on the coke and the drink. But he knew he'd been violent several times stone-cold sober, a fact that made him shiver. He shook his head and squinted as if a bright light was hitting his irises. He remembered. He was embarrassed. He was afraid. *Who was I? Who am I now?* Somebody knew. A brother. A father. A friend. Somebody knew. Somebody who might want to hurt him. He deserved some payback. He knew it. He expected it, really.

Still, he wasn't gonna invite vengeance. It would have to find his ass. Yeah, vengeance would have to GPS him. He wasn't gonna stand around waiting for it by the door.

Dr. Funk found himself playing a riff that was Eddie Palmieri by way of James Cleveland on the electric piano. He loved trying to make mash-ups of different styles. It helped him shift from the past to the present, from bad behavior to good music. He slowed the tempo and the riff became less derivative and more its own thing. Dr. Funk added this new piano piece to the groove, fitting it snugly between the 808, the Fender, and all the other sounds he'd compiled. Suddenly he had a song.

Dr. Funk played it back. He smiled, then frowned. In another era, back when his hair was black, his eyes were innocent, and his teeth were straight, this combination of notes would have translated into money. Greenbacks. Royalties. Record deals.

Dr. Funk kept things old school. He attached a CD drive to his Mac and burned a copy of this new song onto a blank disc. He held it in his hand and savored the tangibility of it. A CD was really just a container. Just like LPs, 45s, cassettes, eight tracks, 78s, and all that. It wasn't music. Music was intangible, of course. But Dr. Funk loved the containers.

That way he could hold music in his hand, like it was eggs or bacon or chicken. Something you bought at a store. Something essential. Something that could feed you. A meal.

Dr. Funk walked over to his "refrigerator," an old metal trunk with a gold-plated lock. He opened it with a key on a chain around his neck and slipped this CD in with the hundreds of meals—maybe a thousand—that he kept inside. Prince had his vault; Dr. Funk had his trunk. Someday, maybe, he'd go in and prepare a feast from all the songs—finished, half-finished, sketched—inside here.

But now Dr. Funk was tired. He walked over to the cot that served as his bed. He'd sleep for a couple of hours and then take an Uber up to Hollywood. He'd play for the tourists over by Ripley's Believe It or Not. Those folks were never lacking for change.

CHAPTER NINE

DINNER WITH AUNT SHERYL

Aunt Sheryl's face was yellow like fall leaves and dotted with freckles, especially around her broad nose. Her eyes were dark and piercing and never as happy as they wanted to be. Her mouth conveyed a faint air of disappointment except on the rare occasions she smiled. Her hair was naturally brown, with dyed-red streaks, and she typically wore it pulled back with an Indian Remy ponytail that she swung coquettishly for her own amusement. Unlike many Cali natives Aunt Sheryl didn't favor tight-fitting clothes, preferring loose, flowing two-piece outfits or brightly colored dresses. Her nails and toes were always immaculate and featured colors not found in nature.

At one point in her thirties Aunt Sheryl put on some pounds, but approaching fifty she'd fixed her diet, danced religiously to Billy Banks workout tapes, and did hot yoga, determined to "get one last good lover before my shit dries up." D remembered one late-night call where she inquired whether he'd loan her money for liposuction, which D reacted to as if it were a Chris Rock punch line.

Still, Aunt Sheryl looked better than she had in years and, from what D had seen on Facebook, had been dating regularly. If Aunt Sheryl wasn't the hottest MILF in LA, she was definitely the one making the most of what she had.

Back in the day she'd treated D with love, practicing her child-rearing skills as she hoped for a little boy of her own. Tonight she served D and Walli salmon, brown rice, and broccoli, a healthy meal very different from the soul food feasts of D's LA memory.

However, the quality of her cooking was the only soothing thing about Aunt Sheryl on this night. She was tense and out of sorts. They hadn't spoken about who might have shot her father yet, which D figured was the source of her discomfort. After Walli said grace and D told a few show-business stories, his aunt mentioned the family attorney had given her a heads-up on her father's will.

"Oh," D said, "anything surprise you?"

"Plenty. When's the last time you spoke to him, D?"

"Not since I was last out here in February."

His cousin piped up: "You took him out to Mr. Chow's and that jazz show. He told me he really had a good time."

"I did too. We went to the Catalina Jazz Club. It's on Sunset if you ever want to check it out."

"What did you two talk about?" Aunt Sheryl's voice had an edge.

"Talk about?" D said. "A lot of things. I know we talked about you and your son. He seemed concerned about you, but that wasn't new."

Sheryl sat fuming. Walli's eyes said he knew what was up but it wasn't for him to say.

"What's going on, Aunt Sheryl? You're acting like I stole something from you."

She got up from the table and abruptly left the room.

"What's this about?" D asked Walli.

"It's about the house. She thought it would just be hers. Uncle Fred isn't around so she thought she would have it. But Granddad gave you half."

"Half? I don't deserve that."

D got up and sprinted up the stairs to her room. The door was locked. "Aunt Sheryl? Aunt Sheryl, can we talk?" He heard her moving around the room and finally the door slowly opened. "I knew nothing about this," he said. "I would never have agreed to this. Never."

"My father was so old-fashioned he was fucking silly," she replied bitterly. "He didn't have confidence in me. Didn't think I could handle our family business. So instead of giving me the house and everything, he gave you half. I just wanted to know if you knew that before coming out here."

"Like I said, Aunt Sheryl, I didn't. I don't want this house. I live in New York. You can do anything you want with it. You have nothing to worry about from me."

She shook her head. "My father had a lot of different faces."

"Yeah, he was a bossy old man."

"That was just part of it. There was a lot to him. A *lot*."

"Is that why he was killed?"

"I think so. I really do."

D embraced his aunt. "I'm not going to let anything happen to you or Walli."

"Okay, that's nice to say. But how are you going to do that in New York?"

As they embraced, D realized he didn't really have an answer.

CHAPTER TEN

A YOUTUBE WAKE

The last time D had been inside Heaven's Gate was just after the turn of the century, when a group of ace 1970s and '80s session musicians gathered to jam. David Williams, Wah Wah Watson, and Phil Upchurch were the guitarists. Stevie Wonder's favorite bassist, Nathan East, held down the bottom, along with Jheri-curled drum legend James Gadson and versatile percussionist Paulinho da Costa. Greg Philliganes and Steve Porcaro of Toto were on the keys. The Waters sisters, who seemed to have sung background on every LA recording of the eighties, stepped forward to lead songs as varied as the Dazz Band's "Let It Whip," Shalamar's "The Second Time Around," the Brothers Johnson's "I'll Be Good To You," to Quincy Jones and James Ingram's "100 Ways." Q, of course, was in the house, sitting with a blond tenderoni. Rumor was that Michael would be attending, but only Jermaine and Tito actually showed up.

The night had been, as far as D knew, a send-off for Big Danny. He was selling the place to two young black entrepreneurs who boasted of Hollywood connections and Ivy League pedigrees. Big Danny was teary-eyed that night, though people thought he was relieved to have the club off his hands.

Well, the two young entrepreneurs never did reopen the place. Word was that they had fallen out over a woman. Another rumor had it that one of the duo's cash wasn't as real as that of his partner. Either way, Heaven's Gate stayed shuttered and, after that night, Big Danny never spoke about it again. D figured he'd gotten some cash and walked away clean. But did Big Danny still own 51 percent of Heaven's Gate as the detective had said? D wouldn't be clear on that until a formal reading of the will.

So it was strange to be back inside the club on this solemn occasion. The candles Aunt Sheryl had placed around the room didn't camouflage the dank smell of spilled drinks. Nor could the floral arrangements beautify a place unfit for daylight. Still, according to Big Danny's attorney and Aunt Sheryl, this is where he wanted his wake held, so there was his coffin, just below the bandstand, a golden-yellow overhead spotlight beaming down upon him.

D sat on the aisle, with Walli between himself and Aunt Sheryl, as he watched people come up and pay their last respects to Daniel Hunter. Sheryl had dressed the body in a silver sharkskin suit, matching raw silk tie, a charcoal shirt, and black Gators. He was to be buried as Big Danny, nightclub owner, not Daniel Hunter, South Central retailer.

D wore a white shirt and one of his dozen black suits—his usual attire since mourning dead family members had almost become his vocation. Sitting before his grandfather's coffin, D wondered if it was time to add color to his wardrobe. His grandfather would never have wanted to be buried in black, so why should D continue to live in it?

He was mulling this when a slightly stooped black man in a brown one-piece ski jumpsuit, blue Cal baseball cap, and a curly blond wig walked past him toward the coffin. He glanced over at Sheryl who whispered, "Yeah, that's Dr. Funk. He and Daddy have been good friends forever."

"Who's Dr. Funk?" Walli asked.

"A great musician," D said. "I'll tell you more later."

Dr. Funk leaned his arms on the edge of the coffin and bowed his head. A low hum began emanating from him that felt as deep as the Mississippi River. The sound vibrated the wood in the coffin. It was a country sound, like birds chirping in a dense forest, but then it changed into the wail of a beast charging its prey. When he turned toward the family, Dr. Funk's grunts became a cry and that cry a hymn. There were words to this hymn but Dr. Funk wasn't singing them. He was pushing through the melody too, reshaping it into something hard and potent as a punch.

As Dr. Funk moved closer to the family, D felt the bench shake beneath him from the force of the singer's voice. His face contorted as he hit the notes, his blond wig wiggling, the gray hairs on his face twitching. His eyes were red, with dark irises. But there was joy in that face too, as if he were a seventh-grade show-off. Dr. Funk took Sheryl's hand and at his touch she cried heavy, luminous tears. He hugged her while still singing, his hymn now a low, soothing lullaby.

D covered his face with his big right palm, because he was crying too. A hand then rested on his shoulder, radiating warmth like a heating pad. He looked up and there was Dr. Funk, more pure sound than person, more light than body. D cried loud and without inhibition, his self-consciousness sucked dry by Dr. Funk. D had long ago sworn off tears, not truly cutting loose since his second brother's murder. Tears, he felt, were a useless, hopeless gesture. New policy today.

When D lifted his head again there was Dr. Funk, his face just half a foot away, singing to and for him, and the old musician was crying too. They looked at each other, suddenly not strangers but relatives united in grief.

And then Dr. Funk closed his mouth and studied D like he was a Renaissance painting. "I see him in you, son," he said.

D thanked him unsteadily and found himself holding Dr. Funk's long, bony hands; the old guy was bowed for benediction, like a sinner to the pope.

It was silent now, save for Sheryl's quiet sobbing and the pounding inside D's ears. Dr. Funk let go of D's hands and the big man slumped backward and blinked away his tears.

Fifteen minutes later D was standing outside Heaven's Gate next to two of his favorite people—the singer Night and veteran music manager Al Brown. Night was talking excitedly.

"Yo, we were driving over and my Twitter feed exploded. It was like Obama got shot. It was *that* crazy."

"Yeah," D said, wiping his face with a tissue. "It was an intense experience. His voice was so fucking powerful. But if I'd known my cousin was gonna share it with the world I would have tried to keep it together." Walli had uploaded a video of Dr. Funk singing and Sheryl and D crying that immediately went viral.

"Shit," Al said, "I'd still be bawlin' if that man had sung to me that way. That's as real as it gets."

The three of them stood in a tight huddle, just as they had on many nights over several tours. A few older folks, true friends of Big Danny, snuck a peek at the celebrity as they entered, but they were there to honor an old friend and didn't swerve from that mission to snap a photo or shake Night's hand. Yet Walli's video had alerted another demographic to the wake. Looky-looks and low-level celebrity-chasers from TMZ or MediaTakeOut or some other parasitic website were arriving with cameras in hand. Night was a star, so lenses were being focused on him. Maybe he would sing to the dead old man too?

"Can you get in contact with him, D?" Night asked while also checking his posture, acutely aware that this courtesy call had become a minor media event.

"I dunno," D said. "Maybe there's a number in my grandfather's things. I'll take a look."

Night was insistent: "D, I need to build with Dr. Funk. I need to talk with that man."

"Don't get your hopes up," Al said, ever the sage. "I worked on a tour with him right as his band was breaking up. He was sliding down-hill fast. He was—maybe still is—a genius. But he's as unstable as the San Andreas fault. What he did for D's grandfather today was amazing. But right now he could be back to eating out of a garbage can."

"I know all about people counting other people out," Night said. "I know how that feels, and—"

"I didn't count you out," Al cut in.

"I know that, Al. But that man is so special. I mean, he's why I pur-sued singing in the first place. If I could just collaborate with him one time, it would be a blessing. I mean that." Now his voice changed and he sounded as earnest as a priest: "I've been wondering what the fuck I'm doing recording in LA. But now I know: I'm here to write with Dr. Funk."

"C'mon, Night," D said.

"No, D, I'm telling you—this is it. You gotta hook us up. You've al-ways looked out for me, and I know this is a difficult time—I know this. But think about it: you could help him *and* help me."

What D didn't need was to spend his time chasing a musical ghost all over the City of Angels. But Night was one of his oldest (and need-iest) friends.

"I'm not making you any promises, okay? I'll do what I can do." D looked across the street and saw more men in shorts and baseball caps carrying cameras with long lenses. "Let's go inside, all right? Too many cameras out here."

As they were walking inside D got a text. *YO! It's Walter G. I see online that you're in LA. Let's hook up. I'm at Soho House every day from one to four p.m.*

Damn. Night. Dr. Funk. Walter Gibbs. The past just wouldn't stay in the past.

CHAPTER ELEVEN

HOLLYWOOD SINGIN'

"**H**ello," Lawrence Pak said with forced professionalism, "can I help you?"

D Hunter was shuffling around K-Pak Groceries like a tourist in some sad reenactment of a historic battle.

"My name is D Hunter," he said. "My grandfather was Daniel Hunter. Some people around here called him Big Danny. He was murdered a week ago. Shot dead. The police say this was the last place he stopped before getting shot."

"So sad," Lawrence said. "Yes, he came in here often. He would stand where you are, buy the paper, and have a cup of coffee."

"Your coffee must be good for him to come here when he has his own store. There's even a gourmet coffee shop next door." D hadn't wanted to come on so strong but the words just tumbled out.

"He was a very loyal customer," Lawrence said. "I just know he came in when my father ran the place, and after my father retired he would still stop by."

D walked over to the coffee machine and folded his arms. "Should I have a cup?"

"Do you like good coffee?" Lawrence asked.

"I never drink coffee."

"Then you probably shouldn't start with mine."

D moved over to the counter. "Did you know my grandfather was a loan shark?"

"Loan shark?"

"He lent money to people in need and charged high rates of interest."

"Oh," Lawrence said, "I did not know that. I am sorry about your grandfather's death. He seemed to be a good man."

D wanted to press harder, but if the guy didn't care to admit he and his family might have borrowed money from Big Danny, it wasn't a crime.

"One more thing," D said. "Do you remember seeing anyone hanging out around here that day? Someone unusual? Maybe someone he spoke with?"

"I am sorry," Lawrence said, "I did not see anyone." This time D believed him and reached out to shake his hand before leaving.

D stood on Crenshaw and peered out at the light-rail construction. So his grandfather stopped in this spot maybe once or twice a month for bad coffee. Probably one of several places if he truly was a money-lender. Clearly this was small change. Big Danny wasn't some mafioso who scared people. It wasn't something you would kill for, he thought. But he obviously carried cash, and that's all a drug addict or some street thug needed to know.

From behind him, a little dog chained up outside the gourmet coffee shop growled at D like he had just stolen artisanal coffee beans. *Wonder what that little bastard knows.*

D drove up Crenshaw to Adams Boulevard and made a left toward a church where he'd read online about a meeting on African American homelessness. It was in the basement of the McCarty Memorial Christian Church, where a small group—mostly middle-aged and elderly women—sipped lemonade, nibbled homemade brownies, and listened to Noel Barnes, a black woman in her thirties with natural hair (a rarity in LA) who worked for a nonprofit focused on the city's growing home-less population.

In the eighties, McCarty had a flock of over a thousand. Some Sundays there were so many in the congregation they couldn't fit all the members inside. Nowadays the regular membership hovered around seventy. This church, which now had cardboard covering broken windows and paint flakes the size of notebook paper, had been a victim of the area's black exodus.

"Black folks are disappearing from this city," Noel said to the audience as D settled in a chair. "Families are leaving Inglewood and Compton and other traditionally black areas for the Inland Empire or back down south. Hispanics and Asians are moving into these neighborhoods. We could get into a long sociological discussion about that, but what people are missing is that one part of this city's black population is in fact growing. Fifty percent of LA County's homeless are black. That's about forty-seven thousand people—the vast majority of whom are black *men*. To put that in perspective: if you combine the total number of Hispanic and white homeless in LA, the number is only about twenty-four thousand. So when we wonder what's wrong with our families, what's wrong with our communities—well, the answer is living on the streets."

After the talk, most of the questions were about how to find missing relatives. They were there looking for hope, just like D. Noel was enlisting volunteers for the city's annual count of homeless, and when D walked up, she held out a form for him to sign.

"Actually, I'm just like everyone else, trying to find a particular homeless man. His name is Maurice Stewart, but he's known as Dr.

Funk. He plays music on the streets. Has keyboards and sound equipment so he's not destitute."

"I see," she said. "Do you have any leads on what part of Los Angeles he's been living in, or any shelters where he may have stayed?"

"I know he played at least once in Santa Monica recently, but I've seen videos of him up by Highland and Hollywood."

"If he's chronically homeless—meaning no regular shelter stays or public assistance—he's probably not using his real name. If he's got instruments, he must have found a secure place. Maybe he has a squat or is sharing a space with a friend. But give me your e-mail and I'll forward you the addresses of some shelters in Hollywood."

As D guided the Electra 225 out of the church parking lot, he thought the visit had been a waste. If Dr. Funk was at a shelter, someone would have put it on front street. The only videos out there were of him performing. He had to have a place. Somewhere off the beaten track, somewhere secure, like the woman said, where he could store his stuff. The musician also had to have access to some dough, since these street gigs couldn't be earning him any real money.

D went up Highland and parked inside the complex where they held the Oscars ceremony every year. This part of Hollywood was LA's Times Square, full of tourists, costumed superheroes, street dancers, hustlers, toy cops, photographers, and drummers. D walked through the mess of people, feeling like he was back in NYC—except there was no El Capitan Theatre or Jimmy Kimmel marquee on 42nd Street. He heard a familiar song waft through the street sounds as he crossed Hollywood and Highland and found himself before a gaudy, tricked-out McDonald's.

There were three black men standing near the doorway, all probably in their sixties, in worn, clean clothes. Two had gray hair. The third, who sang lead, was bald as an eight ball and had a salt-and-pepper goatee. These were doo-woppers, men who knew street-corner harmonies from the days when that was hip hop and slicked-back, processed hair was the gold standard of urban style. They weren't singing Dr. Funk. They were singing the Whispers' classic "Just Gets Better with Time," with one of the gray-haired men killing the bass line with a rich, chocolate baritone. D stood there a while, listening as they then sang "Love Machine" by the Miracles. Both were songs written and recorded in LA back when R&B was in the city's blood. He tossed two twenties in their plastic bucket, thinking his grandfather would have booked them at Heaven's Gate.

CHAPTER TWELVE
BIG DANNY'S WILL

Harriett Wheeler, attorney at law, sat in an ergonomic chair behind the mahogany desk her grandfather had employed when building his South Central law practice. She flipped through sheets of notarized papers dated 2009, when Daniel Hunter and Harold Wheeler Sr. had composed this will over a bottle of bourbon.

The law firm of Wheeler & Walker had been a fixture on Crenshaw Boulevard since 1965, opening its practice in the wake of the Watts riots. Though both founders were long dead, Harriett had followed in the family tradition and kept the business going, though now the firm was called Wheeler & Hernandez and immigration cases paid the rent.

Back in 2009, Harold and Big Danny, pillars of a once-vibrant black community, were well aware the neighborhood that had supported them was evaporating, and that this will, these words on paper, was an attempt to stake their claim on the future for Big Danny's family—if they were willing to grasp it.

Harriett read the document to D, Sheryl, and Walli: "*The house at 2105 West Washington Avenue is to be divided up as follows: my daughter Sheryl has 50 percent ownership, my son Fred has 50 percent. But, in the event he is not in the United States at the time of my death, his son D inherits that 50 percent. The property at 5000 Crenshaw Boulevard, known as the nightclub Heaven's Gate, is owned 51 percent by my grandson D and 49 percent by my daughter Sheryl. The retail properties at 2105 West Washington*

Avenue are to be divided as follows: my daughter Sheryl has 50 percent of both properties. The other 50 percent is owned by Rodrigo Brown."

"Okay," Sheryl said, glancing over at D and her son, "that wasn't so bad."

"There's one more clause you all should be aware of," Harriett added. "It reads, *In the event that Maurice Stewart, a.k.a. Dr. Funk, is in need of shelter, financial help, or emotional support, I obligate my heirs to assist him by any means necessary.*"

D laughed and Harriett wanted to know why this request was funny. "It just seems like Dr. Funk is everywhere and nowhere," he responded.

"Well," Sheryl said, "it don't matter. No one's talked to him in years, right? He left the wake like a ghost. We can't help who we can't find."

"There's a bit more," Harriett went on. "*If my heirs are able to help Dr. Funk in any way, a bond of $50,000 held in escrow will be released to them.*"

"What?" Sheryl cried out, staring at the lawyer as if she was crazy.

"Were Dr. Funk and your father that close?" Harriett asked.

"They were friends and all, but I didn't think they were boon coons," Sheryl said. "That Dr. Funk is a grown-ass man. Why do we need to take care of him? That money should come to us free and clear. Anyway, who decides when we've given enough help?"

Harriett glanced down at the papers. "Well, it says Dr. Funk does."

"This is crazy!" Sheryl was fuming, as if her dead father had kept her from going to the prom. "What do you think about this, D?"

While Dr. Funk was a great artist, D couldn't understand either. Big Danny's cash reward was a powerful inducement to make sure his progeny would look out for Dr. Funk despite their better judgment.

"Wills are a strange beast," Harriett said. "Your parents reveal things to you after they're gone that they could have told you before they went. But people are always in denial. Even on their deathbed, they figure they'll have one more day."

CHAPTER THIRTEEN

THE RELENTLESS BEAT

D hadn't read *The Relentless Beat* in several years. It was almost like hearing Dwayne Robinson talk to him again, except there were no *motherfuckers*, *niggas*, or *bitch-ass niggas* tossed in between the intellectual philosophizing. D looked at the title page where Dwayne had inscribed this copy for his grandfather: *Thanks for the knowledge and laughs.* He had interviewed Big Danny for the book and two-thirds of his commentary hadn't made it into the book "for legal reasons." There was actually a pretty long passage on Heaven's Gate in the chapter on LA in the eighties. On this night, though, D was on his grandfather's sofa reading the chapter on Dr. Funk:

> *Any close inspection of funk music makes clear that this profound black music movement was a merging of James Brown grit, hippie escapism, Eastern religion, free-flowing psychedelic drugs, incipient black nationalism, and big-band horn arrangements that was unique to a particular cultural moment. It was freaky, optimistic, spiritual, angry, spacey, political, self-confident music full of bands led by charismatic figures who bonded a community of musicians and creatives (clothing designers, graphic artists, shamans). Sly Stone, Maurice White, George Clinton are all celebrated as leaders, catalysts, innovators, and dreamers. Perhaps just below them in the pantheon of funk (an observation sure to cause debate) was Maurice Stewart,*

a.k.a. Dr. Funk, whose band the Love Patrol could, depending on the night, rival the J.B.'s. Then again, the next night they could be as experimental as the Sun Ra Arkestra. On one classic LP, Chaos: Phase I, they found the perfect balance of accessibility and invention, setting a standard they never would quite reach again.

Maurice Stewart was born in Memphis, raised in Oakland, and came of age in LA. So the blues and gospel of the South, the progressive thinking of the Bay, and the glittery impulses of Hollywood all formed him. His mother was a music teacher and Sunday school organist. His father was a jack-of-all-trades and master-of-none kind of guy who sold Bibles, drove taxis, short-order cooked, ran numbers, picked up garbage, mopped up buildings, and did whatever other honest blue-collar jobs he could find. His father also sang like Johnny Hartman and belted out Larry Graham's "One in a Million You" like he owned it. So Stewart grew up around several musical traditions within his hardworking itinerant family.

By sixteen he was sneaking into clubs on Crenshaw like Heaven's Gate, becoming a mascot for the musicians, comics, and dancers who frequented those joints. Through those connections Stewart became a regular dancer on Soul Train, and that community of dancers became the backbone of his flamboyant performing troupe.

While attending Los Angeles Community College, Stewart gathered a gang of musicians, dancers, and nonconformists into a group called Funk Unlimited. After graduation, he became a host at Heaven's Gate, which was by then a go-to black celebrity hangout. Stewart shined as he engaged folks in conversation and slipped copies of his demo in the hands of record executives, building a buzz for his growing musical aggregation.

Warner Bros., the Burbank-based label that entered R&B with

Graham Central Station, George Benson, and Ashford & Simp-
son, gave him a deal with immense creative freedom years before
they signed Prince. His first two LPs, Funkin' with the One and
Limits of Control, scraped past goal. But his third, Chaos: Phase
I, released just as big-band funk was giving way to drum machines
and computerized keys, was a grand synthesis of progressive black
music's past and present.

It had hit singles like the joyous "Venus Rises" and the sexy
"Pleasure," but the real magic was in the DNA of the LP, through
album cuts like the majestic, gospel-tinged "Water on the River," the
cleverly arranged "Follow My Heart," and the epic title cut, eight
and a half minutes of funky jazz and soul wailing that immediately
became the centerpiece of Dr. Funk's live show, an unmatched amal-
gam of P-Funk craziness and Earth, Wind & Fire precision.

For the two years following Chaos: Phase I, Dr. Funk and the
Love Patrol were at the peak of the mountain, selling out arenas and
bucking the trends in black music for smaller bands, totally electro
sounds, and the streetwise orientation of rap. It was a glorious balancing act Dr. Funk was pulling off, but eventually he, and it, tipped over.

There has been a lot of tabloid fodder provided by the dissolu-
tion of Dr. Funk and Love Patrol over the years. Drugs, debauchery,
lawsuits, bad haircuts, and mental illness have all plagued him over
the last few decades. If you want the dirty details, TV One's Un-
sung will surely do an episode at some point. But if you care about
the direction of black music, Dr. Funk looms large as a profound
influence on all musicians who've followed in his path. I believe that
one day, as with James Brown and George Clinton, his music will be
rediscovered and his legacy redefined.

So Heaven's Gate figured prominently in Dr. Funk's story. *It's probably why he was able to get in and out without being photographed*, D thought. He and Big Danny must really have been closer than Aunt Sheryl knew. Much closer.

CHAPTER FOURTEEN
SALESMANSHIP AT SOHO HOUSE

Whenever D traveled across Sunset Boulevard, between Vine and Crescent Heights, from Hollywood to West Hollywood, he always noticed the homeless men who haunted its streets, talking to themselves, yelling to the sky (or at passing cars), usually topless in the sun, often pulling a shopping cart, or lying down by a clump of possessions as dingy as their shoeless feet.

Unlike New York, a healthy percentage of these men were white, their skin as red and raw as their black comrades were inky and bronze. D thought homelessness was one of the few forms of Los Angeles existence where black folks were on somewhat equal footing with their white brothers. D wondered if he could find Dr. Funk on a Hollywood street if he looked hard enough, the man's genius camouflaged by dirty, unkempt hair, and the blanket of invisibility walking in LA bestowed on pedestrians.

From what D had gathered, Dr. Funk had no fixed address, regular cell number, or e-mail address. He apparently used burners to return business calls on rare occasions. There was a recent sighting out at the Third Street Promenade in Santa Monica, one of several fleeting musical appearances by a man who once filled arenas with song.

The valet crew at Soho House loved Big Danny's Electra 225, though one of the guys mentioned the bullet hole in the passenger side to his partners in Spanish, thinking D wouldn't understand. Up an ele-

vator and then up a staircase, D entered a wide room that was the heart
of new Hollywood. Because of LA's geography, this private club, located
on the edge of West Hollywood and Beverly Hills, had become the
go-to gathering spot for legit Hollywood players (especially producers
and writers), aligned industries (music, advertising, design), and wannabe men and women of every ambition.

Walking past the long bar and surveying the expensive sofas artfully
arranged around the room, D saw a lot of familiar Botoxed faces from
back in the day. It made him smile. In Los Angeles, relocated New York
players rebooted themselves as producers, TV personalities, lifestyle
coaches, and even gurus of new age wisdom. Los Angeles, compared to
East Coast and Midwest metropolises, felt like a place where the past
was face-lift fleeting.

Sitting in a corner with an expansive view of smog-drenched Downtown behind him, Walter Gibbs faced a slim, chic brunette with blond
highlights. Gibbs had been one of D Security's first serious clients. In
the nineties, Gibbs had been a full-fledged music mogul when hip hop
had overwhelmed R&B, dismissed rock, and gripped out pop's jugular.
D did whatever Gibbs needed done. Protecting rap stars from other rap
stars: got it. Guarding ingénue singers from predatory hustlers: D was
on it. Protecting master tapes from counterfeiters: copy that.

And then Napster appeared in 1999, and all the air seeped out of
Gibbs's balloon. Within three years he, his label, and his management
company were all gasping for breath. So were all his peers. The record
industry strategy of suing customers for downloading was a dead man's
last gasp.

But Gibbs hadn't risen from working-class Queens to a Manhattan
penthouse without street smarts. He'd learned quickly, while promoting
hip hop, that the truth was in the streets and not offices in Midtown

Manhattan. Before most of his peers, Gibbs realized that the new streets were cyberspace.

Gibbs was on Myspace two days after it launched. Instead of suing his customers, Gibbs turned his attention to buying shares in sites that impacted music. Everybody did it now, but Gibbs was there first. Moreover, he no longer just sought out young producers with the hottest joints; he also wooed kids who coded. These, in his opinion, were the new beat-makers. Gibbs leaped into the digital pool and came out looking photo-shoot fresh.

Gibbs downsized his label, using it primarily to manage the catalog (and clear samples), and launched a couple of websites (the most successful of which was www.hiphopluxury.com). The transactional sites kept up the cash flow, as did flipping property in quickly gentrifying Brooklyn. Most significantly, Gibbs gave up on New York. He told friends it made him feel old ("all that history") and dabbled in films and TV, getting an output deal with Netflix for comedy specials and super-low-budget gangsta-themed flicks. In LA, Gibbs knew you were always just a testosterone shot, vegan meal, and hot yoga class away from rejuvenation.

Relaxed in Cali, Gibbs could run game all day long. At Soho House on Sunset, he would lock down a sofa around eleven a.m. and eyeball the room for his next partner.

D slipped onto the sofa next to Gibbs as he talked to Shelia Lynch, the brunette with long legs, a short dress, and a vaguely Middle Eastern accent. The entrepreneur was leaning toward her and explaining his philosophy.

"Sometimes your success is best defined by your enemies," he said. "Pick up the right haters and your core fans embrace you more; their love for you grows in intensity as you are attacked. It what's helped hip hop when Bob Dole and others attacked us. It helped Donald Trump when the mainstream GOP went after him. It's a very useful tool."

"I see," Shelia replied, then glanced over at D. "Is this the friend you were waiting on?"

"Shelia, this is D Hunter, the best bodyguard in the game and a fan of the color black."

"You're in law enforcement?"

"No," D said flatly.

"D doesn't need a gun or a badge," Gibbs said. "He's streetwise. Very little escapes his eye. He's as smart as a laptop and slick as a custom suit. But what really makes him great is that he truly cares about the people he works for. He treats and treasures them like family."

"Thanks for saying that, Walter."

"No doubt. He's protected me from hurting people many times. I mean, I hit hard, Shelia. So I need the Mount Rushmore of bodyguards to have my back."

"You must be a versatile man. Making deals and a street fighter too." D couldn't tell if she was buying what he was selling or being sarcastic. She had a blank smile but her eyes twinkled. Then Shelia turned her attention back to D. "Weren't you in a video on YouTube?"

"Uh-huh. Something got up there. Yeah. My grandfather's funeral." D wanted to excuse himself and maybe go to the restroom or something. That damn video. Fortunately, Shelia's phone rang and she excused herself to the terrace to take the call.

"Thanks for the wonderful introduction, Walter, though it feels like I'm about to retire."

"There's no retiring, D. What would you do? What would *I* do? We're sharks in the water. Who's bleeding? My next meal."

"You mean *deal*."

"I mean *meal*. A deal is just a means to feed you and your family. It's some primal shit. You gotta accumulate chips for when your cash flow dips."

"Walter, your cash flow hasn't dipped in twenty years."

"Oh, don't be fooled, D. Success is an illusion. If you really have two cents and they think you have four quarters, then you have four quarters and people are more likely to give you more. That's really true out here. Everybody's fronting. They're leasing what you think they own. They're being sponsored when you think they're paying. They got a Rolls but they're living on the wrong side of Venice. I know this game. I love this game."

Shelia came back from the terrace. "What are you doing tonight, Walter?"

"Nothing more important than what you're inviting me to."

"There's a cocktail party in Malibu hosted by my business associate Teddy Tapscott. I know he'd be overjoyed for you to attend. And D, please feel free to join us. I'm sure you'd know a few people there."

"If Walter would give me a lift I'd be happy to attend," D replied.

"You must have mad charisma, D, cause very few men in LA get an immediate party invite from Teddy Tapscott. I've been waiting on mine for months."

"Walter, please," she said. "Your social calendar is pretty full from what I've seen."

"Quantity, yes," he admitted, "but what about quality?" Gibbs reached over and touched Shelia's knee and squeezed. "Quality is rare."

This rap sounded incredibly corny to D, but Walter Gibbs had an insincere charm, a way of acknowledging he was full of shit while being earnest in his desire, a technique that had seduced women on both coasts and many a Midwestern city. Shelia tapped his hand as if scolding him but didn't remove it. In that moment an unspoken agreement was made to have sex one day.

When Shelia left (actually, she just moved to another sofa on the other side of the room for her four thirty meeting), D said to Gibbs, "You never learn."

"Why should I learn? I'm free, black, and fifty-plus. The fact that I'm alive and have more than three cents in the bank is a motherfucking miracle. So me trying to fuck everything that moves at this point is a victory lap."

"For a chanting motherfucker, you are still so scandalous."

"Nawn, D. I'm just present. Incredibly present."

CHAPTER FIFTEEN

R'KAYDIA'S MALIBU SOIREE

The house was one of the Malibu spots that, from the Pacific Coast Highway, was just a wall with an elegant door and a buzzer. Behind that wall was a walkway that led to a beautiful white house with big glass windows, elegant external lighting, and foliage imported from across the country.

Inside, next to one of Basquiat's jazz-inspired paintings (this one saluted Louis Armstrong), D found himself in a huddle with Walter Gibbs and Teddy Tapscott, a white man in an expensive suit.

"I've heard of you, D," Teddy Tapscott said.

"Really?"

"You're the Johnny Cash of security. The man in black."

"Okay, I guess that's me."

Gibbs said, "D runs one of the finest security services in the entertainment business."

"You've done a lot of work for Amos Pilgrim."

"I've worked with his client Night, who I consider a great friend. I don't actually work for Pilgrim."

"That's very specific of you, D," Tapscott said. "You sound like a lawyer the way you just split that hair."

"Clarity is a good thing, right?"

"Absolutely, D. Have you moved to LA?"

"My grandfather just passed so I'm out here with the family."

"His grandfather was a pioneering black businessman," Gibbs said in that hypey way he had.

"You should relocate," Tapscott opined. "Lots of work out here for someone in the safety business."

"Safety," a woman's voice interjected. "None of you look safe to me."

Tapscott turned in the direction of the voice and said, "No one is when you're around."

A tall, lean black woman in a sky-blue dress, reddish tanned skin, a ruby necklace, and beige Louboutin shoes strode toward them. She was slim but her shoulders and arms had the taut muscle of a dancer. Her hair was cut Halle Berry short, with amber highlights that played off her copper tone. She had an entitled FOO (Friend of Oprah) swagger. With a glass of white wine in one hand and her other arm swaying under the weight of a glittering gold bracelet, she appeared totally at home and completely judgmental. All the men save D seemed to genuflect, either intimidated by her regal aura or just wisely bowing to the queen. Her name was R'Kaydia Lelilia Jenkins. You could call her Kay when she was feeling generous. But in her mind she was "the R" and she carried herself with the confidence of a Rakim rhyme.

"Mr. Hunter," she said, "you may be the first viral security guard."

"Well . . ." He fumbled a moment for something to say. Finally: "I guess that must be true. That certainly wasn't my goal in life."

R'Kaydia's voice darkened: "It is a tragedy what happened to your grandfather. Have the police made any progress?"

"Not much," D said, unclear where she was coming from or why.

Teddy cleared his throat. Eyes in the circle shifted his way. "R'Kaydia and I were so surprised to see Dr. Funk at your grandfather's wake. They must have been close."

"I knew they had a relationship," D said, "but we had no idea he'd show up. Much less sing."

"Deeply moving, D," she said unconvincingly. "There's no reason to feel shy about your tears. I cried myself when I watched it on YouTube." D doubted that was true but forced a smile.

Teddy cleared his throat again but this time D didn't turn his way. Clearly dude was a puppet. He watched R'Kaydia to see how she pulled his strings.

"It's ironic, actually," Teddy said, "because R'Kaydia and I have been trying to get in touch with him for some time."

"Really?" Gibbs said, finally seeing an opening. "Maybe I can be of service."

"What a sweet offer, Walter," R'Kaydia said, though her eyes shouted, *Fuck off, dude!*

Teddy picked up her cue: "D, we were wondering if you could help us."

"D," R'Kaydia said, continuing the verbal dance, "Teddy and myself are quite interested in helping some of the greats who have either been forgotten or exploited in the past. Dr. Funk was a crucial part of all our lives."

Tapscott added, "I believe there's an incredible movie in his story. I worked on *Straight Outta Compton,* and you saw how well that performed."

"It's not just about a movie," R'Kaydia said. "It's about legacy. How is someone remembered? How is their story framed? Would you take a meeting with us, D?"

"Sounds interesting," he said, trying to sound neutral.

"Good," she replied while touching his arm. "We'll be in contact."

A nicely tanned couple walked up and exchanged kisses and hugs with Teddy and R'Kaydia as the conversation shifted to ski trips to Aspen and the deteriorating Cali shoreline.

D drifted away to the windows and gazed out at the Malibu surf, savoring the Pacific sky and this fleeting taste of privilege. It sure helped to have money if you wanted to enjoy nature. Gibbs then came up next to him, his champagne having given way to a gin and tonic. "So," Gibbs said smoothly, "I see a payday in your future."

"I got a feeling R'Kaydia and her man see one too," D replied.

"Exactly, though I'm not sure that's all they have in mind. But whatever it is, they aren't thinking of breaking me off a piece."

D laughed at the truth of that.

Gibbs continued: "Which means there must be more money in it than I know. Please keep me in the loop, D. You will need a consultant on any deal with those two."

"Believe me," D said, "I'm not signing anything they offer me without your beady eyes in on it."

Gibbs took in the beach and the sky and their glitzy surroundings. "A long way from Brooklyn, right?"

D was happy to be there but remained far from seduced. "You know, it's not really that far. Wherever you go and whoever you meet, there's always a hustle."

"The question is, who's being hustled and who's the hustler?"

D turned to look Gibbs in the eye. "I know you know the answer, my man."

"Word."

"Okay," D said. "Now, can we get the fuck outta here?"

"Not until I find Shelia and discuss the benefits of tantric yoga."

CHAPTER SIXTEEN
MICHELLE PAK INTRODUCES HERSELF

D sat out alone on the porch of Big Danny's house, sipping apple juice and watching cars. It was one of those rare days when his regular all-black attire was sadly on point. The funeral had been, in contrast to the wake, a traditional affair: an old church, proper deacons, women in crowns, a hearty choir. Despite the urging of his aunt Sheryl, D hadn't spoken. After his brothers' funerals in Brooklyn, he had run out of pious things to say and quoting scripture wasn't his thing.

D felt further unnerved because Sheryl had received an e-mail from his father, which said he was on his way to LA from wherever he was in South America. D wondered if he might overlap with his wayward father this time and, if so, where their conversation would start.

He was contemplating his tragic childhood when a gray Lexus and a large moving van pulled up next door at the Jacksons' old house. A curvy Korean woman about thirty exited the Lexus, conservatively dressed except for red horn-rimmed glasses. She walked over to the *For Sale* sign and plucked it off the lawn.

Three movers exited the truck's cabin and hit the ground running. They were Central American men with sturdy, squat bodies and lifting belts around their midsections. With military efficiency, they carried sofas, chairs, and boxes into the house.

Soon a late-model car rolled up the street and into the driveway. There was a small Mexican flag decal on the front window. A family of five got out—a rough-looking father, a portly mama, and three boys all under ten years old. The mother gave the Korean woman a grateful hug, the father supervised the unloading, and the three boys scampered underfoot, anxious to be part of the action.

The Korean woman noticed D sitting there, said something to the Mexican mother, and crossed the lawn and the driveway until she was right in front of Big Danny's porch. "Excuse me, my name is Michelle Pak. Are you part of the Hunter family?"

D introduced himself as Big Danny's grandson.

"Oh, please accept my deepest condolences. My family knew your grandfather very well. They owned stores in the same area that he did. My mother and father both spoke very highly of him."

"That's nice," D said. "He was a good man."

"Can I give you my card?"

"Okay," he said as she walked up to the porch. One side of her card said, *Pak City Real Estate*, with *K-Pak Groceries* on the other.

"You are busy," D said.

"Family business, you know," she responded, seeming both embarrassed and proud.

Good timing, D thought. *And kinda thick.* "You're interested in this place?"

"Well," she said, "whenever you're ready, please let me know. Again, my condolences."

D watched her walk off and then shouted, "Hey, Michelle, what are the names of our new neighbors?"

"Pedro and Miriam Fuentes."

"Thanks," he said as she entered the house next door.

The Central American movers were in the homestretch and D watched two of the Fuentes boys struggling to carry an accordion up the walkway.

Walli stuck his head out of the door. "Ma wants you to come inside and say a few words."

D frowned. "That's really not my thing, Walli. She knows that."

"Nothing spiritual or anything, D. She just wants you to get these people to leave. She really wants to get some sleep."

"Kicking people out a place," D said as he stood up, "*that* I can do."

CHAPTER SEVENTEEN

WESTSIDE CONNECTION TO DOWNTOWN

D, Walli, and Red Dawg sat inside the sneaker shop with bottles of Tecate, sipping and talking. D had stopped by in hopes of rebuilding his relationship with Red Dawg and to see how the hunt for Teo Garcia's head was going. Walli was there, helping to organize the shelves after school, so D didn't get into any of Red Dawg's theories. Instead the conversation shifted onto seemingly neutral ground—hip hop. But no parlay about MCs was ever without drama.

"It's all about flow for me," D said. "People focus on the accent, but the MCs I respect have great flow. I feel like Snoop was the first West Coast MC to really flow. When I found out he was a serious R&B fan it made sense. He was really musical even when he was talking about cappin' a fool. *Unfadeable / so please don't try to fade this.*"

"So Snoop's in your top five?" Walli asked.

"Yeah," D said, "if push came to shove he'd be right there. What's your top five?"

Walli said, "Lil Wayne. Tupac. Kendrick. Rick Ross. Drake, I guess."

"Drake?" D said incredulously. "I hate Drake, though I did like 'Hotline Bling.'"

Red Dawg said, "I respect Drake. He has some bars. But he's always whining about some bitch he got or some bitch he wants or some bitch he needs. I mean, damn, nigga, get a new topic."

"I don't mind that," D said. "After all, rappers have been getting paid off lyrical murder for years. I mean, they perfected that out here. But what I can't stand is Drake's voice. You can talk about women all day and all night, but his voice just irritates me. And when he puts that Auto-Tune on it—ahhh."

"Everyone does that," Walli said. "I'm used to it."

"But Drake uses it to *sing*," D said.

"You call that singing?" Red Dawg scoffed.

"It's what passes for R&B these days," D complained. "MCs sing very simple melodies. It's what my man Night is up against. People get used to Drake singing his three Auto-Tune notes. People today don't even know how to act when someone can actually sing. It's like he's from another planet . . . Walli, do you care about Night?"

"I mean, he sounds okay. He doesn't really put out music anymore, does he?"

"Not often enough."

"He's your friend and all," Red Dawg said, "so I know he's paying a bill or two for you, but Night don't mean shit. Not anymore. Not for years. By the way, you didn't ask me *my* top five."

"You feel left out?"

"Shit, D, my list is more legit than this kid's list."

"How's that?" Walli asked.

"Cause I was up on the rap game before you were born, and I actually rocked a mic or two. You got Drake in your top five. That shows me you haven't listened enough to know the real deal. Plus you're from LA, but the only local MC you got reppin' your city is Lamar. I got Cube number one. Fatlip of the Pharcayde. MC Ren, who is the most underrated dude to come out of LA. The Game, who, to me, is the real Kendrick Lamar, and Mack motherfucking 10."

D nearly fell out of his seat. "Mack 10? C'mon, man. I love that you shouted out Ren. 'If It Ain't Ruff' is a dope track. But Mack 10? You might as well have said Above the Law."

"They're in my top ten," Red Dawg countered.

"That's crazy. Too much Cali love. Walli, do you even know who Mack 10 is?"

"Not really."

"See, D, that's why his list is so weak. He don't know his LA legacy."

"Mack 10?" D said. "Mack 10 isn't even on Mack 10's list. People who really love Ice Cube try to forget he was even in the Westside Connection. Mack 10 is to Ice Cube as Memphis Bleek is to Jay-Z. In other words—what the fuck!"

"Who is Memphis Bleek?" Walli asked.

"Don't worry," D said to him. "He's an MC Jay-Z tried to make a star. But it didn't happen. Look him up if you like, but don't expect much."

"Walli, you need to get up on the Westside Connection," Red Dawg said. "That's real LA hip hop." His cell then rang out with the beat from the Game's "Hate It or Love It." "Time to roll. Walli and I gotta make a run. D, you wanna come? We could use your back."

"Yeah? What kind of run?"

"Downtown," Red Dawg said. "Way downtown."

Red Dawg's van was tricked out with a multicolored mural of Aztec warriors and African tribesmen shaking hands and looking fierce, which made his ride the definition of *not inconspicuous*.

As they started off, Red Dawg plugged in some LA hip hop. He pushed a couple of buttons and the sound of the Westside Connection's

"Bow Down" filled the car. "It's hittin', right?" Red Dawg said. He began to rhyme along: *"Don't fuck with my stack / the gage is racked / about to drop the bomb / I am the motherfucking don."*

"Is this really the first time Red Dawg has shared the glories of the Westside Connection with you?" D asked Walli.

"He's played them before, but I think having you here has hyped him up."

"I don't appreciate you two talking like I'm not here. I mean, this is classic shit." And with that, Red Dawg turned the music up higher and began rhyming along again: *"The Westside connects with me and South Central / And a drag from the zigzag can't fuck with the Philly's."*

Red Dawg drove east on 3rd Street through the heart of Koreatown and then Pico-Union, where business signs appeared in English, Spanish, and Korean. Next they moved past the Staples Center where fans in red and blue were heading to a late-season Clippers game while a few blocks away a self-consciously hip clientele entered the Ace Hotel. When the new condos and gentrified blocks fell away, the car entered Skid Row, and the grim reality of sunbaked, sad-eyed men.

Red Dawg made a left on San Julian Street and guided the car through an alley, stopping next to a battered green door. He sent a text, then said, "Hear how good this is," as he replayed "Bow Down" for the fifth time on their trip.

"Please turn it off," Walli said.

Red Dawg just chuckled in response.

Then a frail middle-aged Asian man in a gray shirt stepped through the green door. He observed them while pulling on his cigarette like a blunt. He nodded at Red and then went back inside, leaving the door unlocked.

"Let's go," Red Dawg said.

D followed Walli and Red through the door and into a storeroom lined from floor to ceiling with boxes. Another skinny Asian man stood next to a handcart piled to his shoulder with boxes that read, *Nike, Adidas, Converse*.

At Red Dawg's request, D pushed the cart out the door while he stayed inside. D and Walli stacked shoe boxes into the trunk and, once that was filled, slid what remained in the backseat.

"How often do you do this?" D asked.

"Depends on how the merchandise is moving," Walli replied, sounding like a veteran retailer.

"Is this one of Big Danny's contacts?"

"I think so. When Red Dawg said he wanted to sell sneakers I know Granddad helped him get it going."

D rolled the cart back into the storeroom and saw Red Dawg and the first Asian man sitting at a table, poring over images of sneakers and talking. Beyond the storeroom he heard a K-pop female vocal group over the speakers. A thirtysomething Asian woman wearing reading glasses surveyed a spreadsheet on her laptop and tapped a foot to the electroboogie beat.

"Let's roll," Red Dawg said, and D followed him out, giving a respectful head nod to the man at the table.

"How's about some Korean barbecue?" Red Dawg asked. "My treat."

"Sounds good," D said.

"But no more Westside Connection," Walli said.

"So what you want to hear?"

"Dâm-Funk."

"Who the hell is that?"

"He's an LA musician," D replied. "He's been playing on the underground scene here for a while. Did an album with Snoop a couple years ago."

"He does a party here called Funkmosphere," Walli added.

"If you can find his music, we'll play that shit," Red Dawg said.

As Walli leaned into the front of the car to manipulate the Internet radio, D said, "So, Red Dawg, this is how you stay in business? Moving counterfeit kicks?"

"I used to buy from the Chinese, but now the Koreans give me a better price, plus they're nicer to deal with."

"My grandpa hook you up?"

"You know Big Danny had serious connects with the Koreans. When I felt like the Chinese were jerking me on price, he hooked me up through some woman he knew."

"Wasn't he killed after leaving a Korean grocery?"

"Yeah," Red Dawg said quickly. "Someone followed him outta that store. I feel that. But believe me, them Koreans loved Big Danny. It was Teo Garcia who did the deed."

Walli located an electrofunk jam from the *7 Days of Funk* EP that Dâm-Funk and Snoop Dogg had released, and the spacey sound filled the car. Red Dawg shifted in his seat. D and Walli traded amused looks.

After about thirty seconds, Red Dawg asked, "You wanna know what I think?"

"No," Walli said, then laughed along with D, who savored the small moment of bonding with his young cousin.

They parked in the back of the sneaker store and began unloading Red Dawg's illegal cargo. It was sundown in LA, the sky a pastel painting of blue and purple. When they were finished, D asked for the keys to Big Danny's grocery store.

"What?" Red Dawg said. "You need some milk?"

"When I came by before I just wanted to help clean up. Now I want to take a closer look around."

"What for? I told you who did it."

Walli came over and stood beside Red Dawg, his placement in the room communicating where his loyalties lay.

"Do we have a problem?" D asked. "I can get the keys from my aunt if I have to, though then I'd really start wondering why you don't want me in there alone."

Red Dawg pulled out his key ring, fiddled with it a bit, and removed three large keys. He placed them roughly in the palm of D's hand. "Have a good time, grandson."

"You want me to come inside with you?" It was Walli.

D shook his head. "I remember where the alarm is."

"The code is 424242," Walli said.

At the grocery store Red Dawg and Walli stood behind D, Red Dawg with his arms folded Run-DMC style, while D unlocked the door. He nodded toward the window where, in black and gray paint, the number *18* had been sprayed over the words *Big Danny's*. D rubbed the numbers with his fingertip, which caused them to smear. Still fresh.

"Okay," D said to Red Dawg, "what's it mean?"

"The 18th Street Gang. A Central American posse from, I think, El Salvador. They're rivals with the Mexican mafia. I guess they wanna expand."

"Why would they put this on Big Danny's window?"

"How am I supposed to know?"

"And that's it? That's all you got?"

"You got a smartphone," Red Dawg said. "Google them. I got some kicks to sell."

Walli looked at his cousin, shrugged, and walked away.

D turned on the lights and walked down the center aisle by himself, past the counter and into the back room, where he switched off the alarm. The air in the back was heavy and full of dust. D sneezed and then sat down behind his grandfather's desk. Before searching around he felt compelled to find out more about the 18th Street Gang. He spent fifteen minutes on Google and YouTube, but none of this new information made him happy. Also known as Calle 18, they were a transnational criminal organization that started in the Rampart area of Los Angeles and had tentacles in every kind of violent and illegal activity under the sun. Extortion was one of their major businesses. Had his grandfather run afoul of them? Had they killed him because he was somehow in their way?

D wanted Big Danny to be a benign Robin Hood. But was his loan-sharking just a cover for meaner deeds and darker alliances? Why else would a seventy-year-old man get gatted like a rap star?

Tacked to a corkboard above Big Danny's desk were fading Polaroids of he and his late wife, a shot of D's father as a little boy in a Dodgers cap, and photo from a Leimert Park barbecue. There was a framed photo of Big Danny with all four of his grandsons taken in front of a Christmas tree in the family's Brooklyn housing project living room. Rah, Jah, Matty, and D (then known to everyone by his given name, Dervin) surrounded Big Danny. Everyone in the photo was now dead—except D.

In the top drawers were the bric-a-brac of precomputer retail: ledger books, vendor brochures for signage and refrigerators, business cards, Bic pens, #2 pencils, W-2 forms, business certificates from LA County, takeout Thai food menus, a pocket calculator, and an LA Lakers calendar from 2009.

In a lower drawer D found a green lockbox. There was no key nearby but D was able to pick it with a credit card. Inside was a Beretta. He popped out the bullet from the chamber and unloaded the clip, finding three more bullets inside. Underneath the gun he found a firearms license and below it the deeds to Big Danny's home, the grocery store, and Heaven's Gate.

At the bottom of the lockbox was another Polaroid. Big Danny sat with one arm around a comely Korean woman and the other hand holding a forkful of kimchi. She had straight black hair, a round face, small full lips, and big, shrewd eyes behind square, businesslike glasses. She smiled demurely at the camera. The woman's face seemed familiar but D couldn't quite conjure a name or a context. The date stamp on the back read, *April 28, 1992.*

D pocketed the gun and the photo, placing everything else back in the lockbox, which he held under his arm as he walked back toward the front door. Why was that photo under the gun? Who was this woman? Did he really know a damn thing about Big Danny Hunter?

CHAPTER EIGHTEEN
BREAK-IN AT BIG DANNY'S

D heard the sound of feet moving quietly behind Big Danny's house. He was lying on the living room sofa in the dark, almost asleep. His body tensed as he rolled off the sofa and crawled quickly into the kitchen. There were whispers outside the back door. In the darkness, he felt around for the drawer where Aunt Sheryl kept the knives. The cabinets had been painted over enough times so that, despite D's care, they didn't open smoothly, rattling silverware as the back door cracked open. Instead of a knife, D found himself with a large spoon in his hand.

Light from the moon illuminated the intruder's face. He was twentyish and Latino with a small tat on his right cheek and a mustache. When he opened the back door D jammed the point of the spoon into the intruder's neck. The man's tongue popped out and his eyes closed. D smelled alcohol on the man's breath when he cracked him with a left hook to his nose.

The guy stumbled backward into a second intruder, and they both dropped onto the grass behind the house. D leaped out the door, landing with both knees onto the chest of the first man. Boozy air escaped his lungs.

The second intruder rolled a few feet away and scrambled to his feet. He was darker than his partner, much slimmer, and had a young man's sneer. D noticed the intruder's NASCAR T-shirt as he reached behind his back. D ran at him, hoping he'd get flustered. But this guy was coolheaded, pulling out his Glock and aiming at D's chest.

D yelled at the top of his lungs to make the man hesitate just long enough so that he could tackle him, knocking the gun and the would-be shooter to the grass. Once he had him down, D pounded his face till his knuckles turned bloody.

"D!" It was his cousin. "Shit!"

"Call the cops!"

"Ma is doing that!"

D used his T-shirt to pick up the Glock and slip it in his underwear band. He found a Beretta, masking tape, and plastic police handcuffs on the first man. He was a few years older than his crime companion, and beefy in all the wrong places. These were not the most fearsome gangbangers D had ever seen. Not even close.

Twenty minutes later D was talking to an African American patrolman named Crowder. "The Mexican gangs have been pushing black folks out of our neighborhoods for a while now. They try to scare folks into selling cheap. Word is that some members of Calle 18 are buying up property out here. I think those two might be down with them."

"That's what's happening around here?" D didn't mention the graffiti on his grandfather's store.

"Anywhere black folks are, they're on the run in this town," Crowder said. "They could have been hired by a realtor or a neighbor. Make the niggas run and get our homes cheap. Bring the relations in or sell it to Central Americans, since they're the low man on the pole these days."

Crowder was fit for forty-five, with hints of gray in his short Afro. He was friendly for an LA cop (or maybe just chatty). His partner Exley, a younger white cop with brown hair, stood by the patrol car, more interested in checking Instagram on his phone than talking with D or the two perps in his backseat.

"I'm sorry about Big D."

"You knew him?"

"He was around a long time. Met him when I was a rook. Last of the old heads in the hood."

"You think this is related to his murder?"

"I dunno," the black cop said slowly. "I don't get paid to investigate murder—just to pick up the bodies and file reports. But these *vatos* move in packs. So if this is just a random break-in, you're probably good. Your statement made sense. You'll be a good witness. But if this is related to your granddad's death, then you need to keep your head up. I'll check in with the detective on the case. He may have questions for your visitors."

Aunt Sheryl sat in the kitchen with a glass of apple juice and a burning cigarette. Walli sat across from her, looking nervous if only half awake. She wore a cranberry-colored robe and a black hairnet. He wore a white T-shirt that swallowed up his body.

She was saying, ". . . These rice-and-bean-eating motherfuckers need to get their asses back south of the border."

"This was just two criminals, Ma," Walli volunteered. "Not all Mexicans are like this."

She wasn't impressed by her son's logic. "They hate on black people. Like that's gonna help them. It just makes us hate them. And that's too bad, because I like me some guacamole." It was a bad joke but it amused her son, who needed a distraction. "Glad you didn't let them in the house," she said to D. "Just need to fix the lock on that one there. Daddy would have let them in. He would have let them walk right into this kitchen and shot them with his twelve-gauge. You know we got one if you need it."

"We have two, Ma," Walli said.

"Two shotguns?"

"Two guns," she explained. "A shotgun and a Beretta."

"Where'd he keep them?"

"One's right here," she said as she reached under the table, flicked a latch, and pulled out a shotgun. Aunt Sheryl held it proudly, reminding D of Pam Grier in a blaxploitation flick. "The handgun is upstairs under Big Danny's bed." She sent her son to go get it.

"Why all the guns?"

"Well, two guns ain't a lot out here, D."

"I found another one at his store. That's three. But I guess that's normal for someone in retail in LA. Guns laws are different out here, I guess."

Walli came down with the Beretta and handed it to D, who found a full clip. He smelled the barrel. Recently fired.

"Does Red Dawg borrow these?"

"I don't know," Aunt Sheryl replied. "Why would he?"

"Red has his own guns, D," Walli said. "He, Granddad, and I would go to a range downtown maybe once a month. Maybe we could go soon? I enjoyed it, though that shotgun has a serious kick."

Thirty minutes, two text messages, and a phone call later, the back door slowly opened. All eyes turned to Red Dawg as he surveyed the busted lock. "Crude but effective," he said before entering. He took a seat at the table and picked up the Beretta, spinning it on a finger, gunslinger-style. "Can you give me some details, D?" After hearing D's story, Red Dawg asked if he got a good look at their tats.

"Not really. I mean, I saw them but they wouldn't have meant shit to me. What about you, Walli?"

"I think they were 18th Street."

Red Dawg slammed his hand on the table.

"Is that the gang that Teo Garcia belongs to?"

"Hell yeah," Red Dawg said triumphantly. "He's definitely affiliated."

"Why does that matter?" Aunt Sheryl asked.

Red Dawg explained his theory of Big Danny's death.

"So you think that fool would have people come kill us too?" she asked, putting out her cigarette and immediately lighting another.

"Maybe," Red Dawg said, "but I'll handle that."

D leaned forward and glanced from Red Dawg to Aunt Sheryl. "Before this goes any further, I think someone had better get real with me. You have a professional hit on Granddad. A real pro job. Not some weak-ass burglary like tonight. I know that Big Danny was doing some shady shit, but I'm wondering how deep this really gets. I don't like living blind, but right now I'm looking and I'm not really seeing. Can someone in this room please help me?"

Aunt Sheryl stood. "Your grandfather was no gangster—if that's what you're saying. He was a black man who stood up and didn't beg. So don't you be talking shit in his house in front of my son. I know your mother raised you better than that."

Red Dawg, being unusually diplomatic, said, "Okay, everybody is a little stressed right about now. Sheryl and Walli, why don't you guys go back upstairs and try to get some sleep. We can't let these fools turn us against each other."

Calmed by Red Dawg's words, Sheryl bade them a terse good night and ushered her reluctant son upstairs. Clearly he was about to miss some real talk at the kitchen table.

"I found a Beretta at the grocery store," D began, "along with this shotgun and another Beretta here at the house. They all licensed?"

"I believe so," Red Dawg said cautiously. "I mean, I ain't seen the paperwork but Big Danny was very by-the-book when it came to guns and shit."

"How many pieces do *you* have?"

"Enough to feed the needy." He smiled and added, "See, I do know some East Coast rap."

"Okay." D plucked the shotgun from the tabletop, bent down, and placed it back on the gun rack underneath. "Big Danny needed this setup to sell groceries and book acts? The only time I've seen a rig like this was in a couple of crack houses back in the day. Honest people don't hook their shit up like this. And you know that."

Red Dawg hesitated before responding. "After his wife died, Big Danny lived here for a year or so by himself."

"I know that. And?"

"And I don't know what he was doing up in here every night."

"Oh, okay. So my grandfather was meeting with the kind of people he needed to have a shotgun handy for? And you're saying you knew nothing about it?"

Avoiding D's logic, Red Dawg responded: "I told you it was Teo. He was probably threatening Big Danny. So he figured he'd muscle up on that bitch."

D was deeply dubious, but figured he'd gotten all he could out of Red Dawg. "All right, I'm going to sleep. You're welcome to stay here. And please don't play with the Beretta."

CHAPTER NINETEEN

R'KAYDIA'S VISION

"So this is it." R'Kaydia held the door open to a small, dark room with a rickety metal chair in its center and a harsh white overhead light illuminating the dark blotches on the floor. "I keep meaning to clean this room up and make it useful, but I think the aura in there is too nasty to be easily transformed."

D peeked inside but didn't enter. The room was a part of hip hop history he'd heard about but had no interest in experiencing in any way, even as a tourist. He said, "I think this whole place could use an exorcism."

R'Kaydia laughed. "That's why we moved here, D. We're in the business of purifying evil spirits." She closed the door and they walked back over to her glass desk.

D couldn't believe that he was in the old Westwood offices of Death Row Records, the most notorious hip hop label of them all. R'Kaydia's Future Life Communications had moved into Death Row's old offices, turning it into the base for her three-year-old entertainment/digital media enterprise, and she'd just shown off the room Suge allegedly used to "discipline" subordinates.

Now this chic black woman, with her glittering white teeth, trainer-toned shoulders, and determined gaze, sat comfortably in the space where Knight had once terrorized the rap game. D had a hard time reconciling this disconnect between past and present, especially as he sat in a soft leather-backed chair trying not to stare at her impressive brown legs crossed under the desk.

"I thought moving into the space would give urgency to our mission," R'Kaydia said. "A large part of our business is managing the estates of artists who have passed. We collect royalties for their families, set up foundations, license their music, writings, and image, and make sure that all their digital rights are defended."

D said, "My mother used to love this song by Adrian Dukes, 'Green Lights.' It was really her anthem when I was a child. I heard it sampled recently in a car commercial. I know Dukes is dead. I've always wondered if his family was benefitting."

R'Kaydia typed on her keyboard. Her eyes surveyed the screen and then "Green Lights" filled the room from hidden speakers. "Vintage," she observed. "D, I will look into it."

"So, you want to help Dr. Funk with his rights?"

"Teddy and I feel his is an underdeveloped legacy. He had an almost unprecedented run of success, followed by an equally long period of silence. In both, there is opportunity. We think we can make him more money than his catalog is earning now and find him new revenue sources. That's the essence of what we do."

"And you and Teddy get a substantial commission on the revenue you generate?"

"Yes," she said quickly, "but let me assure you: we are not just a bunch of scavengers digging through dusty contracts for hidden clauses. The real money will be come from the new revenue streams that we're creating. For example . . ."

R'Kaydia hit a button on her desk and a prism of light appeared atop it, which then morphed into Dr. Funk on the cover of *Chaos: Phase I*. The two-foot-high hologram looked over at D and said, "What up, bruh?"

"Damn," D said.

R'Kaydia stared at him and smiled. "We have the capability to build a life-sized Dr. Funk, along with his old band. We have a deal with his old label for the masters. Las Vegas casinos are excited about the concept. Dr. Funk could share the stage with Elvis or Tupac or even John Coltrane. We could mix old music with these holograms and create dream lineups. The possibilities are endless, as are the financial opportunities. We can make Dr. Funk a contemporary act as capable of selling tickets as anyone performing in the twenty-first century."

D was duly impressed and a little spooked. He'd seen the Michael Jackson and Tupac holograms and hadn't been sure how he felt. Were these ghost performers a good thing? The technology made it possible, but just cause you can do a thing, does that make it right?

In truth, this Dr. Funk image was a definite leap forward from those earlier holograms. He moved fluidly and his features were truly lifelike. This wasn't the ragged-looking man he'd encountered at the wake. This was Dr. Funk with the aura of an incandescent supernova.

"Wow," D said. "Now I guess I have to help you."

R'Kaydia flashed a sly smile. "I just e-mailed you our offer."

D checked his phone and nodded. "Okay. Mind if I show this to Walter Gibbs?"

"Your call," she said. "But go ahead and forward me your banking information, so we'll be ready to wire you our initial payment when he tells you how good a deal it is. We'll expect a written report every week on your progress in finding Dr. Funk. A list of who you spoke to and a recording, if possible, of your interviews with sources. You have three days before the offer expires. Let's speak soon, D."

As D stood up, Dr. Funk said to him, "Don't let a brother down," and then he winked.

CHAPTER TWENTY

IRRITATING AMOS PILGRIM

The late Dwayne Robinson had been D's friend, mentor, and guide to all things black music. The writer had turned him on to the Delta bluesman Robert Johnson, the saxophone giant John Coltrane, the late Cape Verde songstress Cesária Évora, and crateloads of old-school rap records. Dwayne's instruction wasn't just enrichment for his black-suited student. As a bodyguard to music stars, D found his deeper knowledge of music history made him more popular with clients, transforming him from just a big nameless hunk of brown meat into an actual human being.

Tragically, Dwayne couldn't be called upon anymore, having been viciously stabbed to death a few years back, his murder leading D into the labyrinth of rap's origins as chronicled in Dwayne's unfinished book, *The Plot Against Hip Hop*. D had found the two men he thought were directly responsible for the killing, though the case always felt somehow unfinished. This was in part because the man who had *indirectly* instigated the plot was both untried and alive. Maximizing that irony was that for the past couple of years, D had been periodically cashing checks from him.

Amos Pilgrim comanaged D's friend Night, as well as a great many other performers. Decades ago Pilgrim, realizing hip hop's potential for social change, had hired two ex-FBI agents to "direct" the culture as best they could, one in New York, the other in Los Angeles. Things had not gone as planned and he'd lost control of his two operatives, both of whom had gone on to foster chaos in many hip hop cliques.

Many were indicted and a few even died as a result of Amos Pilgrim's agents (perhaps including Biggie and Tupac). That long list contained a woman D had developed feelings for, and who had loved him sweetly, despite his HIV-positive status. So whenever D had to meet with Amos Pilgrim, he barely suppressed his anger. He'd knocked the music manager flat once before, and if Al weren't in the room for this meeting, D would have already leaped across the table and choked him to death. And considering the man's condescending tone, it was still a distinct possibility.

"I'm not offering you charity," Amos said. D sat across a wide black-ivory table with his head titled slightly to the side. Al sat beside Amos's desk, closer to D than Amos, the fingers of one hand drumming lightly on the edge of the desk. "This is a big opportunity, one lots of people in this business would have signed up for in a heartbeat. Yet you are treating this offer like you'd be doing *me* a favor."

D didn't immediately reply. He just stood up and set his hands on the desk, his fingers squeezing the edge. Finally he said, "I've beat your ass before, Amos."

"Yo!" Al shot up, his arms outstretched, his voice firm and smoky, his white hair combed stiff and immaculate. "I didn't set this meeting up to see whose dick is bigger. This is about Night, and giving an artist we all believe in the support he needs. Far as I'm concerned, you two never have to speak again. D, just help us out with Night. That's all I ask."

D still had his hands on the desk and his eyes on Amos Pilgrim. "So he's back on blow?"

"Worse," Al said. "He may be messing with crystal meth."

D leaned in toward Amos. While maintaining eye contact, the

manager slid his chair back. "Damn," D said, "how'd you guys let that happen?"

"I'm a manager," Amos replied, false bravado in his tone, "not a babysitter."

"But isn't that what you'd like me to be?"

"D," Al said softly, "it's my fault. I'm not up to the gig anymore. At least not by myself. Yo, I'm fucking old."

This admission pulled D's attention from Amos to the suddenly frail-looking white man to his right. When Al smiled D's anger dimmed.

"Anyway," Al said, waving at Amos, "fuck him, D."

"Fuck *me?*"

"Yeah, fuck you. You're just the bank. Look, D, Night is a drug addict. Has been for as long as we've known him, right?"

"He wasn't always," D said, remembering Night's days as a street hustler/boy toy for old women and his Italian madam/pimp in the nineties. Back then Night was addicted to sex and had enough ambition to help him justify selling his body.

"Yeah," Al said, "sometimes getting what you want is the most disappointing thing in the world."

D took his hands off Pilgrim's desk and his body relaxed. "So," he went on, firmly back in the now, "you want me to convince him to enter rehab?"

"Well," Amos said weakly, "if that's what it takes."

D sighed and took a step back, now thinking like a manager. "Got it. You want him to finish the record first and *then* go into rehab?"

"D, you know that turning in the album triggers a payment," Amos said. "Even if they reject it eventually, there's a payment for Night. It would be great to use that to get him some help."

"So, finishing the album will help his drug problem, huh? Yeah, right."

Disgusted with Amos Pilgrim and not entirely happy with Al either, D feared the two were simply enablers and ineffectual protectors of a dynamic, fragile man. Their plan was to squeeze whatever music they could out of Night before what was left of his fan base finally stopped caring. D snatched the contract off the desk, gave it a final once-over, and then signed it with one of the expensive pens on Amos's desk.

"Okay, partners," he said, mocking them with every syllable, "I'm down. But I need something—I need some help finding Dr. Funk. I need leads to ex-bandmates, ex-managers, and family. What do you ballers got for me?"

CHAPTER TWENTY-ONE
A RIDE FROM THE P*A*ST

Heading down the elevator from Amos Pilgrim's office, D got an unexpected and largely unwanted blast from his past. It was a text from a number he didn't recognize. It read: *Saw you and your fam on YT. Much respect to your late grandpops. I'm in LA 2. I found Eva. If you're still interested I'm at the Hotel Café tomorrow at 10 p.m. watching her sing. Ride.*

He walked through the garage toward his grandfather's Electra 225, thinking about Ride and knowing against his better judgment that he'd be at that club tomorrow at ten. About eighteen months ago, Ride had run into D back in Brownsville, their old Brooklyn neighborhood, where D had been helping a silly kid tend to a self-inflicted gunshot wound (and stopping his friends from posting the accident on social media). Ride had witnessed that act of charity and enlisted the reluctant bodyguard in an effort to locate his ex-girlfriend.

Ride had just exited the New York State correctional system after five years, though his search for Eva was not a sentimental journey. The ex-con had entrusted her with an ill-gotten $15,000, but when he arrived back in Brooklyn, both Eva and the money were gone. A Facebook search suggested that Eva had split for the West Coast, renamed herself Evelyn, and had used Ride's cash to finance her relocation. D had hooked up Ride with a job as a traveling security guard/roadie for Night. It had started well enough, but the big man's obsession with Eva had ultimately made him unreliable. He'd start questioning singers and musicians in Night's orbit about Eva's whereabouts. Being that Ride was a hulking six foot seven, people didn't always take well to his persistence.

D had lost track of his erstwhile client, but clearly Ride hadn't lost track of D. Of course Walli's damn YouTube video hadn't helped. Last time he'd checked, the video of Dr. Funk at Big Danny's wake had around a million views and had made D a viral celebrity in the way of cute cats, awkward dancers, and Asian girls who did makeup. He'd suddenly gotten e-mails from people from his past (ex–D Security staff Mercedes Cruz from New York), aging mentors (retired detective Fly Ty Williams from Atlanta), and ex-lovers (Emily Anekwe, now living in Jamaica). Somehow his family's misfortune had been forgotten amid the interest in Dr. Funk and the oddness of the venue. All the YouTubers had blithely ignored the fact that they were witnessing a family in mourning.

Or, more precisely, they hadn't identified with his family's pain in any human way. Instead they'd viewed D's tears as just another digital spectacle, no different than the next scene of police brutality or celebrity clothing malfunction (*I see you, Lenny Kravitz*). D couldn't help but read a few of the comments (*What's that big nigga's problem? Burly, all-black-wearing crybaby!*) and saw how gleefully he'd been mocked, his grief ripped free of context and made ridiculous. Some "friend" had forwarded D a GIF of his teary eyes as Dr. Funk sang to him, making it seem like he was a parishioner overcome at the old man's altar. He'd become a crying Jordan meme.

D's solace (or hope) was that it would soon pass and that someone else would become the object of the web's prurient interest. In the twenty-first century you didn't get just fifteen minutes of fame; it was more like one long day of celebrity, as your image rolled around the

globe until everyone was, as Jay Z said, on to the next one. His crying face had probably traveled so far by now that aliens were laughing
about it on the dark side of the moon.

The building where Amos Pilgrim had his offices had once been the
LA home of Motown Records, where Joe Jackson had managed Michael
and young Janet, and the headquarters of the House of Blues, among
countless other music businesses. D, who was usually hyperaware of
black music history, didn't think about any of this as he slid the green
Electra 225 out of the garage on Argyle and took a left on Sunset in the
direction of the 101 Freeway.

Instead he put the address of Willie "Scratch" Williams into his
GPS. Williams was the legendary guitarist who'd played on many of Dr.
Funk's early-eighties solo singles. Al had made the introduction and
the old guitarist had invited him out to his place in the Valley. As he
sat in traffic, D got another text, this one from Red Dawg: *Big Danny's
killer is performing tonight. You wanna come?* What a weird combination
of words. D texted back, *Yeah,* then hit the freeway.

CHAPTER TWENTY-TWO

SCRATCH HAS SOME TAPES

Any trip out to the San Fernando Valley always brought D back to the movie *Chinatown*, a 1974 classic that his surrogate uncle, Fly Ty Williams, a now-retired NYC detective, used to play at his apartment in Queens. *Chinatown* had been the detective's favorite film, a romantic and tragic meditation about a PI swallowed up by an investigation bigger and darker than just a cheating husband. The deeper story in Roman Polanski's film centered on stolen water being used to drive farmers out of the Valley, a plan devised by a nefarious developer to buy up all the land and spawn the region's plague of strip malls. It was a reminder to D that there were multiple levels to every story and what you see isn't always what happened.

Willie "Scratch" Williams had a little house on a side street in the shadow of the 101. Most of the furniture had been purchased in the eighties, from the wood-paneled den to the plastic-covered sofa. The place stank of old herbs and incense, like an unholy alliance of healthy scents gone wrong. Scratch wore a purple-and-gold Laker's sweat suit circa Magic Johnson era and sandals that revealed tough, hard feet with yellowed, uncut toenails. His fingers were long and calloused with nails that apparently hadn't been cleaned since the Forum's "Showtime" days. His face was leathery and drawn, and his voice was equally worn from nights of too much smoke and drink and the fitful rest of unbridled bitterness.

"It's about the tapes, isn't it?"

"Tapes? No, I just want to talk to Dr. Funk. I'm not looking for any tapes."

"Dr. Funk ain't worth shit anymore. Everybody knows he shot his load. I mean, he shot it so long ago he'd need a fistful of Viagra to get his shit hard. But these tapes? They make him young again."

"These are sessions you played on?"

"Hell yeah. Sessions of unreleased songs. Three are pretty finished. A couple half-done but with killer hooks."

"Sounds cool," D said, hiding his curiosity behind a poker face. "Be sweet to listen to but I have no use for them. I'm trying to find Dr. Funk, not his tapes."

"I Googled you. You're tight with that Nightingale."

"You mean Night?"

"Nigga is moderately talented," Scratch said. "He steals good."

"What are you talking about?"

"His song 'Black Sex' is a straight-up lift of chords from a Curtis Mayfield tune. He took an Al Green verse and a Bootsy Collins hook, put the two together, and called it his melody. Now, you give Night-hawk these tapes and that boy will have a new LP in a week."

"*Give?* You're in the charity business, Scratch?"

The old musician reached under his sofa and pulled out a CD that he flipped in D's direction. "Here's a taste. Two songs. Enough to wet your beak. After Nightfall hears them, come back to me with an offer, though a cowriting credit with Nighttime would be a start."

"Wouldn't this be stealing from Dr. Funk?"

Scratch snorted contemptuously. "I worked for that nigga for five years. He got the money and the bitches. I got credits on the back of an album and a check sometimes. Then he threw it all away. Man couldn't handle the white girl. His brain is so fried he should be working for Colonel Sanders. Play these songs for your man Nightlife and maybe we can do something."

A CD? This trip had certainly been a journey back in time. Old clubs. Old formats. Old music. Old men. *Is this my fate?* D asked himself. *Just to be some kind of curator for the last dreams and lingering beefs of old men dead, lost, or endlessly bitter? What about my life? I've lived most—no, all—of my adult life standing in front of people, a wall of human protection, or moving behind them to clean up their sad, ugly messes.*

Between Big Danny's demise and this crazy hunt for Dr. Funk, D wondered if he'd have any time to himself. Going home wasn't the best option right now. Ever since he'd found himself in a shootout with some corrupt Brooklyn cops, life there had been crazy. The honest members of NYPD blue saw him as notorious. A local rap posse he'd tried to help was giving him the side eye. He'd only just moved back to Brooklyn two years ago and his landlord was already trying to price him out. Sometimes D felt jealous of his mother's fading memory because he was tired of looking back, yet that's all Cali seemed to be offering. Looking back at people, places, and music that latched onto him like scales, making him scratch other people's itches but not his own.

CHAPTER TWENTY-THREE
NIGHT IN THE VALLEY

In a dictionary of soul vocals, the words "Green, Al" would have provided the definition of "singing low." That is, contrary to the stereotype of the shouting, yelling singer, Reverend Green would get close to the mic and lower his volume, forcing the listener to lean in, to really listen to the sweet nuances of his sound. That technique had become a lost art, out of place in an era of sexting penises and booty portraits.

Yet here was Night, in a Sherman Oaks studio navigating a new slow jam, keeping the music quiet and his voice low, letting it simmer on a hot stove of passion in the style of good Reverend Green. It was a mature, controlled fire Night was bringing. He may not have finished his album by the deadline, but there was tremendous growth in Night's delivery. Life might not be good, but his friend's learning curve was spiraling up.

"That's beautiful, Night," D said. "Truly beautiful."

"Yeah," Night replied softly, "it's getting there."

"You all right?"

Night spoke haltingly, with a lack of confidence D found alarming. "To be honest, D, I'm not sure what I have left in me. And you know what? That's fine. I'ma artist. You gotta dig to have something worth giving."

"I feel you on that," D said, trying to be supportive, but Night sounded tired and a bit incoherent.

"The part that's fucking me up right now is that the people at the label ain't hearing it."

"C'mon, man. They didn't hear your last album, but you wound up with a Grammy for best R&B song."

"You know how in debt I am to that label?" Night countered. "I didn't make a record for like seven, eight years and they advanced me money for two LPs I didn't deliver. I need to sell some Beyoncé numbers just to get even."

"So what do they want you to do? Go to Sweden and work with Max Martin?"

"You laughing but it ain't funny. If I let them I'd be on the plane now with a list of the best long-stay hotels in Stockholm."

"Ne-Yo and Usher went electropop and look what happened to them," D said, putting out a rock-critic vibe. "Made their real fans angry and not one sixteen-year-old downloaded their new shit."

"That's why I wanted you on board as my manager. You've seen mad motherfuckers crash and burn."

D was about to reply when Night's eyes shifted toward the control room. "Hey, Sy, how you doing?" he said.

Sy Sarraf was a lean, olive-skinned Persian with a slim nose, Dolce & Gabbana shades, a purple V-neck T-shirt, and a dangling gold medallion that waved at Night like a sailor docking at his home port. Through the intercom Sy replied, "Happy as always, my friend."

"Just take a seat," Night said, and Sy reclined on the long brown sofa behind the board. Before D could ask, Night told him, "Sy is my herbalist. I mean, he's legit. He mixes up teas and shit for energy, calmness, and all that. When my throat gets rough he mixes up a mean lemon, honey, and tea thing that soothes it."

"Herbalist to the LA stars?"

"We are out in Hollywood, D."

"No, we are in the fucking hot-ass Valley, Night. That's where we are. Now, this Sy guy. Just herbs, right?"

"For me, D. That's all I need from him."

"Okay, let's see what kind of potions he brought you today."

Night had met Sy at the Equinox on Sunset where the Persian and a couple of homeys were lifting weights. At first Night was a bit suspicious, since that Equinox location had an active gay pickup scene and lots of steroid-enhanced pectoral muscles. But Night saw that Sy was friendly with the scores of tight-bunned, heavily made-up, ab-obsessed women who sashayed through. He was a regular at the Nice Guy, Craig's, and the other trendy Hollywood hangs where the city's moneyed youth partied and awaited a Kardashian-like moment of social media fame. Sy claimed multiple businesses, one of which was supplements. So Night had asked him to stop by the studio with a medley of pills for various ailments. Al was dubious about Night's new friend, but not hostile, so D likewise remained courteous but cautious in greeting him. He'd met a lot of high-end drug dealers in his club security days, and Sy definitely had the pedigree.

"It's all about energy, isn't it?" Sy said. "We all need the strength, endurance, and power. We know what we have to do and what we want to do. But without the energy there's no intensity and without intensity, what can you really get done? That's what I help people achieve, D."

Night had clearly bought this line, seeking something medical and magical to get his album over the creative hump.

After Sy left, D examined several pill bottles and looked up the ingredients on the web, which led him to believe it was all organic—but then, so were the coca leafs in Colombia.

"I'm not doing drugs, D."

"Really. I heard you were poppin' Viagra like cough drops."

Night laughed. "Okay, you got me. I've been known to pop a gentle blue pill."

"Or two."

"Yeah," Night admitted. "Or two."

"But all joking aside, you got to watch what you're taking and watch what Sy is giving you. You can get dependent on anything. It may not be shit from the street, but over-the-counter these days can actually be worse. This stuff he gave you all seems well and good. I just don't wanna see you strung out on oxycodone or some other white-boy opiate. You feel me?"

"Of course," Night said, but D didn't believe him. He knew addicts could be like vampires. The motherfucking thirst was never too far from their minds. Whether it was sucking blood or a crack pipe, the sun couldn't stop that thirst from rising up. He'd been hired to keep Night stable. He would do his best, but memories of his days babysitting tortured singers made his soul sour.

CHAPTER TWENTY-FOUR

SERENE POWERS IS NO JOKE

E va sang with husky sensuality and a coquettish vibrato that blended full-blown woman with nubile teen. This alluring vocal combination was enhanced by black leggings, a velvet jacket with matching bra, and a taut brown midriff. Her hair was a crimson-and-black natural. Her milk-chocolate skin shined under the stage lights and her round eyes were inviting. D now understood why his old client Ride was so enthralled with her, especially while he'd been sitting in an Upstate New York prison cell.

As D checked the room, he didn't see the huge ex-con among the stylish young Hollywood crowd at the Hotel Café. At six foot seven with large shoulders and the haunted face of a `horror-film victim, Ride stood out everywhere he went, but in this modest, music-loving LA hangout, he'd have been impossible to miss.

D hung out by the small bar in the back of Hotel Café listening as Eva sang soul covers interspersed with hooks from hip hop hits. It was like Eva and her band—a white guitarist with a brown five o'clock shadow and a short Asian keyboardist/laptop manipulator—were trying to sound like a DJ doing a live remix. D smiled when Eva wailed on a cover of Dr. Funk's "Pleasure," a much-sampled soul jam, when suddenly he felt someone staring.

If Ronda Rousey was dark brown with a short Halle Berry cut, wore aviator glasses and a beige hoodie, well, this would be her. The woman, who was standing across from the bar, radiated palpable power. Her muscles were at rest but D could sense she was dangerous. He figured he could take her if it came down to it, but it wouldn't be pretty.

D received a text from Ride: *I'm outside. Eva sounds good, right? See ya soon.* The crowd, small but very much into the singer, applauded as Eva stepped offstage.

D replied: *Why didn't you come in? I'll be right out.*

When D glanced up from his phone the black Rousey was gone. He paid for his two ginger ales as the next act set up. Eva, her two band-mates, and a couple of friends walked out of a back door that took them onto busy Cahuenga Boulevard.

As D stepped through the hotel café's front door, which was actu-ally in an alley off Cahuenga, he heard a scream. When he reached the boulevard he saw the black Ronda Rousey kick Ride in the kneecap and drop him to the street with a short left. The big man stumbled backward, his body falling atop several Hollywood stars.

"Oh no," Eva shouted, "you didn't have to do that!"

The black Ronda Rousey, looking quite calm, said, "I can't stand seeing a man put his hands on a woman."

"He wouldn't have hurt me," Eva said.

"It looked like he was already hurting you," she replied.

D bent down to see how Ride was doing. Black Rousey, calm and cool, stared at D.

"Ride, can you get up?"

"Nawn, D. That bitch fucked up my knee."

"Ride!" It was Eva. "I can't believe you'd roll up on me like that."

"Like what? Like you run away from Brooklyn with my money and I wouldn't try to find you?"

"Who is this guy?" the guitarist asked Eva.

"Who am *I?*" Ride said. "I'm her man." He tried to rise up from the ground but groaned before falling back on his ass.

"Stay down, Ride," D said. "I'll call an ambulance."

"C'mon, man. You know my pedigree. Get me out of here."

D braced himself to lift the big man off the ground. Eva stood five feet away, talking with her bandmates, clearly unsure what to do vis-à-vis Ride.

D watched black Rousey move up the block toward Hollywood Boulevard, seeming pleased with herself. She turned, nodded at D, and then kept on going. "Who was that?" he asked.

"I have no idea," Ride said. "Please get me out of here before five-o comes."

D put Ride's considerable weight on his shoulder and moved him slowly in the direction of Sunset. He felt Eva take a couple of steps behind them and then stop. Ride had his head down, embarrassed on every level.

Forty minutes later Ride was stretched out on a faux-leather sofa with a bag of ice wrapped around his bare knee. He balanced a Dos Equis on his forehead. A plate of rice and refried beans sat on his chest. "You sure you don't want a beer?" he asked.

D declined the offer. "You don't feel grabbing a woman by the arm is putting your hands on her?" he asked.

"Like I said, D, I just wanted to talk to her. But she kept walking. I mean, she knew I would show up."

"You called her?"

"Well, she should have been ready, you know."

A little Latino boy, around seven or so, walked into the room with a bottle of mango juice. "*Mi madre* wants to know if you'd like this," he said to D, his small, curious eyes surveying the man's all-black ensemble.

"Tell your mother thanks, but no, I'm leaving in a minute. What's your name again?"

"Emilio," the kid said.

"Well, Emilio, I want you to do me a favor."

Emilio glanced over at Ride to see what he thought. Ride gave him a small nod.

"Emilio," D continued, "I want you to make sure my friend here stays in the house and doesn't do anything else silly tonight. Can you do that?"

"I'm not sure," he said sagely. "*Mi madre* says he *estúpido*. Says it all the time."

"Does she?" Ride asked from the sofa, suddenly worried.

"No," Emilio said with a giggle. "I always fool him."

"I'm sure you do," D said.

The 225 was parked down the block from where Ride was staying, not far from the Korean spa his grandfather took him to years ago. Though the area was technically Koreatown, the blocks in this part of the neighborhood were overwhelmingly Latino. So it was weird to see a black woman leaning against the car, especially the black Rousey.

"You've already beat the shit out him."

"He okay?"

"Nope."

"You like Korean barbecue, D Hunter?"

"And you are . . . ?"

"My name is Serene Powers."

Serene ordered all the food at Chosun Galbee, getting the combo steak and shrimp for them to share, as well as a beer for herself and a

Korean tea for D. They were quite a sight among the Korean families and couples surrounding them. He was a large black man wearing all black; she was wearing a beige hoodie and boots, tight jeans, and a black T-shirt with the image of a scowling Ice Cube.

"So," D began, "you must be ex-military."

"Maybe."

"I bet I could look you up on a mixed martial arts website and get your whole bio."

"So why not do that now? If that's all you want to know, just pull out your phone."

"I won't find out why you are following me on Google."

"Why do you think, Hunter?"

"To beat Ride's ass wouldn't be my first guess."

"That was a bonus."

"Do you know the whole story of those two?"

"Unless Eva bled his ass dry and bashed his mother's head in with a hammer, I don't need to. Did she do any of that or did she just leave his ass?"

"She left him. But also took money that wasn't hers."

"Emotional violence is not my concern, Hunter. If she's not Hanni-bal Lector, I don't care. Putting his hands on her was, is, and always will be unacceptable to me."

"You could have kept on following me," D said. "There's a lot of technology for that. So what do you want?"

"I thought we should meet. I read up on your family after I saw you and Dr. Funk on YouTube. Any man who cries that openly is all right with me. Plus, based on what happened to your brothers, I know you earned those tears."

"Now I get it. So this is about Dr. Funk?"

"How much do you know about him?"

"I know his music. I know he's a legend."

"His music lies," Serene declared.

"I've been around musicians and artists long enough to know that their work is the best part of them. So I don't judge their character based on creativity. But you saw that video—if he's done bad shit, I'm sure it hurts his soul."

"Kelly Lee Minter."

"Who?"

"Kelly Lee Minter. Use your phone, Hunter. Then call me."

"I have your number?"

"I'll text you, Hunter. Enjoy the food." She put a fifty on the table and walked out.

CHAPTER TWENTY-FIVE

OLD MEN PLAYING DOMINOES

D was back on his grandfather's sofa. He was reading the *LA Times* Calendar section, enjoying holding the print edition that his grandfather had continued to subscribe to. It had been awhile since he'd held an actual paper and it felt weird, like he was living life out of sync. Still, he found it comforting to read the newspaper after spending the morning on a deep Internet dive.

He hadn't found much online about Kelly Lee Minter, but she seemed like a real music fan who had even published a Dr. Funk fanzine. Her funeral in Richmond, California, was notable for the presence of a lot of Bay Area musicians. There was one testimonial from a childhood friend about how sweet and "musically inclined" she was. Judging from a couple of pictures, Kelly Lee Minter had been a cute, sandy-haired Creole girl with some baby fat, buckteeth, and a taste for Spandex. She was definitely Dr. Funk–affiliated, but none of the items gave a cause of her death.

Unlike most of the women in the Unified Women's Mixed Martial Arts rankings, Serene Powers didn't have a nickname. But in the featherweight division she had ten wins and five losses and, according to one MMA site, "had the tools to be a contender but perhaps not the dedication," since she'd become less active the last two years. "When Serene fights it's clear she's got the power(s) to wear a champion's belt. But perhaps because it comes too easy for her, Serene has become an erratic presence on the circuit, popping up at odd tournaments after long absences, flashing skills but sometimes seeming distracted. She's a mystery inside an enigma."

One profile of Serene reported that she'd served with the United States Army in the Middle East and later taught English and physical education at an all-girls academy in the Bay Area. There was also mention of a boyfriend who, apparently, was a chef of some sort. So there was a Bay Area connection between Kelly Lee Minter and Serene Powers. Maybe she knew the family, though she seemed to be in business and not simply out for revenge. She'd taken Ride down and hadn't sweated a beat. She clearly knew some nasty tricks. *Hope it doesn't come to me having to take her one-on-one,* D thought.

Walli walked into the living room and placed his laptop on the coffee table. "I got something to show you."

"More memes making fun of me?"

"Nawn. Grandpa and Dr. Funk."

D put the paper down and glanced over at the computer. "What?"

"Awhile ago Grandpa asked me to get a VHS tape digitized. I just got it done the other day. I'm sorry it took me so long."

"Lemme see."

On Walli's computer screen, Big Danny, looking to be in his late sixties, sat across a card table from Dr. Funk, who looked much healthier than he had at the wake. They were playing dominoes in a dark room. The camera seemed to be on a tripod and was as static as the two men were animated.

"There's film out there," Dr. Funk said. "Shit, I got VHS tapes somewhere with all of Jackie's TV appearances. The man was bad. I mean, everyone talks 'bout Michael Jackson being influenced by James Brown. That's not even half the truth. You see, Michael Jackson came out of Jackie Wilson, from his posture onstage, to his leg movements, to his spins. It's not even a question."

"You gonna rely on a damn VHS to prove that to people?" Big Danny probed.

"I've got it in here somewhere."

"Nigger," Big Danny said, "you must know that people don't even remember what a VHS or a VCR is. You might as well bring out a Betamax."

"I got those too," Dr. Funk said.

"You are missing my point."

"Mine is that people need to honor Jackie Wilson."

"Mine," Big Danny said, "is that you sounding old and silly."

"You know about Jackie Wilson. Don't act like you don't know about Jackie Wilson." Dr. Funk had a bit of a twang in his voice, a Memphis-meets-Oakland blend that crept through in his singing, but was also present in his speaking voice.

"Wilson was great. I mean, you didn't even talk about his voice. Man, he could soar like a bird. I'm with you on that. But a VHS? You can't prove anything with a VHS."

"I got a VHS player."

"A VCR, you mean?"

"A VHS player. In fact, I got two of them bad boys. Right up in here somewhere," Dr. Funk said. "Shit, I used to give them out as gifts. I'll give them one of 'em. So whenever I need to explain about Jackie Wilson, I can just pop my VHS in, and—*bam*—there he goes in a shining sharkskin suit and his process and Jackie doing a sideways split like his heels had ball bearings in them."

"That's a nice description there, Doc," Big Danny said, "but nobody is interested in a goddamn VCR. That thing isn't even a museum piece. A museum might want a Motorola Hi-Fi. A museum might even want an eight-track player. But a VHS, a VCR? C'mon with that. Ain't no one want a Datsun. And a VHS is a Datsun. Nigger, you better get some CDs or get gone."

"Jackie Wilson is one of the reasons I do music," Dr. Funk said, ignoring Big Danny's logic. "The man's been lost. *James Brown this* and *James Brown that.* On any given night Jackie Wilson would loosen his tie, open up his shirt, and then, like those punk rockers, dive right into an audience. Right into the arms of some chubby gal. Let me tell you what Jackie Wilson taught me. Jackie Wilson said it to me backstage when I was a kid and playing my guitar for anyone who would listen. He said, *Look at Jimmy Ruffin. Look at the mistake he makes every show.*"

"Jimmy was from Detroit too?"

"Yeah."

"Had a couple of hits."

"Yeah. People don't know Jimmy Ruffin now, and this is probably why. So at the second show of the day, I watch Jimmy Ruffin. He's got a little something onstage—but he's no Jackie Wilson. So I watch the show, then go back to see Jackie. I say, *I don't see no mistake.* Jackie Wilson says to me, *Jimmy only sings to the pretty girls.* I say, *That don't sound like a mistake to me.* Jackie Wilson laughs and says, *Watch me.* So I watch him and he's doing his thing. He's doing 'Baby Work Out.' Dancing his ass off. And then I see it. He's at the edge of the stage and these women are screaming. They're pulling his sharkskin suit off. They're ripping at his creamy white shirt. The man's clothing bill must have been crazy. But I see it. I see it."

"What did you see?"

"Jackie Wilson is singing to the homeliest, most unattractive woman on 125th Street. I mean, he is laser-beaming his eyes into her and that woman is ecstatic, like the Lord has just anointed her. I mean, this sister is shaking."

Big Danny was not impressed. "Making an ugly woman come is genius? Ain't that a singer's job?"

"After the show Jackie Wilson quizzed me. Did I see? I told him that by singing to the homely girl he made every other not-so-fine woman in the room think, *Damn, I have a chance with Jackie Wilson.* And the fine girls? They respect that too. They know they fine. They know they have a shot at Jackie but they love that he's so generous with his affection. Then Jackie Wilson says, *See, Marv Johnson only sings to the fine women. Singing to fine women only gets you so far. The homely women feel excluded and the fine women resent that she ain't the fine woman he's singing to. Anybody here really remember Marv Johnson?*" Now Dr. Funk got excited. "And that's my motherfucking point, Danny. There was a science to what and how Jackie Wilson did what he did. Cause and effect. It was scientific. I got it. Jackie understood and taught me this stage shit was one plus one."

"Well, you know what? I think Jackie Wilson may have cursed you and anyone else he told all that to."

"Curse? Nigger, it's that kind of knowledge that helped make me millions. I mean, I didn't hold onto the damn money, but at least I made it."

"You see all that love, man? Sexy shit is a curse," Big Danny said. "God gives you a certain power. A spiritual kind of power. But it can be dangerous to your soul too. You know I'm right, Doc. You use that power to get into a woman's panties. But the power is about more than sex. There's a price to pay for shortchanging that gift."

D had forgotten that Big Danny had a lot of preacher in him. He believed deeply in God and no matter how late he was up on Saturday night, on Sunday morning he always made it to church.

"Danny, you pussy-hound," Dr. Funk said with a laugh. "When did you get so damn holy?"

"Look at it. Just look at it. All these one-name singers: Jackie, Sam, Marvin, Teddy. Look at Al. These young singers. D'Angelo. Maxwell. Miguel. That fool who hit fine-ass Rihanna upside the head."

"Chris Brown," Dr. Funk said. "He a silly kid. But then he also got two names."

"Cursed. Every last one. Your man Jackie Wilson died of a stroke onstage. Probably singing to some old lady. Sam Cooke: shot in a motel office without his pants on. Teddy P. paralyzed in an accident with a questionable individual. Michael Jackson: enough said there. D'Angelo made a naked video and the hellhounds chased him down to Virginia. And you, Doc. I found you wandering around LA like the ancient mariner. You ever think it's a curse for misusing your power?"

"Better blessed for a minute than never blessed at all."

"You know who was truly blessed? Mr. James Brown."

"Of course," Dr. Funk said. "That's news?"

"The difference," Big Danny went on, "is that Jackie made a couple of good records. Only a couple. James made a million great records. Jackie was really brilliant onstage. Maybe he was as good as James Brown. Maybe he really was Michael Jackson's true model. I could see that. But a good show is like a deep breath. You take it in, it fills your lungs, and it goes out. On to the next one. Jackie Wilson was a good, deep breath. Really fills your lungs. Keeps your ass alive. But he didn't endure. He was just a way to get to the next breath. But what if that breath was recorded? What if that breath wasn't just a breath, but a sound? A sound that's distinctive. A sound that's more than just a voice or a performance, but both? Well, that's immortality."

"If Jackie Wilson had signed with Motown, we wouldn't be having this discussion. He would have been as big as Michael or the Temps or Marvin."

"But he didn't," Danny noted. "James Brown could perform all right. But he had a band. He had a sound. They had what we call a *brand* and James Brown owned it. He owned himself as much as any black man could back when we were just feeling good about being black."

"African American," Dr. Funk said.

"What?"

"African American. You missed that memo." He was being petty because he knew Big Danny had him.

Big Danny said, "I'm black. You black. I ain't been to Africa. My wife took me to an Ethiopian restaurant. Made me eat with my hands. I don't even use chopsticks, so why would I eat with my hands? At least with chopsticks you can stab the shit that looks questionable."

They both laughed at that. Dr. Funk poured Big Danny a taste from a bottle of whiskey and the debate resumed.

"You wanna know what really irritates me about James Brown?" Dr. Funk asked. "The man became a crackhead when he was what, fifty or something? How you become a crackhead at fifty? That don't make a damn bit of sense. I did coke when I was in my twenties and thirties. That's when doing coke made sense."

"C'mon," Big Danny said, "give the man some grace. When he was James Brown with capital letters, when he was the hardest-working man in show business, when he was soul brother number one, that man was as clean as the board of health. He didn't get all cracked out until he was on the downside. Once a performer realizes he's no longer the Godfather of Soul, well, crack's gonna happen.

"James Brown was his own thing," Big Danny continued. "He was never a love man. Not a true one. Too sweaty to compete with Jackie

Wilson or that pimp Sam Cooke. Sam Cooke. He was the anti–James Brown. He was so handsome all he had to do was stand there, open his mouth, and the women would fall right out. You know what's shame, Doc? Only British artists understand that now. That fine-ass Sade in them tight-ass dresses. Got a narrow-ass range and a fine-ass frame."

"That big white girl Adele. Don't move a muscle. Guess she's worried about jiggling. But she can sang. And that's the whole thing right there—"

The tape ended.

"That's it?" D asked.

"That's what he gave me," Walli said.

"Are there other tapes?"

"No. Sorry. I looked all over after he died. This was the only one."

"Okay," D said, "let's watch it again."

CHAPTER TWENTY-SIX

D AND NIGHT GO TO FUNKMOSPHERE

It was good to be out rolling with Night with Big Danny's top down under the Los Angeles moon. It had been awhile since the two old friends had hung out. Moreover, it was even better that they weren't heading to Soho House or the Nice Guy or that whole Hollywood scene D had never warmed up to. Instead they were on their way to a club called the Virgil, where a local label called Stones Throw was hosting a party.

D didn't know much about the label but Night did. "Yo, Stones Throw put out J Dilla's *Donuts*."

"Classic material right there."

"Madlib is down with them. MF Doom did the *Madvillain* LP with them. Aloe Blacc was originally on Stones Throw. And that white boy Mayer Hawthorne, though he can't really blow, has made some dope records for them."

"So it's an old-school indie label."

"A new-school indie label," Night corrected. "They put out a lot of vinyl—even do cassettes. It's owned by a DJ named Peanut Butter Wolf. He's spinning tonight."

"Who's the party for tonight?"

"New music from Dâm-Funk."

"I heard of him. He did some tracks with Snoop. My little cousin is into him."

"*7 Days of Funk*. Some underground shit. But I liked it. You know, I've been in a rut but so much is going on out in LA creatively. You got Kamasi Washington, Terrace Martin, Thundercat, and so many other dope musicians."

"They're in Kendrick Lamar's camp?"

"Yeah," Night said, "I need to plug into that energy."

D was happy to hear Night talk music like this. Self-awareness was a rare and great thing in an artist. He knew he needed to open up his process and let in some fresh air.

"So this is a networking opportunity?"

"Maybe, Mr. Manager," Night said. "Worse comes to worst, we meet LA hotties."

The Virgil was out in Silver Lake, a part of the city D had never spent much time in. Despite it being an LP release party, the vibe was more neighborhood hang than showbiz spectacle. This wasn't Hollywood—this was LA, home of break-dancing Filipinos, skateboarding Chicanos, bohemian blacks, and cool-ass white folks who rarely ventured past Highland at night.

Night and D walked through the two sides of the Virgil, enjoying the spirit of the community in the house and feeling a bit like tourists anxious to pick up on the local customs. The place wasn't packed but it was full. Dâm-Funk was playing keys and singing, backed by just a drummer and bassist playing a modern funk, a style inspired by Prince, electroboogie, and eighties groups like One Way. D recalled it was a style Dr. Funk had been flirting with just before he faded into obscurity.

Somebody from Stones Throw spotted them and soon Night and D were sitting at a corner table with Madlib and PB Wolf, talking music and having drinks. That's when D noticed a familiar face in the crowd. It was that Korean real estate woman from the day of the funeral, looking cute in black-and-white Chucks, skinny jeans, and a purple-and-black, on-and-off-the-shoulder Prince T-shirt, chatting with an Asian man and woman. D wasn't going to say anything to her until he saw her dance. *Whoa, she's got a lot going on back there.*

Still, he hesitated. In the last two years his T-cell count had become damn near normal. He only took two pills a day and sometimes even forgot to take them, something inconceivable a few years back. But the mental block hadn't totally lifted. The whole drama of explaining that he was HIV-positive and seeing the look on a woman's face—the fear, disappointment—suppressed his lust.

So D talked himself out of speaking to her and, sadly, felt relieved. But then she walked over to the table.

"Hey, guys," she greeted Peanut Butter Wolf and Madlib. Seems she was a regular in the Stones Throw/Funkmosphere scene. Night shook her hand too and gave her that I'm-a-hot-singer-so-you-should-probably-want-to-fuck-me look. She took it in but didn't seem impressed. "Oh, hi," she said when she spotted D. "I know you, right?"

"Yeah, we met the other day. You sold the house next to my family's. I'm D Hunter. Michelle, right?"

"Oh yes," she said. "You were having the wake. I'm so sorry. Hope I wasn't inappropriate that day."

"Not at all."

"Mind if I sit down?"

"Ahh, no."

Night saw D's discomfort and smiled. "I can make more room."

Michelle slid into the booth next to D, who was surprised and suddenly very shy.

Fortunately, Michelle held her own: "I love that area of LA. Did you guys grow up there?"

D gave her a condensed version of his childhood trips to LA and his grandfather's life and times, which led Michelle to lean in close. D grew uncomfortable but excited.

"We were one of the first Korean families in Arlington Heights," she said, referring to the once predominantly black middle-class area. "My family owned a number of stores on Western, and we even have one or two on Crenshaw."

"It was rough between blacks and Koreans in LA back in the day."

"Yeah. My father and mother didn't speak much English, so there were some misunderstandings. It took them some time to get comfortable."

"They got hurt by the riot in '92?"

"I was only five at the time, but I know it had a big impact on my parents. To this day it's a sore subject in the house."

"Hey," Night said, "sorry to interrupt, but let me slide out. I'ma get up and jam with Dâm-Funk. If that's all right with my manager."

Madlib and PB Wolf stood up too. A buzz rippled through the crowd as Night and the Stones Throw crew approached the stage.

"This is great," Michelle enthused. "You must really enjoy working around so much music. I wish I could get paid to do that."

"It can be fun. But it's not as stable as real estate."

"Oh, yeah. But stable isn't everything. A girl can't spend all her time selling."

Michelle's friends Lana and Joey Chao soon came over, introductions were made, and music chatter continued. Joey peppered D with questions about Night's new LP, which D gracefully dodged.

Then Night appeared onstage with Dâm-Funk and band, plus Madlib on a drum machine. Together they worked out an eccentric electro version of "Black Sex." As the crowd surged to the stage, D took Michelle by the hand and, accompanied by her two friends, guided her to the wings stage right.

Michelle didn't pull her hand back, just looked up at him with soft eyes. He let her hand go once they were situated. Lana whispered something in Michelle's ear as they shared a giggle and started swaying to the music.

After all the drama around his grandfather's death and the search for Dr. Funk, it was great to be full of music, hearing his friend blow pure and sweet, feeling the buzz of a new woman checking him out (and feeling her back).

Later that night D, Michelle, Night, and the Stones Throw crew stopped at an all-night taco stand before hitting a bar in Little Tokyo, where Mexican hipsters, Japanese homeboys, and millennial beauties in horn-rimmed glasses and floral dresses chatted and slipped outside to smoke. D kept an eye on Night, aware that this was just the kind of environment that could seduce his friend to the dark side.

"I see you, D," Night said at one point, reading his mind. "But I got this. Keep your eye on that fine Asian chick, okay? Or I will." He let out a chuckle.

Sitting at a table with the Chaos, Michelle told D about clubs, music, food, and the city. D realized he'd never spent any real time with Asians of any ethnicity. He'd lived in a white, black, and Latino world back in New York. As he watched Michelle he figured this was a good time to expand his horizons.

"I gotta go," she said around one a.m. "I have to show some houses at nine."

"I'm glad we met under different circumstances."

"Me too." She reached into her purse and pulled out a business card. "Please pass this on to Night. If he wants to buy or rent in LA, I have many attractive properties."

D felt a touch deflated. Was all this hanging out just a ploy to get Night's business?

Michelle read D's mind: "Let me have your phone." Dutifully, he handed it over.

As she typed, Night leaned over from his conversation with Madlib and said to D, "Looks like *you* need the bodyguard."

Michelle gave D his phone back, along with a deep hug, before leaving with Lana and Joey.

"You through macking girls, D?" It was Night again. "Madlib and I got some ideas. I figure, as my manager, you'd want to know."

"Indeed," D said with a smile, "I do."

CHAPTER TWENTY-SEVEN

NARCOCORRIDOS IN BOYLE HEIGHTS

O nstage at La Zona Rosa on East Cesar E. Chavez Avenue, El Komander and his band were performing a song that favorably compared today's Mexican drug god, El Chapo, to Jesús Malverde, a 1900s bandit who was the patron saint of twenty-first-century outlaws. El Komander wore a black cowboy hat, a bedazzled black denim shirt, jeans, and pointy black boots. His band members, even the accordion player, wore black masks like bank robbers. Women crowded the stage in clingy dresses and heels, reaching out toward El Komander, who basked in their adoration while singing a narcocorrido filled with murder and blood.

D was absolutely the proverbial sore thumb: a tall black man in an ebony ensemble amid ten-gallon hats, cowboy boots, and a bar decorated with Mexican flags. The crowd at La Zona Rosa in Boyle Heights was about 99 percent Mexican or Mexican American. D stood at the bar sipping on a Tecate, trying not to make eye contact with anyone.

Red Dawg had disappeared into the crowd ten minutes before, vowing to "be right back" as the corridos moved dancers around the wide, wooden dance floor. To D's R&B/hip hop–raised ears there was zero rhythmic complexity in the music. Folks were moving enthusiastically to a rudimentary shuffle beat. D did dig the accordion that provided the melodies—it was an instrument he'd never heard live before so the novelty of it amused him—though he wasn't sure how long before that would wear off.

The bartender had his back to D, but was scoping him in the bar's mirror. That wouldn't have bothered him so much but the tattoo on the back of the bartender's head was of Diablo's skull with piercing eyes and a gleeful smile. When the bartender turned around, D saw that the skull was a reasonable facsimile of its owner's own rugged face. "Yo, holmes," he said. He was a solidly built man, his bare arms bearing tats (D recognized Jesus near his elbow), a leather vest revealing a hairy chest, a glittering gold cross, and round, mountainous pecs. The mustache on his lip was salt-and-pepper but the soul patch on his chin was snow white. He looked to be an extremely fit sixty. He wasn't hostile, but not warm either. "You want another beer? Maybe something stronger?"

"Another Tecate would be fine, amigo."

"You gonna dance?" the bartender asked. "I'm sure a lot of people here would enjoy seeing you out there."

"I bet."

"I'm not being disrespectful, holmes. I see you vibing to the music. You like the corridos?"

"I'm learning to enjoy them."

"You from Nueva York, right?"

"The accent, huh?"

"Yeah. And you guys from there stand a certain way."

"I guess. You must know Nueva York well, huh?"

"The part I know, I know. But this is LA, holmes. You may see what you see in this place. But you don't know who knows who, who owes who, and who owns who." He paused and let that sink in. Then he said, "I saw you come in here with Red Dawg."

"He's an old friend of my family."

"Big Danny, right, holmes?"

"Yeah."

"I heard what happened to him. I bet you and Red Dawg are trying to find out who capped him. I respect that. I know I'd want to know who did my papi. I respect that. Anyone would. But respect only goes so far. You ask the wrong person and the beat could drop like a Dr. Dre track. Your head will be ringing and you'll never know why."

"What's your name, amigo?"

"Antonio."

"I'm D Hunter. I am not Red Dawg's friend; I'm Big Danny's grandson. Glad you are so concerned for a stranger's safety."

Antonio's eyes widened and then his face softened. So did his voice.

"This ain't the first time we met, D. I recognize you now. I believe I met you back one time I had some business with Big Danny. You were just a kid and I had a lot less hair and no gut."

"Were you a cop, Antonio?"

"I was the motherfucking long arm of the law, holmes. I was 1-Adam-12 with an accent. I was the real Erik Estrada and a lot more handsome."

"You miss it, huh?"

This bid for familiarity was just a bit too much for the bartender. "This ain't *Behind the Music*. I got no sad stories for you, holmes. That is, unless you don't pay attention to your surroundings. Then you could get hurt."

"Why do you care?"

"I liked Big Danny. He carried himself well, and whether you wore a cop's badge or a bandanna, he was straight with you. I see you his kin, so that gives you a bit of rope. But Red Dawg? I don't give a fuck about that liar."

"What's he lied about?"

"If Red Dawg says he's breathing air, check his breath for carbon dioxide. But Big Danny, he was a decent human being and looked out for that fool. But see how he ended up . . . And people knew and liked him. You? Nobody around here knows you. Nobody gives a fuck. Enjoy your beer."

From behind, D heard Red Dawg's voice: "D, we should leave."

"You're ready?"

"Yeah. We have to go."

Red Dawg moved quickly through the bar toward the front door. D followed in his footsteps, trying to not bump into anyone but sure there was trouble at his back.

Once outside, D headed past the doormen and a few folks standing outside smoking. He didn't see Red Dawg so he went to the parking lot around the corner from the club.

Red Dawg was standing next to Big Danny's ride looking anxious. Suddenly, three cholos—two plus-size and one pinto—rolled up on him. No words were exchanged. They all just started scrapping. The two big guys grabbed Red Dawg and threw him against the car while the little man wailed at his gut.

D grabbed the puncher around the neck and spun him hard, so that he bounced when he hit the ground and then rolled over holding his damaged elbow. Next up: which of the big men would roll on him first? There was a moment's hesitation—the little man had been in charge and the duo weren't sure how far to go without him.

"Let him go!" D snapped, hoping they'd just follow orders. No dice. The cholo on the right loosened his grip on Red Dawg and shifted his body toward D. But before he could take a step, D kicked his right kneecap. He went down like a chopped redwood.

The third man, the biggest of the posse, now had to make a decision: let Red Dawg go and back off, or flex on D and see what happened.

"Let him go!" D barked again, optimistic but prepared to scrap. The big man shoved Red Dawg aside like a nuisance (which he was) and took a step toward D. Clearly he saw D as a worthy opponent.

"Hector, back off!"

D glanced over his shoulder to see Antonio standing there with a baseball bat in hand and two bouncers by his side. Hector eased up a bit.

Antonio walked over to D but kept his eyes on Red Dawg. "D, I see you found your amigo."

"What up, Antonio?" Red Dawg said.

"I was just telling your amigo here that you never know who knows who in East LA." He reached down and picked up the smaller man, who was still clutching his elbow. "You see this man?"

"I do," D replied.

"He brings in sportswear from Mexico and does business with your friend Red Dawg."

"The bitch owes me!" the small man yelled.

"Fuck you," Red Dawg said, "I don't owe you shit."

"Sounds like *he said, she said,*" Antonio observed.

"Who you calling a *she?*" the small man asked.

"Must be you, since you were stupid enough to answer."

"So what now? Po-po?" D asked.

Antonio laughed, then leaned over and punched Red Dawg dead on the jaw, knocking him to the ground. Then he turned to D. "Take him home," he said. "But remember, you are known by the company you keep."

On the ride back Red Dawg was quiet, rubbing his jaw and moving it around slowly, hoping it wasn't broken. D turned on the car radio and Gerardo's "Rico Suave" popped up.

D chuckled. "Here's some real LA rap for your ass."

Even in his embarrassed state Red Dawg tried to laugh, but it hurt like hell.

"You like, huh?" D said.

"Fuck no," Red Dawg mumbled. "But he did have some hot bitches in that video. He was from the Valley."

"One-hit wonder," D said.

"Abso-fucking-lutely."

"So, what the fuck happened back there?"

"I got jumped."

"Yeah. Sounds like you earned the ass-whipping, my man."

"I don't owe that dude shit. He just can't count."

"Did you find out anything about Teo Garcia?"

"Nobody's seen him."

"That's what you said before we got there. So you didn't find a thing. But I guess I did, which is that a lot of motherfuckers got problems with you."

"You know it's cause I'm a Blaxican."

"No, I'm thinking it's because you an Assican."

"You ain't funny."

D pulled the car over to the curb.

"What?" Red Dawg said.

"I'm beginning to think maybe my granddaddy got capped for some bullshit *you* did. I'm beginning to think he was busy cleaning up some mess you got into when he either accidently got shot for you, or he was there when they really wanted to do *you*. Maybe it's you who's in trouble with Calle 18."

"Fuck you, D. You don't know shit."

"I know that the detective thinks you're holding out on me, and that the cholos back there think you ain't shit. My granddaddy is the only person who seemed to give a fuck about you, and now he's dead."

Red Dawg pushed the car door open and D watched him stomp away into the East LA night. Antonio was right—he really didn't know who's who or what's what in these Cali streets, and he wasn't sure how to fix it.

CHAPTER TWENTY-EIGHT

THE DETECTIVE DRINKS COFFEE

The morning after Red Dawg's misadventure, D thought it was time to check back in about the official investigation. He left five messages before Detective Gonzales called him back.

"There's still an ongoing investigation into your grandfather's homicide, Mr. Hunter," he assured D while slurping his coffee.

"That's good." D held his phone in his left hand, since his right was soaking in a bowl filled with ice. "Are you aware that we had an attempted break-in at the family home?"

"Yes. A report on that was passed on to me."

"Do you think there's any connection between my grandfather's murder and the break-in? I mean, these guys might be Calle 18."

"Not that I can see, Mr. Hunter. I looked over the statements of the men you subdued—great work, by the way—and it seems like a crime of opportunity. Someone told them there was a lot of jewelry in the house, and that just a woman and a boy lived there."

"Is it because my grandfather was a loan shark that they believed that story?"

"These two are new to LA. They haven't been over the border very long, so I don't believe they had much insight. They heard a story, got an address, and saw an opportunity. They are wannabe bangers. That's all."

"Who'd they get the address from?"

D heard the detective flipping through papers.

NELSON GEORGE 3 151

"Not sure," he said after a moment. "Their stories contradicted but they did agree they heard about your home at a bar in Boyle Heights."

"La Zona Rosa?"

This got the detective's attention. "You hang out in Boyle Heights, Mr. Hunter?"

"No, detective. Just heard of it as a good place for music."

There was a long pause before Gonzales spoke again. "I went through their statements carefully, Mr. Hunter. If I thought there was a link to the murder, believe me, I'd pursue it. Speaking of which, have you had any luck in getting Red Dawg to talk about who your grandfather loaned money to? We didn't find anything on his computer, but there must be some kind of record in his files."

"I'll try again, detective," D muttered with little enthusiasm.

"Good. Mr. Hunter, I don't believe there was any grand conspiracy to kill your grandfather. Somebody was in debt to him and didn't want to pay or didn't want anyone to know the reason he needed to borrow money—that's what this is about. Maybe the shooter was afraid your father could have blackmailed him. That's a motive."

"Do you believe Red Dawg knows who killed him?"

"He may know. He may know and doesn't realize that he knows. Where are you going with this? Did he say something?"

"Could he have been involved himself?"

The detective picked his words carefully. "At this point I can't completely rule that out. But my impression is that if this man was loyal to anything or anyone, it was to your grandfather. Unfortunately, he's not the brightest light in the ballroom, so maybe him seeming suspicious is just because he's confused about how to act when he's trying to do the right thing. Anyway, I gotta go, Mr. Hunter. I'll keep you posted. Make sure you do the same for me."

CHAPTER TWENTY-NINE

TEO GARCIA HAS A STORY

D was out by the garage contemplating washing his grandfather's Buick when he heard someone ring the doorbell. Walli, who was upstairs in his room, yelled, "I got it!" out the window. D figured it was one of his high school pals. D knew Big Danny would have hated seeing his car with a speck of dust but worried that meticulously washing and drying it the way his grandfather had always demanded would be an all-day affair.

So when Walli stuck his head out of the backroom and said, "Someone's here to see you," D was relieved at not having to wash the car. That was until his cousin added, "Says his name is Teo." Based on Red Dawg's description, D grabbed a monkey wrench from the garage before heading inside.

"Is he alone?"

"Yeah," Walli said. Registering the concern on D's face (and seeing the wrench in his hand), Walli whispered, "Should I grab the shotgun?"

"No," D replied as he headed toward the front door, "just stand by the kitchen table while I answer the door. If I need that thing I'll let you know."

D peered through the frosted yellow glass of the front door to find a calm, middle-aged Mexican man wearing a cowboy hat with empty hands at his sides. D opened the door and stepped outside, so he'd be within arm's length of Teo.

"I'm D Hunter."

"I'm Teo Garcia. I hear you've been looking for me. Thought I should find out why."

They sat at the kitchen table, D in the chair where the shotgun was handy and Teo across from him, sipping water, his hat on the table. If Teo meant do to do D harm, he was pretty relaxed about it. Walli was standing by the front door, keeping watch in case someone nasty rolled up on the house. All he could see right now was a plump Latina playing with her iPhone in a parked Prius.

"So," Teo said, "Antonio at La Zona Rosa is an amigo. He told me he spoke to you and that you were a decent man but confused by some bad information."

"Please, Teo," D said, "unconfuse me."

"First of all, Red Dawg hates me. He's jealous that I made a music career for myself and found a new way to express myself while he stayed in the store selling sneakers. He's just a jealous man."

"So you had nothing to do with my grandfather's death?"

"Okay, you know I had history with Big Danny, and some of it not good. But *hermano*, I was a stupid, selfish kid who went to jail for stupidity. That's just the truth. But I hold no vendetta against Big Danny. None. If you don't believe me, I have my wife outside. I may sing gangsta corridos and praise bad men in songs, but my wife Juanita knows my heart. She will testify to my respect for your grandfather, especially after I really understood how he supported me. It's Red Dawg who now has a vendetta against *me*. He is trying to justify hurting me. He threatened me after Big Danny's murder so I have kept a low profile. I am a successful singer, D. I have a wife. I have a life. Red Dawg has nothing and he hates me for that."

"Are those amigos from La Zona Rosa looking for me?"

"No. I have spoken to them. They aren't happy with you, of course, but they are not out looking for you either, and I would never tell them about this house. Now, Red Dawg—I think they wouldn't mind seeing him again. And to be honest, amigo, I wouldn't mind if they found him."

"Well," D said, "I can't help you with that. But lemme see if you can answer a question: who killed Big Danny?"

"I do not know who pulled the trigger or why. But Red Dawg is blaming me and that has to stop. It *will* stop. But our problems should not be your problem. I will not let them be your problem, and you shouldn't let me be yours."

"Okay," D said.

Teo reached into his pocket and placed two tickets on the table. "I'm part of a big show at the Hollywood Palladium next week. I know you work with the singer Night. I am a big fan. I'd be honored if he could attend."

"Okay." D took Teo's hand when he offered it from across the table.

D was still sitting at the kitchen table when Aunt Sheryl came home from the beauty parlor an hour later. He and Walli were eating takeout tacos from a Mexican food truck.

"Ma," Walli said, "you'll never guess who came by today."

Sheryl stopped cold when he told her. "Oh my God. Are you all right?"

As D relayed the encounter, Sheryl grew increasingly skeptical. "You act like you believe him."

"He told a good story," said D. "You heard from Red Dawg since I last saw him?"

"No."

"The store is closed," Walli said. "I rode over there this morning."

"Where do you think he is, Sheryl? He needs to know Teo stopped by. Where does he live?"

"Walli knows," she muttered, then exited the kitchen and headed upstairs.

"When you're finished," D said, "let's go visit Red Dawg."

CHAPTER THIRTY

A SOUL SPINNER IN PICO-UNION

The green Buick rolled smoothly down Crenshaw as it had before on countless days and nights. But behind the wheel was a younger Hunter, a fact very much on D's mind as he came to the intersection where Big Danny was murdered. Since he'd arrived in Los Angeles, D had avoided that spot where Crenshaw met Wilshire.

But now, after all the conversations about his grandfather's death and the many false and confusing leads, he finally felt psychologically equipped to face it. Of course there were no markers for Big Danny, no recognition of his life and death. He was just one of 280 murders in LA this year. Big Danny was just a statistic. D understood this was the way things were in LA, the US, and the world. For black lives it had been like this since the first Europeans felt it was necessary to call themselves white.

When D reached the corner the light was green, so he didn't linger or get sentimental. Not a tear or a solemn moment or even a sigh. Not even a look at Walli, who sat quietly in the passenger seat. Just a quick glance around—cars, a truck, and the odd pedestrian—and he turned right. After all that anxiety the moment itself was a nonevent, like the death of an old man in a big American city.

Red Dawg's place was just past MacArthur Park, where K-Town became Pico-Union and all the store signs shifted from Korean to Spanish. Despite Red Dawg's many years of service to Big Danny, Aunt Sheryl and Walli knew surprisingly little about his home life. He definitely had a woman, but they weren't sure if she was his wife or his baby mother. Aunt Sheryl had come across pictures of a baby boy in the house a few years back and she suspected he had more than one kid.

"We did a lot of things together," Walli said, "but he could disappear for several days at a time. Just close up the shop to handle personal business. Big Danny told me not to pry. But I did look on social media. He had a couple of photos on Facebook and some posts about sneakers. No Instagram or Twitter that I could find."

D turned the 225 onto Alvarado and then onto a block of cheap apartment complexes, none newer than the late eighties. A couple of teens rolled down the block on kid's bikes. Three middle-aged Latinos sat smoking in a tight circle in front of an apartment building. Turned out that's where Red Dawg lived.

The trio stared at D and Walli as they exited the car and continued watching as they walked toward the building. D nodded in their direction. No verbal or physical response. D and Walli were moving past them toward an outside staircase when a voice asked, "You looking for the mestizo?"

One of the men, slender except for an imposing beer gut, wore a black bowling shirt with white lettering across the breast that read, *Southern Soul Spinners*. On the back, in the same white thread, was an image of an adapter for playing 45 rpm records on a turntable.

"Yeah," D said. "He a friend of yours?"

"A neighbor," the man replied. "Nobody with such bad taste in music could ever be a true amigo." His previously silent compadres laughed.

D said, "You don't like hip hop, huh?"

"If it ain't a 45 I don't touch it. Anyway, he ain't home and it's been awhile."

D told Walli to head up and knock on Red Dawg's door.

"What," the man said, "you don't believe me?"

"Red Dawg is a resourceful man. He might be back. By the way, my name is D Hunter." He walked over and reached out his hand, unsure what would happen.

The man smiled and nodded at his two friends before shaking D's hand. "I'm Ruben Santiago. You related to Big Danny?"

"I'm his grandson."

"Yeah," Ruben said, "you got the look. Not to mention you driving his money-getting green monster."

"You knew him?"

"Me, him, and Red Dawg had some epic card games."

Walli came downstairs with news that no one had answered his knock.

D asked Ruben, "Didn't he have a woman?"

"She's gone. He came home one morning when I was outside washing my car. He was bloody. He was scared."

D figured this had to have been after the fight at La Zona Rosa. "So he got his woman out of town and went underground?"

"Seems so," Ruben said. "When you rolled up wearing all black I thought you were some fly hit man called the Undertaker or something. But I saw in your face you were kin to Big Danny. This one," he gestured to Walli, "has his blood too."

"Anyone else come looking for him?" D asked.

Ruben's eyes traveled up and down the block, as if he thought someone was watching. "I seen some cars with some vatos trying to look slick roll by. But Red was gone, so . . ." He offered a shrug.

D gestured to his bowling shirt. "What's up? You a musician?"

Ruben reached into his back pocket and pulled out a flyer for a party. "I'm the DJ. Come through. Soul music. No crap rap. Just good songs you can hold your woman tight to."

Red Dawg was hiding in LA or maybe had left town, though D doubted that. No need to go hunt for him. He'd turn up or he wouldn't. Having Red Dawg out of the way was just one less thing D had to worry about.

CHAPTER THIRTY-ONE
A FARMERS MARKET MEET-UP

D thought the farmers market on Fairfax might be his favorite place in Los Angeles. A maze of shops and restaurants with roots in the 1930s, it provided a cozy sense of human interaction that he sorely missed as a New York native son.

He missed the closeness of strangers. The murmur of old and young voices engaged in conversation and spiked with questions reminded D of negotiating Broadway and Houston on a summer Saturday afternoon. He'd never known how much New York's endless chatter was a part of him and it wasn't until he sat at this table at Lotería Grill, a Mexican restaurant with great chicken mole, that he realized how comforting all the noise was.

He'd been raised in chatter and its absence in LA had left him slightly unsettled. So while D sat eating chicken mole, he let his ears entertain his soul. This late lunch meeting had originally been sched-uled at some fancy Beverly Hills spot but D wasn't having it. If she wanted to meet it had to be on D's turf, and the farmers market on Fairfax was where he felt most comfortable.

Still, when R'Kaydia, fine as she was in a red strapless dress, silver bracelets and matching necklace, walked toward him with her hair in a natural curl, circling her bronze face like a halo, he worked hard to hide his excitement. But when she greeted him with a bright smile, D felt his heart sink as he realized, and then accepted, that he'd now have to talk to one person and not just listen to many.

"You turned down my offer." She sat down, staring at D both sexy and hard. "You don't wanna work with me?"

"I'm getting on board as Night's comanager. My attention and loyalty goes to him first."

"Walter Gibbs told you not to sign it, didn't he? You taking advice from a silly hustler like that? He's probably still mad because I didn't fuck him when I was twenty-five."

"Walter's an old friend but I make my own decisions. Plus, things changed. My grandfather left Dr. Funk some property. I have to find him anyway. I don't need or want your money to do that. If I find him and he wants to meet with you afterward, I'll hook you two up."

R'Kaydia pouted. "Sounds like I shouldn't have tried to hire you. I should have just asked for your friendship instead. That would have been easier. People tend to like me. Do you like me, D?"

"Not really," he said, then laughed. "I'm just joking."

"Oh," she said without smiling, "an unnecessarily honest man. I guess I can respect that. Tell me, when did I become *unlikable?*"

D repeated that he had been joking, but R'Kaydia seemed genuinely hurt. *Thin-skinned*, D noted. "What I mean is that I don't know you very well."

"Well, I'm not sure I like you either."

"I'm okay with that."

"Do you always wear black?" It was a question D had been asked hundreds, maybe thousands of times. But his answer was simple and always the same: "Yes."

"What, you flunked undertaker school?" That drew a smile from D. "So," she continued, "no red, no blue, no green? You must think it makes you look serious or intimidating, huh? Don't you get bored with all that sameness?"

D tried to muster some enthusiasm for this conversation. But since this beautiful woman really seemed to want to know, he struggled not to give a rote reply.

"I don't do it for how it looks," he said. "I do it for how it makes me feel."

"And what's that feeling?"

"It makes me feel grateful. Grateful to be alive. Every day is a blessing and an opportunity."

"Colors do that for me. You look at nature and you see color. The sky. Birds. Animals. Trees. The ocean. Life is vivid, D. You're living in California now."

"Black is a color too," he said defensively. "Black is the truest color there is."

R'Kaydia sat back in her chair. "You are the most philosophical bodyguard I've ever met."

Now D had had enough jousting. He'd told R'Kaydia his decision. He'd reach out to her when he had something to reach out about. He was tired of explaining himself. Plus, he felt patronized. "Listen, R'Kaydia, my enchilada is getting cold, so I'm gonna eat it now. If you wanna keep talking, feel free."

D figured he'd offended this moneyed Hollywood lady enough that she'd leave. Instead she stood up and got in line at the Lotería counter. She ordered a watermelon juice and then came back over to the table. She stood next to D sipping on her straw.

"Stay in touch, D," she said.

And then she was off, moving smoothly through the families and the shops in the farmers market, disappearing from his sight, though, he had a feeling, not from his life.

CHAPTER THIRTY-TWO

A KOREATOWN NIGHT
WITH MICHELLE

Michelle told D not to bring his green monster of a ride. They'd be making moves on an LA Tuesday night, and waiting on a valet would kill the vibe. So when the homeless black man walked into the middle of Wilshire Boulevard, weaving through the lanes and indifferent to oncoming traffic, D was sitting in the backseat of a Prius. The Uber driver, a midtwenties black man in a straw hat with long seventies sideburns, was singing along to Drake's *Views* as he had been since picking D up, and continued mimicking the Canadian's Auto-Tune vocalizing as he waited for the homeless man to move.

Perhaps it was Drake's whiney delivery or an earlier ingestion of herb, but the driver seemed unfazed by this nuisance. D tried to be equally blasé, but the homeless man looked like too many faces he'd seen—another brother who'd lost his big-city mind with no future but incarceration or an early death. It wasn't how D wanted to start the evening.

Michelle was waiting inside the expansive, stylish lobby of the Line Hotel; she guided him back to Roy Choi's trendy Korean restaurant, Pot. The tables were white and long. The menus were on newsprint. The music was classic hip hop. The crowd was young and vibrant. A

Central American couple next to them ordered and then began doing the Dougie between tables. D approved of the vibe.

Michelle wore a black J Dilla T-shirt with *Donuts* written across her chest. Her hair was up in a bun, she wasn't wearing a lot of makeup, but she had on some fetching perfume that wafted across the table like an embrace. D was impressed with her ability to code shift, moving from identity to identity without hinting which one was really her. As much as D loved this particular look, he wondered if daytime Michelle was the real Michelle; was the person sitting before him just her wearing a fun uniform?

"So, how's Night's album going?"

"Good. A lot of songs. A lot of directions."

"You're involved in narrowing them down?"

"Along with the rest of the team."

"Well, it sounds like an amazing job. A lot better than keeping screaming girls away from Night."

"Better, yes. Easier, no. At least I knew how to handle the fans—"

"And the groupies?"

"Them too. But being a manager is like being a politician. It's not my natural move to the basket."

"You'll learn," Michelle said. "It took me awhile to become a saleswoman. It's trial and error. My father used to be great. You probably know there were a lot of bad incidents between the first generation of Korean merchants and African American customers."

"Yeah," D said. "Same things happened in New York. You ever see *Do the Right Thing?*"

"Of course."

"Well, there's that Korean grocery store right across the street from Sal's Pizzeria."

"Haven't seen the film in a while but I remember that," she said.

"I was surprised. It was good of Spike to include us, though they didn't have much to do."

"At least they didn't get burned down."

"Seoul to Soul, or something like that, right? I think John Singleton had something like that in *Boyz* too. I'm happy our presence in African American areas was acknowledged. But we weren't central to any of those movies."

"But if those movies were made now, how do you think those same Korean characters would be doing?"

"We'd own everything," she answered without hesitation.

"Oh shit."

She laughed at his reaction. "Well, maybe not everything. But a nice chunk of wherever we were."

"You're serious."

"Of course I am."

"Well, considering I'm in Koreatown, which is booming like crazy, I guess I should be asking you what the black characters would be doing. Odds are that Doughboy would be dead. I'm pretty sure Mookie got priced out of Bed-Stuy a long time ago. That spot where Sal's got burned down? A condo for sure."

They were both amused by this revision of film history but D wanted to circle back to her family history. "Anyway," he said, "you were gonna tell me about your father's skills."

"Well, he listened to everyone and picked up the slang. He'd say *cuz* to gangbangers and they'd laugh and not steal as much."

"I guess they figured he was trying to fit in."

"Apparently he even got good at dice," she said.

"Craps?"

"I dunno the name of the particular game but he'd do it with them.

It made things easier—at least that's what they told me, cause I was very young then." It was clear that even though Michelle was sharing with him, it wasn't easy for her.

"Looks like it all worked out," D said smoothly, then waited for Michelle to inquire about his own family, a narrative of ghetto tragedy he hated relating. There was no way to talk about the death of his three brothers without putting a serious damper on any evening. Debating how much to tell, how much to lie about, and how much to omit made each new human interaction a challenge. Plus, the fact that D carried the HIV virus made the whole getting-to-know-you phase of any new relationship a dark, tangled journey.

For the most part D kept details to himself, hating to see the cycle of sadness, horror, bewilderment, and sometimes disgust inspired by stories of his family and his health. Though he came across as big and strong mentally, D was actually a collection of fragile pieces liable to shatter at an intimate touch. He didn't want people, certainly not a beautiful woman, to perceive him as a walking, talking HBO documentary on urban despair. Yet here he was again, sitting across from a lovely lady on the verge of changing forever how she saw him.

D was saved, for now, by the arrival of Michelle's nighttime party partners, the Chaos. Joey managed several restaurants (when he wasn't DJing) and Lana was a veterinarian. Like Michelle, they were doing what their parents wanted, but they used the nightlife east of Western as a release. The Chaos drank several beers with them and then they all took an Uber to a club on 6th Street to see Awkwafina, a half-Korean/half-Chinese MC from (of all places) Queens, New York, who had a good flow and an amusingly deadpan way with her punch lines.

The crowd was all in their mid-to-late twenties, well dressed, and 80 percent Asian with a sprinkling of Latinos and whites. D thought

Awkwafina was cool and was impressed with the crowd's response, especially how they knew the words to her rhymes and sang all the hooks. In the digital age, when audiences were sliced and diced into microscenes, Awkwafina was satisfying an audience starving for its own voice.

Down the block they grabbed a quick bite at a hot-pot joint. Afterward, as they waited for another Uber, they saw a minivan pull up and let out three middle-aged businessmen in suits and four young Korean girls who entered the club next door.

"Doumi girls," Michelle said.

"What's that mean?" D asked.

"Men pay $120 for them to join them in singing rooms," she explained. "The taxis pick them up and take them to clubs like this. They are private clubs where you have to speak Korean to get in. This is the side of Koreatown outsiders never see."

"Seems to upset you."

"Yeah. What's that movie, *Six Degrees of Separation?* In this neighborhood there is much less."

Another Uber took them downtown to Little Tokyo where they went to Tokyo Beat, a ramen bar in an outdoor mall that on Tuesday nights was home to a fun electrodance party. This crowd was younger, postcollege, split evenly between white and Asian with a few hipster black kids in the mix. A series of DJs manned the turntables. D really enjoyed Mousey McGlynn, a performer who alternated singing originals with snippets of radio hits while programming electrobeats.

But the evening didn't really turn up until midnight when a crew of Chicago footwork dancers took control of the space in front of the DJ. Two black dancers in their thirties and an eclectic crew of younger white dancers began moving in frantic sixty- and ninety-second bursts to beats programmed up to 160 per second. Turned out this was a crew who met at Tokyo Beat every Tuesday to get down and show off. Michelle and D shared a ramen bowl while the Chaos Snapchatted the dancing Chicago footwork to their global posse.

The Chaos had an apartment near Little Tokyo. So after last call at one thirty, the quartet stopped by their one-bedroom condo and smoked some strong Cali chronic out on the balcony. When the Chaos went inside to find munchies, D and Michelle stood close.

"So," she said, "what did you think?"

"I saw another LA tonight. Thank you." He passed her the last of the joint. She took a final hit and then put out the roach on the railing. "Don't you have to go sell houses in the morning?"

"In about four hours. Sunglasses, eyedrops, mouthwash, a shower, some quality perfume, and no one knows what I did the night before."

"I bet your mama knows everything," D teased.

Michelle snorted. "She *thinks* she knows everything. So nothing new there."

Michelle leaned over and kissed D, their mouths smoky. Her smaller body pressed against his.

"Nice," he said finally.

"Yeah, cause you never know."

D and Michelle shared one last Uber ride, heading to Hobart Boulevard in Koreatown and Michelle's walkup apartment, where, in her extremely neat bedroom, he didn't tell her anything but was as careful as you could be while having fun.

CHAPTER THIRTY-THREE

WALLI'S ILL-FATED LOVE AFFAIR

D was doing mountain climbers in the living room. He'd pushed the living room coffee table up against a wall and shoved his grandfather's old easy chair into a corner, laying his yoga mat over the moldy old shag carpet. He was going at it, his arms anchoring him as he drove his legs toward his chest. A *15 Minute Hell* ab workout played on his android.

If you did this right—and didn't cheat with short sets—a workout of mountain climbers, bicycles, and various twists generated dripping sweat, heavy breathing, and active stomach muscles. D was on his last thirty-second burst when a call interrupted him. Irritated, he glanced over at his phone, but picked up when he saw it was Walli.

"What up?"

"D, can you come pick me up at school?!" He sounded unsteady, agitated, fearful. "There's been a shooting. I don't want Ma to know yet."

Twenty minutes and a couple of run red lights later, D was standing outside a crime scene tape along with TV news crews, ambulances, and black, Mexican, and Asian Angelenos. A young Mexican girl was crying into the arms of a black male teacher. A tough-looking Asian kid with tats peeking through his white T-shirt puffed a cigarette. One of the cops policing the perimeter was Crowder, who had come by the house the night of the robbery.

"Hunter, right?"

"Yes, officer. I'd say that it's good to see you again but this is a terrible situation."

"It's happening all the time, one way or another. Your nephew almost got shot."

"My cousin—is he all right?"

"I got him over there. We haven't taken his statement yet. You keep him calm, okay?"

D found Walli sitting on a curb, teary-eyed with specks of dried blood on his J Dilla T-shirt. At his feet was a crumpled bouquet of gardenias. Some broken petals covered his sneakers. Walli appeared to be in shock. D had seen this look before; he sat down and pulled the teenager close.

"The police take your statement yet?"

"No. They told me to wait here."

"Okay," D said. "Tell me everything. Then we'll figure out what to say to them."

It had been about a woman—well, actually, a teenage girl. Her name was Carmen. They'd been classmates his sophomore year in English. Walli had noticed her round hips, thick black hair, and sharp sense of humor. In his junior year they sat next to each other in history class and bonded over Cesar Chavez and began a private Snapchat flirtation neither their parents nor classmates were aware of.

Black and Mexican friendships, while not forbidden by their parents or even rare among classmates, were still fraught in a neighborhood quickly transitioning from black to brown. Walli and Carmen used the relative privacy of social media to leap over the barbed-wire fences of race. No Bloods, Crips, or Mexican or Central America gangs breeched their Snapchat sanctuary.

Walli kept any tension between Latino and black classmates out of conversations with his mother, who'd been fragile since Grandpop's murder. Talk of cafeteria fights at school sure wouldn't calm her. And Carmen? Why even go there with his mother? A real-life/virtual Mexican girlfriend? A shouting match waiting to happen. Today was Carmen's birthday. Sweet seventeen. Walli was going to surprise her and show the school what he felt in his heart—that explained the gardenias.

Unfortunately for Walli, his goal of cementing black/Mexican relations ran afoul of a multinational group of gangbangers. He was coming around the corner toward school when he saw Carmen coming from the other direction. For Walli it was a slow-motion teenage dream coming true. Then cue the scary music (in this case a bomb-ass Dr. Dre track) as three baby Crips, who might have harassed Walli for the hell of it anyway, spotted the gardenias.

"Hey, fool!" called out the oldest and tallest of the three. "Those for me?"

Now Walli had two options: try to ignore the three young Crips and incur their wrath; or joke with them and risk their ridicule and the snatching of the gardenias. Either scenario would happen in front of Carmen.

Walli chose to ignore the baby Crips, hoping only one of the trio gave a damn about him and that the other two would be too busy looking at girls to fuck with him. Alas, the girls the other two locked in on were Carmen and Tarsha, a cute black girl standing nearby.

Carmen saw Walli and smiled. She saw the gardenias and giggled. Then her vision was blocked as the oldest of the Crips, probably eighteen and actually quite handsome despite a few scars on his face, got in her way. Worse for Walli, this kid was smooth. Had some actual game. Walli moved to the side to get a better angle and, damn, he saw Carmen laugh at something he said.

The other two Crips attempted to engage Tarsha, who wasn't

charmed and tried to get past the duo and their lascivious intentions. Carmen started to look nervous and glanced Walli's way, weighing whether or not to involve him. After all, she was an attractive girl in an LA hood; negotiating with gangsta lotharios was the price of that ticket. Walli's young manhood was now challenged. He'd have to walk over there if he was to ever respect himself, much less have Carmen consider him as a true boyfriend candidate.

Things escalated when a red Impala creeped toward the school's entrance. Inside were three Latinos. Walli noticed them heading in his direction and recognized the kid in the passenger seat from history class. Teddy, maybe? A big burly man behind the wheel rocked Locs. The car pulled next to Carmen and the baby Crips. Walli's former classmate yelled, "Get away from our women, nigga!" and then the Crips cursed them back.

D asked, "Who shot first?"

"The older guy in the back of the car stuck a gun out of the window," Walli said. "At first he didn't shoot—I guess he was just gonna scare them. Then the older Crip grabbed Carmen by the arm like he was gonna kiss her. That's when I ran over."

"You grabbed the Crip?"

"More like ran into him."

"You pull him down?"

"Ah, well, I actually kinda just, you know, bounced off him."

"But he let Carmen go?"

"Yeah. Then the shooting started. I saw the older Crip shoot first."

"No you didn't."

"I did."

"You didn't. You fell to the ground. You covered your head. You heard the shots but you didn't see who shot who. Okay?"

"Okay."

"Where's Carmen?"

"Ambulance took her."

"Was she hit?"

"Just got blood on her from somebody. But real scared."

D noticed Crowder approaching. "Remember," he said, "you didn't see who shot first. You don't have any theories. You just tried to help your friend. You hit the ground and covered up."

Walli stood up, still shaking.

D didn't want his cousin identifying gang-banging shooters for the LAPD. "Oh Walli," he said, "give me the flowers."

Two hours later Sheryl held Walli in her arms, tears streaming down her face as she realized how close she had come to losing her son. In retelling the story, Walli and D neglected to mention the flowers or Carmen. It was just the tale of one classmate trying to help another.

Sheryl in midrant: "Those fucking Mexican motherfuckers! Bitch-ass drive-by bitches! Taking over our neighborhood. Scaring good folks away."

D knew she was excitable and a touch prejudiced, but he hadn't ever seen her like this. She glared out the window at the Mexican kids playing soccer next door. D wondered if he should grab the shotgun from under the kitchen table before his aunt went postal.

"Ma," Walli said, "the police said the people shooting were from El Salvador."

"I'm tired of *all* of them. They came in and overran this neighborhood like roaches in light."

"Well," D said, "black homeowners sold to them."

"You ain't from here, D, but you see how they do. I'm sure that's why Dad had that shotgun under the table. You saw them fools try to break in here. Fuck them all."

Walli and D sat on the sofa, prepared to wait out her fear. This was something that had been eating at her, eating at lots of old-time black Angelenos, and the high school shootout gave it voice. Moreover, it had turned his lovely aunt into a temporary Donald Trump supporter.

"It's time to sell the house. I've had enough of this shit. My little boy ain't gonna die in these damn LA streets. They took my father. They ain't taking him."

"I know a broker," D said.

"Better not be no taco eater."

"She's not."

CHAPTER THIRTY-FOUR

SUN HEE PAK TELLS A STORY

After working out at the Equinox on Sunset Boulevard (Walter Gibbs hooked him up) and grabbing an omelet and green juice at Caffé Primo next door, D cruised along and made a right at Western. Soon he found himself in Alternate LA. Down a long stretch of the avenue the store signs were written in Korean, Spanish, English, or trilingual. D was in a sun-drenched Blade Runner reality that made him wonder what country he'd entered.

Big Danny had been no stranger to Western Avenue as he made alliances there that helped him cut corners at his grocery store and nightclub. If he had any problems with white distributors on anything from cigarettes to gummy bears, there were Mexican, Korean, or Japanese businesspeople who had the hookup. It wasn't always brand-name material, but changing wrappers solved that problem. D had vague memories of wandering through a Western Avenue swap meet, trailing Big Danny as he haggled with a Korean man. Now he wondered if these various deals involved some form of loan-sharking.

He was a little early for his meeting, so he checked out some of the shops at the Koreatown Plaza Mall, impressed by the range of products being sold. Once again D had the feeling that he'd traveled a great distance by just taking that right on Western. On the second level he walked past a large Korean supermarket and then stopped in a bookstore, leafing through a lifestyle magazine which featured a four-page spread of Korean B-boys sporting the hottest urban gear. *Hip hop, you don't stop*, he thought.

Next to the bookstore were the stained-glass offices of Pak City Real Estate. The reception area consisted of two sofas. D lounged down on one, while a Latina in her forties sat in the other with a little girl. The woman read from several legal-looking papers while the daughter played on her mother's phone. On the wall behind them was a huge map of Los Angeles. It could have been any anonymous office anywhere in the city, except for the music: a man passionately crooned an Air Supply–type ballad in Korean.

Behind the reception desk sat a cute, chubby, college-aged Korean woman, who was focused on her phone. D cleared his throat. "Hi, my name is D Hunter. I have an appointment with Michelle and Sun Hee Pak."

"Oh yes, we were expecting you. I'm Michelle's sister Alice. Take a seat and I'll let her and Mom know you're here." Instead of phoning, Alice got up and walked down a corridor into the back.

D felt the Latina's eyes on him. He smiled. Her eyes shifted away as if he had a bad disease. Then both their heads turned when they heard the unmistakable voice of a scolding mother emanating from the back. The words were in Korean but the tone of parental disapproval was universal.

It went quiet for a moment and then the scolding resumed. Alice emerged from the back and said, "Michelle will be out to get you in a minute," and then went back to her iPhone.

A minute later, Michelle appeared from the back, a forced smile upon her lips.

"Nice to see you again," D said. He leaned over to kiss her cheek, but she stuck out her hand for a stiff handshake instead.

"Come on back," she said. "My mother is looking forward to meeting you."

D found himself sitting across from stern-faced Sun Hee Pak, a petite, formidable, middle-aged woman in a blue-and-green floral dress. Michelle meekly stood next to her mother.

"You are related to Daniel Hunter?"

"He was my grandfather."

"You do have his eyes," she said, then added, "His lips as well."

"Oh, I guess I do. You were friends?"

"He helped me survive the '92 riot."

Michelle looked at her mother with wide eyes. "That was his grandfather?"

"My daughter knows this story but must not have been paying attention to her mother," Sun Hee said as Michelle avoided D's gaze. "Your grandfather was both practical and wise."

"You mean he knew how to keep a secret," D said.

Sun Hee Pak smiled and then continued: "Daniel came to this area when it was still mostly Mexican and made friends with many Korean merchants in the area. This was a difficult time for such relationships. So many of us did not speak English well. So we had a hard time communicating, particularly with black customers. You probably know of instances where Korean shopkeepers shot black customers."

"I knew there were several black people murdered by store owners," D said flatly. "And that no one was brought to justice."

"Yes," Sun Hee admitted, "it was tragic. It made it difficult for us to find common ground with blacks and Mexicans. So hard. We were strangers. We were afraid. Whites told us blacks were violent. The police told us blacks were animals. So, often, fear overcame our reason. We didn't see black people as human and blacks didn't respect us. Terrible time. We met your grandfather at a swap meet. He was negotiating with a friend of ours who was importing sneakers from China."

"Counterfeits?"

"Imports from China," she repeated with a laugh. "He was the first black person to reach out his hand in friendship to my husband and me. He listened to us as we struggled with English. He told us slang words that made our customers laugh. He told us things to order that we would not have known about, like pig's feet."

"That's definitely crucial information," D said, now smiling too.

"The day of the Rodney King verdict Daniel was next door meeting with Mr. Joo, who was a wholesaler. Afterward he came to say hello to us when the footage of the Reginald Denny beating appeared on live TV. It was not very far away from where we were. Daniel asked me, *Where is your husband?* He had gone downtown to renew our retail license. He said, *Do you have a gun?* I told him my husband kept one by the cash register. He told me to go get it. He went out to his car and came back with a gun as long as his arm. I said, *You think we'll need it?* He said yes.

"We closed the shop and shut off the lights. Then it started. I heard shouting. I heard glass shatter and car alarms go off. It wasn't dark yet but the sky turned gray and the sun—the sun was blocked by smoke. He sat on a garbage can in front of the store. He had both guns. Mr. Joo next door also stood outside his store with a gun. Some of the other shop owners climbed onto the roof of the strip mall."

"When night fell the shooting started. I told Daniel to come inside. In the dark, who would know looter from protector? It was a sleepless night. No word from my husband. Was he alive or dead? I told your grandfather to go look after his store and his family. But he would not leave me by myself. He promised he would get me home to my girls. Soon as the sun rose we got in his big car."

"I'm driving it now."

"Oh really?"

"Yeah. It attracts attention—I'm sure it did back then."

Sun Hee laughed. "Yes. Hard car to miss. I was terrified already . . . and to ride in that boat . . ." She shook her head. "It wasn't funny then. But your grandfather—very fearless. At first I was sitting with him but it was too scary. Too much smoke. So many angry faces. I climbed into the backseat and covered myself with a coat. The police stopped us one time and looked inside. I stuck my head out and I believe the officers would have shot Daniel if I hadn't told them I was not being kidnapped. One policeman kept his gun on us and the other went to the car. I told him, *People are dying and you're worried about us—he is taking me home!* Finally they let us go."

"As bad as that was," D said, "you two are lucky it wasn't one of those rednecks on the National Guard. He wouldn't have even asked. He would have just shot you both."

"Well, Daniel got me home safely. I was so thankful."

"But the drama wasn't over, was it, Mother?" It was the first time Michelle had spoken in a while. "I was a little girl but I remember. Are you going to tell D that part?"

Sun Hee snapped at her daughter in Korean. It was the same tone D had heard between them earlier. Michelle was acting like a petulant adolescent and Sun Hee a scolding mother. Maybe, D thought, it was time to leave. It had been a good story. He loved hearing that Big Danny was a hero. Yet there was a private war going on here between mother and daughter that D wanted no part of. Michelle was a hottie, no doubt, but D didn't like how she'd turned him into an audience.

"My husband was at home," Sun Hee said. She stared at D with sad eyes. Michelle's face went smug. Sun Hee continued: "He'd been attacked. His car had been damaged. His phone stolen. Instead of thanking Daniel, he slapped me."

"Oh."

"And I slapped him back."

"Your grandfather's presence made my father angry—" Michelle started.

"It was mostly embarrassment," Sun Hee cut in. "He was upset he wasn't there for me, and that two little black kids had carjacked him. He never forgot it. How could he? That riot redefined our lives. By that, I mean the whole Korean community. The Koreatown you see now was built up from those ashes."

"Fire forges steel," D observed.

"Every year, when the anniversary comes around, I know it's difficult for him," Michelle said.

"You are driving your grandfather's car?" Sun Hee asked.

"Yeah," D said. "It's in the garage."

"I would like to see it."

Downstairs, Mrs. Pak stood a few feet away from Big Danny's car, taking it in silently.

"He really kept it well maintained," D said, filling the silence.

Sun Hee took a step forward, bent down, and peered inside.

"I need to wash the windows," D said.

Sun Hee didn't reply. She just straightened back up and turned around, her eyes red and wet.

"Mom, what's wrong?"

"Nothing," Sun Hee replied. "Michelle will make sure we get a good price for your grandfather's home and I will make sure your aunt has a fine house to move into. I promise you that."

"Thank you," D said.

Sun Hee turned and walked toward the elevator.

"What was that about?" Michelle asked quietly.

"Weird, right?" But D knew what was up. He hadn't been sure upstairs. But the way she'd looked at the car and her riot story had nailed it. Sun Hee Pak was the woman in that photo with Big Danny.

CHAPTER THIRTY-FIVE

R'KAYDIA HAS GAME

Al had called first and D mumbled an excuse to blow off the meeting. Night called ten minutes later and pleaded with D to show up. One of D's goals in life was to be in Amos Pilgrim's presence as little as possible, but his friends/partners seemed to feel this was a meeting about money, and since they all needed some (and he was now a co-manager), D had to be there.

He was on his way to Amos's Sunset Boulevard office when he got a text from Al to instead head over to Westwood and the offices of Future Life Communications. R'Kaydia's office. *Oh shit.*

When D entered, R'Kaydia had just shown Night and Al the infamous Suge Knight room next to her office, while Amos sat at the desk messing with his smartphone. Amos nodded; D grunted.

R'Kaydia came over and gave him a theatrical hug, like they were the oldest, dearest friends. "So good to see you, D," she said. Amos watched this and smiled, and right then D knew that Amos understood their entire business history.

"You two know each other?" It was Al.

"We've worked together," she said, "albeit briefly. But in this business, worlds always collide."

D sat in the chair farthest from R'Kaydia's desk. He'd seen her magic act before.

Ten minutes later, Dr. Funk was singing on the desk and Night was geeking out. D glanced at R'Kaydia and yawned. In response she pressed a button on her desk and a hologram of young, pre-drug Night popped up next to Dr. Funk, chiming in on the chorus.

R'Kaydia then pushed another button and Dr. Funk's old band the Love Patrol appeared behind Night and Dr. Funk looking freaky, florid, and fantastic. The music flowed from the Dr. Funk classic to a funkified remix of Night's big hit, "Black Sex."

"I got Questlove and the Roots crew to recreate the track and had this LA funkster Dâm-Funk mix it," R'Kaydia explained.

"It's lit," said Night.

"It's the future," said Amos. "It's the visual equivalent of the DJ mash-up. We can create the concerts you always wanted to see. Dead giants collaborating with living stars. All-star jams from all kinds of eras."

"Live, or is it Memorex?" asked Al. "People today don't really know the difference anyway. People will still pay, I guess." The vet wasn't really buying the digital spectacle but he wasn't going to be too negative. Night looked toward D for his input.

At that point Amos spoke the magic words: "In order for this thing to work, R'Kaydia has to make a very generous publishing deal with the copyright owners."

"How much?" D said, turning his head toward R'Kaydia.

"I'm prepared to offer $250,000 for the exclusive use of Night's songs in the hologram space for ten years. The agreement would start from the project's launch date."

Al asked when that would be and was told two years.

D piped up: "I assume there's a bonus if Night signs now. And I assume you'd want him to be a rainmaker to attract other artists to sign on. So it sounds like $500,000 to $750,000 is a better starting point for negotiations."

Everyone turned toward R'Kaydia. "Yes to $500,000, D. Of course we couldn't have a better ambassador than Night. He's got mystique, great music, and is a sex symbol."

"Thank you," Night said.

"You are all welcome," R'Kaydia replied. "Amos and I will sit down and work out all the details."

"So," Night asked, "do you have Dr. Funk under contract?"

R'Kaydia smiled. "He's proven difficult to reach."

"D's got the hookup," Night said. "Right, D?"

"Night wants to work with him, so I've been looking for him," D responded. "But R'Kaydia already knows that."

"Well, now that search is even more important." Amos spoke the words but it was R'Kaydia's eyes that sparkled.

"Night," she said sweetly, "there's more to it than just these holograms. As you may know, my partner Teddy Tapscott was a producer on *Straight Outta Compton*, and he's got Universal interested in a Dr. Funk biopic. If D can get us in touch with Dr. Funk, this could be a big win for you."

All eyes fell on D, who slumped in his seat and sighed.

CHAPTER THIRTY-SIX

MICHELLE PAK MEETS AUNT SHERYL

At first Aunt Sheryl eyed Michelle Pak suspiciously. Without a word her eyes asked, *How come we aren't using a black broker?* D didn't want her to know he had a romantic interest in Michelle, so he stuck to the facts: she had just sold the house next door, had a roster of buyers interested in the area, and, since she wasn't black, could probably get a better mortgage from whatever bank we went to. It was logical and sad, but even as Sheryl cursed the racist bankers she acknowledged D had a point.

At the kitchen table, D couldn't help but smile when Michelle ended up sitting in the chair where, with a flick of her finger, she could have access to a Mossberg twelve-gauge shotgun. Aunt Sheryl was clearly not comfortable with this seating arrangement, especially since D sat squarely in front of the shotgun muzzle.

"My family has had a variety of businesses, but real estate is our major focus," Michelle explained. "We offer full service. We can sell this house for you and, if you wish to stay in the Los Angeles area, we can find you a new residence and help relocate you as well."

Aunt Sheryl picked up Michelle's business card. "Your family name is Pak. I know some Koreans named Park, but I've never heard of Pak before."

"There's a weird story with that," Michelle said. "When my father came over from Korea, his name was Park. Park is like Smith or Jones in

America—extremely common. But the immigration officer, for whatever reason, put down *Pak* on the immigration form when he entered the country. My parents didn't realize the mistake until it turned up on all our paperwork. My parents couldn't really speak English, so we started as Pak, not Park, and it became difficult to change, so my mother decided we should own it."

"I bet that lazy immigration officer was Mexican."

"Aunt Sheryl," D scolded.

"I believe the officer was a white male," Michelle said. "It's just bureaucracy at work."

"I guess that's true," Aunt Sheryl conceded. "I have a lot of customers who work for the city. I know they spend as much time on Facebook as business."

"Our business," Michelle said.

"That's right," Aunt Sheryl said.

"You are an independent businesswoman, and I know how hard that can be. My mother runs our real estate business and she doesn't tolerate laziness."

"So you work for your mother?"

"Yes. My father founded the retail business but my mother got us into this."

"Working for your mother—I know that's a bitch. Not saying that she's a bitch, but, you know? I mean, my mother was as good a woman as could be, but she still worked my nerves. Too much advice. Too much *I told you so.*"

Michelle smiled uncomfortably. "It's challenging. She has her way of handling things."

"Set in their ways," Aunt Sheryl said. "Trying to change them is like pouring mouthwash down a sewer. It's gonna smell how it smells."

NELSON GEORGE 187

And that was that. Michelle's practiced, professional demeanor cracked under Aunt Sheryl's honest, kinda country views on life. "You are so right," she finally said, smiling. "Working for your mother is very, very hard."

With that kinship established, Michelle and Aunt Sheryl did a quick walk around the house while D stayed at the table, slipping on his Bose earphones to listen to some of Night's new tracks.

Fifteen minutes later the women were back, ready to talk business. As D took off his earphones, he heard Michelle ask: "Where are you interested in relocating to?" Her glasses were perched on her nose and her fingers hovered over an iPad.

Aunt Sheryl took a drag from her cigarette and puffed out some smoke. "Hmmm, I have heard Lancaster's nice. Got friends out there."

D asked, "Isn't that in the middle of the desert?"

Michelle didn't even need to click on her little computer. "It's the Inland Empire," she said. "There's been a huge amount of development over the last five to ten years. Many African American families—young families with people in your son's age range."

"A lot of my friends have moved out there," Aunt Sheryl said. "A lot from this neighborhood. Prices are reasonable. They have big houses and condos. It's a little hot, but that's what AC is for."

"Fifteen percent of the population is African American." Michelle was now reading off her iPad. "Which is the fifth-highest concentration of African Americans in Los Angeles County. There are 32,000 African Americans in Lancaster, and 9,500 households are African American. That's a healthy percentage."

"That's a long drive, Aunt Sheryl. What about your business?"

"D, it's been shrinking. Has been for a while. Less heads in the neighborhood. But I could get a chair out there in Lancaster at this salon I know, and then keep my spot here three or four days a week. I could stack the appointments so I'd be working all day as opposed to sitting around and waiting like I do now."

D smiled. "So you've actually been planning this for a while?"

"Hell yeah. I was gonna wait until Walli was in college, but I've had it."

"I will get you a good price for this place," Michelle reassured her. "More than enough to get a bigger place out there. There's so much demand for homes in this part of LA that it'll move quickly."

"I like how you handle yourself, Miss Pak. How soon can you get all this going?"

"I can have potential buyers over to see your house tomorrow, and I will send you a link to Lancaster properties as soon as I get back to the office. Two bedrooms, right?"

"Shit, if we can afford it, look for three. We need a guest room for my nephew here. I can't wait to see if he's crazy enough to wear all black out in the desert."

CHAPTER THIRTY-SEVEN

IN THE ANTELOPE VALLEY

Lancaster is about seventy miles north of Downtown Los Angeles and on the edge of LA County. Along with neighboring Palmdale, Lancaster is the anchor city of the Antelope Valley and is noteworthy for an aerospace wall of honor called Boeing Plaza and a patch of highway that plays the William Tell Overture when cars cross it. D was curious about the musical highway but figured he'd try that route on the way back to LA.

First order of business was finding his aunt's new house. He went through the center of town along Sierra Highway and drove for about twenty minutes before he found himself on a street of well-separated two-story homes with large garages and sad bits of shrubbery. Aunt Sheryl's house was bigger than Big Danny's, but it had no porch, no trees, and you had the feeling the whole neighborhood was built five minutes ago. There was no history on this block and no stories in the homes. The land was just desert with cement on top. D figured it would be a serious battle keeping dust out of the living room.

As he pulled up he noticed a young black man in a do-rag driving past in a blue Audi. He was playing something by Future that D didn't recognize, which meant D was old, though the fact that he actually recognized Future's voice worried him.

Aunt Sheryl had given him a key but when D walked in he felt uneasy. The living room was filled with new Ikea and Crate and Barrel furniture. A flat-screen TV was hanging on the wall. The place felt as modern and faceless as the family home back in LA was old and comfy. But his aunt thought character was overrated and that new appliances were God's gift.

She and Walli were in the kitchen stocking the new refrigerator and shelves with groceries, having just completed their first shopping trip as Lancasterites.

"They got some nice malls out here," she said.

"Yeah," Walli said, "we ran into more black people while shopping here than we've seen by us back home in years."

"I even saw two of my old customers. Getting paid out here already," Aunt Sheryl said.

D took a seat at the spanking-new kitchen table, which his aunt pointed out had no gun rack underneath. The purchase of this house had happened lightning-quick, less than two weeks after Aunt Sheryl first met Michelle.

Sheryl reached into her purse and pulled out an envelope, which she tossed onto the table. Inside D found $1,500. "Your girl Michelle helped us find a buyer for most of the furniture. That's your share. You know that Korean girl did us a real solid. If she was black I'd say jump on that."

"But she's *not* black," D responded.

"Too bad."

"But Ma," Walli said, "you like her though."

"I do. But I know how hard it is to be a black person in this country and so does D and so does any black women he would marry. Michelle don't know and ain't never gonna know. Walli, your cousin is a hard-working man and I can see he's growing. Be good for him to have a partner."

D was taken aback by his aunt's comments and told her so.

"Don't be surprised. I see you, D. You moving to another phase in your life. A good woman would really help you get there. That Michelle is smart and knows how to use two coins to make three. But is she really ready to put up with what comes with a black husband and a baby or two in this fucked-up country? Shit, I am seriously black, and some-times I can barely get through the day."

"I don't know why we're having this conversation," D said. "We've just gone out a couple of times."

"Oh," Aunt Sheryl teased, "you're getting defensive."

D could tell he was blushing. It was weird. In the middle of every-thing going on he was catching feelings for Michelle. This conversation made him deeply uncomfortable. "Walli," he said to escape his aunt, "show me the rest of the house."

First they checked out Walli's room, which was much bigger than what he had back in LA. Through the window was a vista of electrical towers behind a block of similar two-story buildings. On the wall was a framed photo of Walli with his grandfather and D, right next to post-ers of Blac Chyna and Zendaya. Aunt Sheryl's master bedroom had its own walk-in closet and a private bathroom, plus a brand-new bed with a canopy covered in leopard print. Her new carpet was thick and the view overlooked the street and her neighbor's homes.

Finally D was shown the guest room, which he could use whenever he wanted. He stood in the doorway and regarded the bed with its dark wood posts and sturdy frame. It was his grandparents' bed. "She couldn't toss this out, huh?"

"The appraiser from the vintage shop really wanted it," Walli said. "But I guess not."

D sat on the bed, which was covered in kente cloth sheets his grandmother had sewn together back in the Afrocentric nineties. It squeaked, which made D remember being told it was the bed his father had been conceived on, a detail that used to gross him out but now felt like an essential connection to his family's past. Without this bed, neither he nor any of his brothers would have existed.

Walli had gone back to his room to grab his computer to show D some genealogical material he'd found online about the Hunter clan. But when Walli returned D was stretched out on the bed, snoring and dreaming.

CHAPTER THIRTY-EIGHT
HOT IN SHERMAN OAKS

It was one of those pink-, sand-, or slate-colored apartment complexes rife in the Valley with a faux-Spanish water fountain in front, balconies for every apartment on each of its four floors, and a gated entrance to underground parking. Out back was a courtyard with a family-size pool, a smaller wading pool, Jacuzzi, barbecue pit, and worn deck chairs.

The furniture in the apartment was imitation Crate and Barrel, including a sofa, TV, dining table, bed, kitchen gear, and washer/dryer. The AC went from mild to freezing if you tapped the thermostat. The two windows looked out onto Woodman, a busy street that had exits on and off the 101. *Welcome to Sherman Oaks*, D thought. It was a short walk to the studio down Ventura Boulevard, so he wouldn't be totally dependent on a car. There were some minimalls in the direction of Ventura where he could grab provisions, along with cleaners, a Peruvian restaurant, and some other small businesses. Along Ventura itself were plenty of spots to eat, some yoga studios, and, down by the 405, the Galleria Mall with an ArcLight Cinema and 24 Hour Fitness.

D had never spent much time in the Valley and sure hoped his stay would be short-lived. Night was staying in the same complex, where he could keep an eye on him. And Amos Pilgrim was footing the bill, so D was only paying for utilities, cable, and Internet. Though the apartment defined bland, this journey west had morphed from sad family gathering to legitimate business trip. Living in this faceless joint would definitely focus D on the task at hand.

Now that he was here, Night and Al wanted to play him everything they'd cut in the studio, a marathon listening session D couldn't wait to start. Anything that kept him out of his apartment was fine.

On overbearingly hot summer days, Ventura Boulevard's pavement scalded walkers. Which is why D was hopping between patches of shade, from the side of a building to a bus stop to the long shadow of a palm tree.

D knew he must have looked silly to the passing Cali motorists rolling through Sherman Oaks. But he was determined not to give up walking just because he was in LA. He felt his back tighten up when he spent too much time in a car seat, plus the stubborn New Yorker in him refused to concede the ability to walk places, something most LA locals had given up long ago (if they'd ever had the walking itch at all).

Even today, stupid as it was, D braved the blazing sun and ninety-degree midday heat in charcoal shorts and T-shirt, walking past a Guitar Center and a big new Ralphs to the recording studio on Ventura, where inside, Night sat in front of the board. He was tweaking a few of the hundreds of small knobs before him.

Sometimes he nodded his head to the beat. Sometimes he sang softly to himself, especially on tracks where he hadn't yet laid down lead vocals. Nothing Night played was actually finished. Some were just keys and a drum machine. A couple felt like they were played by a full band, though Night had overdubbed most of the instruments himself. There was one song that had the feel of a LinnDrum-driven Prince track. Another had a DJ Premier feel, like three old vinyl LPs had been grinded up in a blender. Night had even dipped his toe into trap music, with its spacey sonics and a mush-mouthed MC who rhymed *lit* and *shit* twice in four bars. D's ears perked up when Night played a cover of Dr. Funk's bodacious funk jam "Venus Rising," which he had slowed down to a midtempo simmer.

By the time the epic listening session was done, Night had played twenty-four tracks, the product of three years of writing and eight months of recording in this San Fernando Valley studio. He swung his chair around and gazed at D, who reclined on the leather sofa while staring at the ceiling.

"That's a lot, right?" Night asked.

"Yup," D said, thinking hard about what to say to his old friend. "It's a lot."

Al, who'd been coming in and out, entered with takeout Chinese food and a six-pack of Mexican beer. He surveyed this awkward moment and laughed. "Come on, guys. Stop being politicians and get on with it. I'm too old to sit around with you two bullshitting."

"Okay," Night said, "it's a little scattered, huh?"

D sat up now and looked his friend in the eye, determined to be as honest as possible. "Night, there's lots of good shit here, but yeah, it's all over the place. If I didn't know you, I'd say you have no musical direction, don't know who you are musically, or even who your audience is." Then he paused and added, "But I know you do."

Truth was, Night did and didn't. He'd been heavily influenced by the late-nineties neosoul movement, and like a lot of artists of that generation, his output had been maddeningly sporadic with splashes of brilliance. His last album had been released only three years ago but it had done well for the Internet age, selling nearly half a million copies of actual vinyl and CDs, plus a couple hundred thousand downloads.

But the supporting tour had been spotty. He sold out multiple nights in New York, Chicago, Los Angeles, and DC, but outside of Atlanta, sales down south had been so poor he basically played two nights below the Mason-Dixon line—in Atlanta and Miami. Booking "soft ticket" dates (i.e., outdoor festivals and state fairs) where people weren't paying to see individual acts helped cover expenses, plus he did some lucrative shows in Japan and the United Kingdom.

The fact that he was now a niche artist struggling to build true national appeal messed with Night's head and sent him flailing around, flirting with *this hot sound* and *that new producer* like so many vintage acts do when they become desperate to stay current.

But Night didn't say all that. He just muttered, "Just trying new shit, you know. Experimenting. Not all of it works yet."

"Well, how much of your past do you want to walk away from?" D asked. "You are known for a sound. It's not the most current sound, true. But there's several hundred thousand people in the world—maybe a million or two worldwide—who like it. You gotta move forward. Nobody's life stands still. But right now I'm hearing you zigzag between the past and a bunch of things that sound like now."

"Go on," Night said.

"You need to pick one or two of these songs and decide which one puts your flag in the ground. You gotta pick that sound, that song, and build around it like it's a number one draft choice and you own the franchise."

Night burst out laughing and Al chuckled too. "I told you," he said to Al. "I told you this nigga is growing up into the new Yoda."

"Huh?" D replied, not sure if he was being complimented or caricatured.

"D," Al chimed in, "you used to be a silent-bodyguard type. But I guess all those nights hanging with Dwayne Robinson rubbed off."

A little embarrassed, D said, "I'm just speaking from my heart."

"I feel you, D," Night said. "And I think you're right. But I'm not sure which are the right choices."

"Give me an iPod with all the tracks and let me live with it a few days."

"What did you think of the Dr. Funk cover?"

"Pretty amazing. Really well arranged."

"Thanks. After I saw that footage at the wake I had to touch some of his music."

"It felt good. I'm sure the good doctor will be flattered."

CHAPTER THIRTY-NINE

EVERYONE HAS A STORY IN LA

"**I**t's been handled."

Red Dawg was on the wrong side of the glass in the visitors room of an LA County correctional facility, smiling as wide as the Pacific coast. It wasn't until yesterday that D got a heads-up from Aunt Sheryl about Red Dawg's location. Ten days earlier he'd been picked up on an outstanding warrant following a fight outside a Koreatown bar. Aunt Sheryl told D that Red Dawg didn't want him to know until he was ready. And now he was.

D stared into the face of a stupidly happy incarcerated man and asked, "*What's* handled?"

"The situation regarding Big Danny. It's been taken care of."

"That's it?"

"And you were right," Red Dawg said. "I was wrong. It wasn't who I thought it was or why. Walli knows the whole story. This ain't the place to go into details but I wanted to say to you face-to-face that Big Danny can rest easy and that I did the right thing by him."

"The right thing?"

"Yeah. By Big Danny. By your family. Even by you, D."

"Does Aunt Sheryl know?"

"Only Walli knows the whole story. Talk to him. By the way, the next time you walk into your grandfather's store, look up. The sky's the limit, cuz." Then Red Dawg tapped the glass with his knuckles, gave a thumbs-up, and walked away.

* * *

A few hours later D sat across from Walli in Lancaster, sipping on bottled water, listening to his cousin relate a secondhand story.

"It was a robbery. A straight-up robbery. The guy knew Granddaddy loaned people money. He figured he'd have cash on him so the guy was clocking him. He must have seen the Korean grocer slip Granddaddy some money. He was going to move on him in the minimall but there were so many people around that he lost his nerve. So he got in his car and followed Granddaddy. He was some kind of addict. He got more frustrated as he followed him. At Wilshire Boulevard he just snapped. After he shot Granddaddy he even forgot to get the money."

D just looked at Walli blankly. "Is there more?"

"This is what Red Dawg found out in County. The guy who shot Granddad was inside. He was bragging to people and Red Dawg heard and had the man *handled*."

"Red Dawg believes this is what and how it happened?"

"Yeah, I guess."

D sighed. "You got the keys to the grocery store?"

"I can get them from Ma."

"Do that."

"What's wrong?"

"Everything. Get those keys for me."

D sat, shaking his head as Walli exited the room. Dumb motherfucker got a man shanked because of his typically ass-backward reasoning. Some junkie stickup kid wouldn't have worried about those chai latte drinkers at the café. He certainly wouldn't have driven halfway across LA to rob his mark. Red Dawg heard a story, put two and seven together, and got someone hurt. Proud of it too.

But maybe the keys would actually lead to something useful. D snatched them from Walli's hand and headed toward the door.

"Ma wants to know if you're staying for dinner."

No reply. D was out the door and gone.

At the store, in the drop ceiling, right over the detergent, D found an old ledger book with a blue cloth cover and the heft of a well-worn Bible. On the second page there was a list of names:

Robinson
Wills
Valenzuela
Park
Koufax
Piazza
Drysdale
Garvey

Flipping through the book, D saw that each of the names had its own section. *Robinson* had the largest section—ten pages. In the left-hand margin was an address on Vermont. In columns below the names were various marks (*1B, 2B, 3B, HR, E1, E2*). There was only one page each for *Koufax* and *Drysdale*. But *Valenzuela* was eight pages and *Park* was five.

D put the ledger down and smiled, his grandfather's mind revealing itself with visions of Saturdays spent in the left field bleachers at Chavez Ravine. These were the names of Dodger greats: Jackie Robinson, Maury Wills, Sandy Koufax, Don Drysdale, Fernando Valenzuela, Chan Ho Park, and Mike Piazza. Big Danny covered a bunch of ethnic

groups with the names of players he both celebrated and castigated—
presumably these were groups he had loaned money to.

Piazza = Italians

Koufax = Jews

Drysdale = Caucasians

Valenzuela = Mexicans

Robinson = blacks

Park = Koreans

That was the easy part. Figuring out the meanings behind *1B*, *2B*,
E1, etc., was harder. He suspected the base hits were loans and the
errors were late payments or defaults. But within these sections, under *Robinson* and *Park* and the other Dodgers, there were no names, just addresses.

Under the *Robinson* heading he began randomly checking addresses on
Google. Some were stores. Most were homes or apartments in Ladera
Heights or Baldwin Hills or some other well-established black neighborhood. Some addresses appeared several times—multiple loans
perhaps—but with no dates next to them, so it was hard to know when
these loans were made or the length of the repayment term.

D scanned the few addresses under *Koufax* (all were around Fairfax
north of Beverly) and *Valenzuela* (scattered around Crenshaw, South
LA, and Koreatown). To his surprise, not all the addresses under *Park*
were in Koreatown. In fact, most of them were in beautiful Hancock
Park, an area of palatial homes, treelined streets, and a golf course.

Hancock Park began just two blocks west of Koreatown but, in
terms of architecture and mood, it was on another planet from bustling,
hustling Koreatown. The neighborhood was overwhelmingly white, solidly Jewish, and moneyed, with a population on the plus side of the baby
boom. That Big Danny was loaning money to anyone with a Hancock
Park address shocked his grandson.

D Googled one address and found a traditional brick New England home with a large lawn and a Mercedes sedan in the driveway. In the ledger there was an *HR* designation next to four entries, and then lots of *E1, E2, E3*, suggesting this customer borrowed big and then paid back slowly, compounding interest. Why would Big Danny keep lending this loser money? Did he send Red Dawg after him?

The next morning D was sitting in a car down the block from the Hancock Park address. Wisely, he had ditched his grandfather's gaudy ride for a rented white Prius, which he hoped would make the presence of a big black man on this street just a bit less conspicuous. It was seven thirty. D was hoping he'd catch whoever lived there on their way to work.

He knew he couldn't post up there long as, Prius or no Prius, his big black face would eventually get noticed and he didn't want to explain his presence to the LAPD. At eight fifteen a car finally pulled out of the garage and headed in his direction. D slid sideways and ducked down even as he craned his neck. Lawrence from the convenience store rolled past him in a gray Lexus. *So that's why Big Danny stopped there so frequently.*

He pulled out his phone and prepared to call Detective Gonzales with this serious tip, one that could break open the case. Then D stopped what he was doing and put his cell down on the car seat. A well-dressed, middle-aged Korean woman walked out the front door to inspect her hedges. She seemed to be surveying the work of a gardener. It was Sun Hee Pak. Or was it Park?

CHAPTER FORTY

MICHELLE AND D
TALK ABOUT HER FAMILY

"**S**o," D said into his phone, "I have to ask you something."

Standing outside a decrepit home on Wilshire Boulevard, Michelle was taken aback by his tone. "You sound so serious, D. What's the matter?"

"Sorry, but I'm worried I'm gonna offend you."

"Now I'm really concerned. So what's this serious question?"

"Does your mother have a gambling problem?"

There were two men hovering near Michelle—the owner of the dilapidated property and the broker standing in the doorway—so she walked down the block. "Who told you something crazy like that?"

"I just found my grandfather's ledger book and I think he lent your mother money."

"And why would my mother borrow money from him?"

D gave her a short rundown of Big Danny's illicit activities and how they related to her family's home. She listened carefully; D could hear her breathing hard.

"You have it wrong, D," she said. "It couldn't have been my mother. She would squeeze a dime until it bled silver."

"What about your father?"

"My father . . . yes."

Gambling might be a way of life for some in Korea, but Jung-ho didn't really catch that particular disease until he got to America and fell in with a self-consciously cool group of Korean businessmen. Jung-ho wanted to fit in because this group had the ear of Mayor Tom Bradley and the city's establishment. These guys held a weekly poker game in the back of a restaurant in Chapman Plaza in Koreatown and eventually he got himself dealt in. Young Joon Jung, owner of various bars and restaurants in K-Town, befriended Jung-ho (meaning he beat him at poker) and secured him a role in the local chamber of commerce. The contacts he made were gold and they gave him additional ambition. (He moved into Hancock Park because the mayor's official residence was there.)

Unfortunately, at the poker table Jung-ho had more tells than a gossip blogger. He lost so consistently that the other businessmen wouldn't play if he didn't show up. "I figured he borrowed money from somewhere," Michelle admitted. "I guess he went outside the Korean community to keep it out of local chitchat. Ma must have found out."

"Found out?" D said. "You and I both know that my grandfather told her. From what I could figure out, it appears he was way behind in his payments. Why he didn't pay on time is not clear. Maybe he felt he had nothing to lose, so my grandfather couldn't really hurt him."

Michelle was now way down the block from the house she was supposed to be looking at. But her eyes were watering. Too much family information. Too much dirty laundry. She liked D but he shouldn't know all this. "Well," she said finally, "I don't know what happened between all of them. You don't know either. My father has been very ill the last few years. He stays at home. I see where you are going with this, D, and I don't appreciate you suggesting that my father may have had something to do with having your grandfather murdered."

"I didn't say that, Michelle."

"I'm not stupid." She was hot now. "Have you been hanging out with me just to investigate my family?"

"Of course not. I didn't know your family borrowed money from my grandfather. I just found this out."

"I don't believe you," she said, and then walked away.

D met Mrs. Pak at a coffee shop in the Korean mall on Western. He had asked her to come alone. She had a cappuccino and he ordered a bottle of still water.

"So . . ." she began, wondering if something was wrong with the sale of Big Danny's house.

D pulled his grandfather's Polaroid out of his pocket and slid it across the table to her. She leaned over and glanced at it. Without looking back up she said, "I told you we were friends."

"That looks like a date, Mrs. Pak."

Now she sat up and stared at D with what was supposed to be a poker face, but D saw right through to her hole card. "Your grandfather's dead. Is this how you honor him? Going through his possessions and asking nasty questions?"

"Mrs. Pak, before I came out here for his funeral, I thought I knew who he was. Now I realize I knew very little about him. I just feel like you might be able to tell me things no one else would know."

"We were close, yes. But we were not lovers. So don't make this into some silly soap opera. He loved his wife very much and I have always honored by husband."

"But you were close," D pressed. "Is that why he kept this picture hidden in his desk?"

"I don't know where he kept it."

"Did my grandmother know how close you were?"

"I was not in their home. We did meet a few times. She was a lovely woman, as you know. We weren't friends but she was always courteous."

Despite Sun Hee's discomfort with these questions, D sensed that she was open to talking. She definitely knew things D needed to know, but she wasn't just going to volunteer it. "I understand," he said softly, "that your husband was upset after the riot. I was—"

"My husband is a very honorable man," she interrupted. "But not so strong. Sometimes I needed advice or information about dealing with the city and Daniel always helped me. That was the bond. My husband knew he was helpful, especially once I got into the real estate business. So we all got along."

"Okay. Can you think of anyone who'd want to harm him? Anyone he might have mentioned? Maybe someone who owed him money?"

"You know," she said, "in the Korean community many people of my generation and older either didn't trust American banks or could not get approved for loans. So they borrowed from friends and acquaintances instead, keeping their financial needs within the community. It is a good system if people live by their word. But not everyone does. You would be surprised how many shootings happen within our community over unpaid loans."

D just listened, wondering where this was going.

"Loaning money without the force of the law is an uneasy business. It can make you do terrible things, or at least make people worry that you will. I told Daniel this when I found out what he was doing. I told him several times." Sun Hee Pak stood up and stepped toward D. "But I was just a friend giving advice."

"Thank you for your time. I am sorry if you feel I was accusing you. I meant no disrespect." D felt sheepish and in over his head.

"You are a good grandson." She placed a hand on his shoulder, then her face hardened. "But you are not a good boyfriend for my daughter."

She walked away. D picked the photo off the table and slid it into his shirt pocket.

The next morning, D watched Lawrence Pak drive off toward Crenshaw. Thirty minutes later, Sun Hee Pak headed off to her office on Western. Instead of leaving, D exited the rented Prius and walked up to the front door of the Pak residence. He buzzed twice, stood around for a minute, then noticed the security camera above the door. He smiled and waited. The door finally opened.

"Come in, young Mr. Hunter." Jung-ho Pak moved aside and let D in.

The living room felt formal, with plaques, family pictures, and flowers positioned just so around a fireplace and a lovely wooden table. Jung-ho guided D through it toward a large kitchen filled with the aroma of toast and eggs. A small TV played Good Day LA. A cigarette burned in an ashtray. Jung-ho, who had a polite but rigid presence, wore a blue Dodgers T-shirt and gray slacks. He offered D coffee and toast. D could see a lot of Michelle in his soft, gentle eyes. Compared to the lion that was Sun Hee, Jung-ho had the air of a lamb content to graze upon someone else's grass.

"It's quite hard learning to be an American," he said. "Obviously I had to master the language. As you can hear, I may have missed a few lessons. Once you get a grasp of the official language, you then must learn slang if you want to work in retail. Our stores were in black neighborhoods. For a long time I thought blacks were all named Cuz."

Jung-ho Pak's easy humor again reminded D of Michelle, without the hard edge of his wife or the uptight intensity of his son. D liked him immediately, which he certainly hadn't expected.

"Is that why you let them set up the dice game in the parking lot?"

"Well, it is one thing to master English, but one plus one still equals two all over the world. People wonder why immigrants move into retail— well, numbers don't need translation. So, to answer your question, I got good at counting dice. Some of those gangbangers were scary. But since a lot them hadn't gone far in school, they began to use me to keep the games honest. If I didn't have a family, I would have opened a gambling spot."

"Is that how you met my grandfather?"

"No. We actually met at a seminar about minority small businesses organized by Mayor Bradley's office. I must have looked a bit confused, cause Big Danny introduced himself. He even knew a few words in Korean. Unlike a lot of blacks who seemed threatened by us, Big Danny was willing to give advice and make deals with Koreans wholesaling goods from Asia."

"Like at the swap meets?"

"Yes. I was able to cut him a few deals. In fact, he was the first and only black person to invite my wife and me to their home. They were probably our first American friends."

"As I understand it, the '92 riot strained your relationship."

"What do you mean?" It was the first time Jung-ho lost his amiable smile. "Strain? No strain. In fact, it all brought us closer. He helped my wife survive danger. What more can one ask of a friend? Where did you hear that?"

D lied: "I guess I heard it from my aunt."

"Tell your aunt that isn't true. She was just a child then—what would she know? We stayed in communication until his death. If there was strain it was between Red, who worked for him, and my son. If it had just been business between Big Danny and me, there would be no strain. But young men can be disrespectful to each other for no good reason."

D considered that for a moment. Then he said, "The police don't have any leads about who might have killed my grandfather. Do you have any ideas?"

"I have thought about this often. He was in business for many years in a very tough area. I know I had many serious run-ins. I was threatened; I am sure he was too. I remember that Chicano rapper who shot at him."

"I spoke to Teo. Right now I don't think he did it."

"Oh." Jung-ho shook his head. "Big Danny was well liked. But he carried cash. These new people in the community—Mexican, Central American—they don't have the same connections. Not like those of us who have lived here decades. Only a new person would assault or attack him. Can I show you a picture?"

Jung-ho retrieved a photo album, the pages sticking together from plastic coverings that looked like they hadn't been separated in years. He opened the album gingerly and pointed to a picture of he and Sun Hee having dinner with his grandparents. The table and walls matched the background of the picture in D's pocket of Big Danny and Sun Hee.

"Where was this?"

"It was a chicken and waffle place. Rocky's, maybe?"

"Roscoe's House of Chicken & Waffles."

"Yes, that's it. We had dinner there. Very popular. Always had a line out of the door."

"He took me there every time I'd visit when I was a kid," D said. "He must have really liked you guys."

Driving back to the Valley, D found it hard to believe Jung-ho Pak had hired a contract killer to hunt down his grandfather. Didn't mean that Big Danny and his wife didn't have an affair or that he didn't owe a lot of money to Big Danny. But it was a huge leap to believe he'd pay for murder.

D's head began throbbing. He pulled over to the curb on Highland and put his head against the steering wheel. He wasn't a fucking detective. He was just a big man in black clothes. Threatening from a distance, but truly clueless up close. *This is embarrassing*, he thought. *Damn embarrassing*.

His phone buzzed and the text read: *Need to speak to you. In person. Chan Dara off Sunset. An hour. Amoeba after!*

Back in the nineties, the Chan Dara chain had a reputation for hiring extremely cute, flirty Thai waitresses in short skirts. There was an air of disrepute that hung over the spot, like you might get invited to a brothel after eating your curry. But when D arrived he found that the owners had cleaned up their act. There were now as many male waiters as female, and the women, while not unattractive, didn't make anyone think of wild nights in Bangkok.

Gibbs picked up on D's disappointment, noting, "These days it's just about the noodles and veggies here, my friend. In fact, the place is gonna close at the end of the month. Without the sexy girls, it's just another place in LA serving pad thai. But don't you worry, you'll be glad you came."

After they'd ordered, Gibbs asked how it was going with R'Kaydia, so D related how he'd tried to get her out of his life, but that through Night, she'd slipped back in.

"Yeah," Gibbs said, "she won't be easy to shake. Not with all that money on the table."

"Do tell."

"The pitch she made about the hologram and music is just a small part of her business. You see that house she and her man Teddy live in? You don't pay for that with just music these days."

"So?"

"So there's what I know and there's what I hear. What I know is that R'Kaydia is tight with Mark Zuckerberg's team, and her company is developing software for Facebook that would allow users to create holograms of Facebook posts that would pop up right off your laptop or smartphone."

"Wow," D said. "A big deal."

"Yup. The fees for developing that technology are paying R'Kaydia's bills. Everything else is chump change. We're talking up to thirty million dollars from Facebook. But there's a problem, and this is where you come in: a key Facebook executive has a funk band and he idolizes Dr. Funk. So much so that he wants Dr. Funk to play at his thirtieth birthday party in two months. Well, R'Kaydia and Tapscott told him they could get the doctor for him. But, so far, it ain't happened.

"Now what I hear is that this Facebook executive is so pissed that he's threatened to pull all the funding for this hologram development gig. So R'Kaydia is freaking out. That Facebook prick's ego could cost her millions."

"How true is the *what I hear* part?"

"I dunno, dawg. It's second- and thirdhand."

"Hmmm," D said, "so I'm probably not the only person she'd have out looking for Dr. Funk?"

"A Facebook deal worth millions at stake? Hell no. She's probably got all the PIs in LA on it. But, of course, you're the only motherfucker seen on YouTube being hugged by Dr. Funk."

"So she's really desperate, huh?"

"How many multimillion-dollar deals you fixing to lose, D? I've lost one or two. It ain't pretty. It's a lifestyle changer. No new home. No new cars. No new women—and you'll damn well lose the one you got."

D mulled this over for a minute. Then he said, "You got any new business to discuss with R'Kaydia?"

"Nawn. Doubt she'd sit with me these days."

"Okay. Does she still go to clubs?"

"There's a Sunday pool party at a Beverly Hills hotel that DJ Rashida throws. She's hot to death too. Used to spin for Prince."

"And . . . ?"

"Anyway, this guy Legendary Damon promotes it, and he attracts a posh crowd. I can make sure he invites her this Sunday. I know him from New York."

"Do that."

"What's your play?"

"Have Legendary Damon tell her Night's coming too. Tell her he'll be debuting a cover of a Dr. Funk song."

"You got a plan, huh?"

D wasn't sure how much he wanted to reveal. "I got a hunch. This has been a crazy hunt for Dr. Funk, but I'm thinking I may have been looking in the wrong places for the wrong thing."

"You're getting very philosophical in your old age."

After dinner, the two New Yorkers walked across Sunset to Amoeba Records, a block-long cathedral to the world of predigital music and film culture. Rows of CDs, LPs, DVDs, posters, cassettes, and even some eight-tracks filled the cavernous store. For D and Gibbs, whose memories of music were connected to long, lazy afternoons digging through vinyl in bins, Amoeba was as back-to-the-future as it got. They strolled through the R&B, hip hop, and dance sections, recalling, reminiscing, and reminding each other of artists, songs, clubs, and moments from years ago that seemed like yesterday. Good times then; a melancholy journey now.

Gibbs hopped into an Uber in front of Amoeba (he was meeting Shelia back at Soho House for drinks) while D ambled down Ivar. Leaning against a wall in a nearby parking lot was a shirtless black man with Army fatigues for pants and no-name sneakers on his feet. He had on Apple earbuds and the white cord reached into his pants. He grooved to the music like it was the most jamming song ever made. D couldn't help it—he found himself transfixed by this sadly fascinating sight.

The man came out of his dancing groove and looked at D.

"Sorry for staring, brother," D said. "What are you listening to?"

The man plucked out an earbud but no music came from it because they were plugged into nothing but the lint in his pocket. "You got twenty dollars?"

"Twenty dollars? That's ambitious." D reached into his pocket, found five, and handed it over. "That's all I can spare."

The man took the money and asked, "If I was who you were looking for, how much would I get?"

"I'm not sure. But it wouldn't be twenty dollars. Have a good night."

"Every night with music is a blessing," the man replied, putting his earbud back in and returning to the music inside his head.

CHAPTER FORTY-ONE

WALLI'S FIRST POOL PARTY

Women in bikinis, some wearing flip-flops, a great many in wedge-heeled scandals, lounged on deck chairs, while shirtless men, a few actually in Speedos, hovered around preening under the California sun. There were six-packs on the men. There were six-packs on a few women too. There were middle-aged men with Viagra-generated erections who dipped in and out of the water to highlight their chemically enhanced wears.

On a cushion by the pool sat Walter Gibbs in trunks and a Notorious BIG tank top, with a full setup (vodka, juice, ice), and two lovely young women (one black, one Thai) ordering liberally off the food menu. Not far from Gibbs, in a shaded cabana, R'Kaydia wore a floppy sun hat, round Jackie O. sunglasses, and an elegant pale-blue two-piece bikini. With her were Nikeva and Daisha, two wavy-haired ladies on the Creole side of black, who sipped champagne and wore slightly more conservative outfits. They were R'Kaydia's running buddies, married-well ladies happily young enough to still turn heads.

R'Kaydia herself had eyes for a large, well-muscled, bronze-skinned trainer type across the pool with more tattoos than a Maori warrior. Her gaze shifted at a rising murmur of female voices and the lifting of smartphones, which meant a celeb was entering the pool area. Night, in Warby Parker shades, a white tank top, a gold medallion, baggy shorts, and Nike flip-flops, smiled for the ladies as D, looking as large and serious as always, remained a step behind in a black polo-shirt-and-shorts ensemble that R'Kaydia found silly. Always the bodyguard, she mused, even as he tried to step up in class.

She wondered who the skinny kid was trailing in their wake and gawking at the poolside women like a cub who'd never been fed. The teenager looked familiar but R'Kaydia couldn't place him. Based on his clothes and demeanor he probably wasn't from the West Side. *Whatever,* she thought as she waved Night over. Her Instagram was going to be on fire this afternoon with pics of her cozied up with this sex symbol.

Night had been shocked when D invited him to a Los Angeles hotel pool party. Not that he didn't want to go—he'd already hit the Roosevelt Hotel Sunday gig and the Do-Over at Lure a few times. But D insisting he come out and perform was a major surprise, a sign that perhaps he was emerging from mourning for his grandfather and was really ready to help Night hype his career.

Night loved that D had brought along his cousin Walli. Taking a kid out of the hood and letting him see a bigger world was always cool. Taking him to see a multiculti rainbow of sexy-ass girls sipping cocktails in swimsuits under the Cali sun was a gift this young man would never forget. (Also, Sy Sarraf would be coming by with a supply of "vitamins," perfect for a relaxing Sunday.)

Walli was fixated on a tanned bottle-blonde in a red bikini and high heels sipping a mojito when D asked him, "You see that woman hugging Night right now?"

"Uhh, yeah?"

"She look familiar?"

"Ahhh."

"Please focus, Walli. You have all afternoon to eyeball the blonde."

Walli squinted. He pondered. No women who oozed so much money had ever been in his vicinity before. But then he said, "She does seem familiar."

"Maybe she came to speak to Big Danny at the grocery store?"

"Grocery store? I didn't see her there. What kind of car does she drive?"

"Car? I dunno, why?"

"Maybe she came to talk to Granddad at the house. I remember a woman driving a slick car who came to the house one night. A white Maserati. I watched it from my window. Could have been her. I only saw them in the hallway for like a second—I had a lot of homework. But her car I remember. You didn't see many cars like that in our neighborhood."

This was inconclusive to D. A woman like R'Kaydia probably had three or four different rides. "Okay then, let's go say hello."

R'Kaydia and her two friends were fussing over Night like he was an expensive pet. D and Walli joined them briefly but ended up sitting down with Gibbs, and now the three women sat laughing at the singer's stories and terrible jokes. D looked for signs that R'Kaydia was uncomfortable in Walli's presence, but her eyes only strayed from Night to the well-muscled man across the pool.

While everyone around him chilled, drank, and recklessly eyeballed tanned flesh, D did calculations. His Hail Mary pass that Walli would link R'Kaydia to Big Danny hadn't connected. Now he had to see if she drove the same car that Walli had spotted outside the house. Even then, it wouldn't necessarily prove that she had anything to do with Big Danny's murder. But it would at least establish contact between R'Kaydia and Big Danny in her search for Dr. Funk.

His grandfather would have stonewalled her, and she would have quickly grown frustrated. Could that anger have triggered her to have Big Danny killed? Or maybe she intended to scare him and things went

NELSON GEORGE ✸ 217

wrong? And what about Serene Powers—could she have been the killer? She was definitely capable of taking a man out. But what if she thought his grandfather was somehow protecting Dr. Funk? Was she a cold-blooded murderer as well as an avenging angel? D wished he had a way to contact her. He presumed she was watching him—but how could he make her come out of the shadows?

These questions occupied D's mind while Night engaged in conversation with R'Kaydia and her girlfriends. Soon the women got up and walked toward the hotel. D turned his gaze toward the muscleman across the way, who took a sip of his mimosa and then headed inside too. D waited a beat before excusing himself, reminding Walli not to drink any alcohol, and then entered the hotel.

He sat on a lobby sofa and pulled out his cell phone, pretending to check Facebook. One of R'Kaydia's friends emerged from the women's restroom. He let her pass and then strolled in that direction. Trying not to look conspicuous, D cracked open the door to the ladies' room. Lucky for him it was empty. In the men's room a couple of dudes were taking leaks.

He was going to head back to the pool when he noticed the door to a stairwell. He cracked it and heard two voices. He opened the door wider and, on the level below, he spotted two people pressed together, swimming trunks down and muscles flexed as they furiously fucked against the wall. R'Kaydia certainly seemed to be enjoying herself. Good for her. But maybe this guy with the wide back, the bright tats, and the tight butt wasn't just a boy toy.

D left R'Kaydia and her friend to their business and walked back out to the pool. His little cousin, now shirtless, was about to join a game of pool volleyball. D caught his eye, smiled, and nodded. Walli went in and was quickly surrounded by a beguiling swirl of girls in bikinis.

"Your cousin there has a boner that could break concrete," Gibbs observed.

"As he should," D said.

"So," Gibbs asked, "how's the investigation going, holmes?"

"Picking up bits and pieces. Did you see that guy who followed R'Kaydia into the hotel?"

"I saw the guy you followed who was following her. They probably booked a suite."

"They went a lot more basic than that. You know him?"

"Jake G.—he's a stuntman. Doubles for the Rock and Vin Diesel, and sometimes for Mexicans, Latinos, the odd Mongolian, and various mixed-race bad guys. I used him in a couple of videos."

"A man of action," D said.

"Yeah, I guess. He designs stunts too."

D was taking this all in when R'Kaydia, looking refreshed, appeared poolside and sauntered over to them. "When do you think Night is going to perform that song? I may have to go meet my husband soon."

"No problem," D said with a smile, "I'll make it happen."

Twenty minutes later Night held a microphone and was standing next to DJ Rashida's booth as she clicked on an iPod Mini that played an instrumental of Dr. Funk's "California Sun." As Night started singing, the girls swooned. So did the gays boys. The straight guys crossed their arms in the hopes that excited women would, later on, literally fall into their laps. The odds of that improved when Night flowed into "Black Sex."

"He's definitely still got his audience," R'Kaydia commented. "When is the album coming?"

"He's got a ton of songs, but we're still figuring out what goes on and what doesn't."

"Will that Dr. Funk cover be on it?"

D looked around. "Judging by the reaction, it should be."

"You think he could perform that song with a band in about a month or so?"

"No."

"No?"

"Like I said, R'Kaydia, we're in the middle of trying to finish a long-overdue album. The label wants it for Christmas. That's gotta be the priority."

"The performance would be worth a lot of money. Six figures for a couple of songs."

"Who for?"

"A Facebook executive who's a good friend of mine."

"Is he an investor in your hologram company?"

R'Kaydia didn't seem to appreciate this line of questioning. "He might be. But yes, it would be a great help to me and my business, especially if Dr. Funk hasn't been found by then."

"So you want Night to be a living hologram, huh?"

"I don't like your tone, D. I've tried to be helpful to you and to your client. But you haven't really been working with me. Why is that?"

"Listen, R'Kaydia, come back to me—or Amos, if that makes you more comfortable—with a real offer and specific dates and I'm sure we'll seriously consider it."

"Enjoy the rest of your Sunday, D," she muttered before walking off.

After R'Kaydia and her pals paid their bill and moved into the lobby, D grabbed Walli, who had just downed a Jell-O shot with a slender college-age, chocolate-brown woman named Felicia. "Time for you to earn your keep, Walli."

A few minutes later D and Walli stood by a window in the lobby where they could see the valet stand. R'Kaydia, Nikeva, and Daisha handed the valet their tickets. D said, "Tell me if you see that car again—the white Maserati."

When one of the valets drove up with a pearl-colored Maserati, Walli said, "That's it."

The three women kissed each other's cheeks and then Nikeva got in the car.

"Damn," Walli said. "Sorry. Maybe *she* was the one at the house?"

D watched R'Kaydia and Daisha chat as they waited on their cars. A valet dropped another pearl-colored Maserati in front of the hotel, and this time R'Kaydia got in quickly and sped off.

"Wow," Walli said.

"Let's see what the other woman drives."

To their surprise, Daisha also had a pearl-colored Maserati.

"So," Gibbs said to D when they were back by the pool, "have you learned anything new?"

"I believe there was a relationship between R'Kaydia and my grand-father that she's been hiding from us."

"You calling R'Kaydia a murderer?"

"People have been killed for much less than thirty million bucks."

"But what could your grandfather have done that would get his cap pulled?"

"I have no idea," D admitted.

Like a lonely puppy, Walli had now rejoined them since Felicia was sitting in the lap of a hairy, middle-aged Persian man who was pouring her champagne. Night had also joined them, along with Sy Sarraf, the herbalist.

D glanced at his downhearted cousin and said, "You look ready to go."

"Yeah."

"You got a good lesson today, Walli." It was Gibbs. "Girls you meet at pool parties tend to float around."

The party had already hit one peak but the sun was still shining and the pool area was being refreshed with another wave of party people. Jake G., R'Kaydia's lover, was chatting up a pale, slender, surgically enhanced brunette over by the DJ booth. D pulled out his phone and Googled him. Turned out the man's real name was actually Jake Gee and, yes, he did some personal training along with his stunt work. D scanned his credits for something he recognized, and it turned out Jake had been a heavy on *Banshee*, a Cinemax action joint in which he'd played an ethnically ambiguous terrorist.

"I'll be right back," D said, then strolled over to where Jake and his companion were sitting. On closer inspection he recognized the brunette as Ashley Mae, a contestant on *The Bachelorette* (D always checked the lineup of women at the start of each season).

"Excuse me," D said, "Are you Jake Gee, the stuntman?"

"Yeah."

"Well, my name is D Hunter. I'm a manager for Night, the R&B singer who performed a bit earlier."

"Loved him," Ashley Mae said. "What a sexy voice."

"Well, we're starting to develop ideas for his next video. Thinking of doing something involving action. I saw you kick ass in *Banshee*. I know your rep. Thought maybe we could toss ideas at you and you might help choreograph them."

"Oh, Jake is so good at stuff like that," Ashley Mae said. "He's even helped us with stuff on *The Bachelorette*. He's so gifted." She gently rubbed his arm like a proud friend.

Jake blushed and D half expected him to say, *Aw shucks*. He seemed bashful. Very different vibe from what he'd seen in the hotel staircase.

"Thanks for the compliment, Ashley," Jake said. "Sure, my man, I'm definitely interested. Hit me up on Facebook and we'll meet up."

"Thanks, Jake. Talk to you soon."

Before heading out, D stopped by where Night was cavorting with Gibbs and Sarraf. "You cutting tonight?"

"Most def. I should be over there by nine or so. Think I've finally figured out the sound. Watching people react to the Dr. Funk song today was cool. Thanks for suggesting it."

D surveyed Night's companions. "You sure you don't want a ride home now?"

Night smiled. "I'm a big boy, D. I know what not to do. I'm not getting in the way of my money."

"Okay, no problem. See you tonight."

CHAPTER FORTY-TWO

AFTER HOURS AT HEAVEN'S GATE

On the freeway riding out toward Lancaster, D turned on the radio and found some jazz, happy to be listening to Charles Mingus's "Goodbye Pork Pie Hat" after an afternoon of trap music and electrobeats. Walli was quiet as the film noir sound of Mingus's arrangements filled the car. D figured he was still thinking about the women at the pool, but his young cousin had weightier things on his mind.

"Hey, D," he said more to the window than the driver, "I'm really glad you took me with you today."

"Glad you enjoyed it, Walli. I think it's an LA rite of passage to be at a pool party filled with beautiful women. First of many parties like it for you, my man."

Walli now gave D his full attention, turning toward him with sad eyes. "You know, you are not what I expected."

"What did you expect?" D asked. "You've known me your whole life."

"But, you know, you always came in and out. When you were here you were busy and mostly you hung with Grandpop. So I didn't really know you."

"I'm sorry if you feel I neglected you, Walli. But that will never happen again. We're family, and we need each other more than ever."

"Yeah, I see that . . . And I need to tell you some things."

"Yeah?" D smiled, thinking they were going to have a man-to-man about women.

"Red Dawg told me not to. He told me you weren't really interested in Grandpop or Ma or me. That you were just hanging around to get paid off Grandpop's will."

"Fuck that fool," D said. "What is it that you want to say?"

"When Grandma died, Red Dawg tried to get Grandpop to retire and let him run the grocery store and all that loaning business."

"It's called loan-sharking."

"Yeah," Walli said, "so Grandpop got angry. He was real stubborn and they had an argument. Before Grandpop got shot, Red Dawg and him hadn't really been speaking."

D quickly cut through traffic and pulled over to the side of the road, causing much honking and some cursing, but this was a conversation he needed to have stationary. "You understand your grandfather's code?"

"A little bit."

"But you didn't tell me that because Red Dawg warned you not to? Is that right?"

"I'm sorry. I know I should have let you know that. But, you know, Red Dawg has been like a brother to me, so—"

"Okay, I got it. Anything else I should know, Walli?"

"Well, this isn't about Michelle. This is about another woman."

"Just tell me."

"This woman came to the grocery store about a three months ago asking about Dr. Funk. She got real nasty with Grandpop, accusing him of being immoral or something crazy like that. She was yelling so loud that Red Dawg came over from the sneaker store and stepped to her, but she punched him in the face! Almost broke his jaw."

No doubt that was Serene Powers.

"Did she touch Granddad?"

"No," Walli said, "but he was definitely shook."

"Did he file a police report?"

"I don't know."

"That detective would have mentioned it. I assume neither Red Dawg or your mother told the police."

"I'm not sure if she even knew about it."

"What about the K-Pak connection? You tell the detective about that?"

"No. Red Dawg said he'd handle everything."

"And not one of you thought I should know about that woman who threatened Granddad, or this shit about the grocery store?"

"Sorry, D."

"Y'all are sorry all right," D said. "I can't wait to talk to your mother."

Forty minutes later D was sitting in a chair in his Aunt Sheryl's new living room as she stood over him, holding a TV remote in her hand, her voice raised. "I'm your elder. Don't be questioning me, D. You have a lot of nerve. You may scare them fools out on the street but I will slap the black off you!"

Asking his aunt pointed questions hadn't gone well. First she became angry with Walli for spilling the beans to D. Then she got defensive with D and subsequently downright irritated. D lowered his voice, hoping his aunt would take the hint.

"I'm just trying to find out what truly happened to Granddad—that's all. But the truth is that you all decided I wasn't trustworthy or not even a real part of this family. You treat Red Dawg like he's your blood. What about me?" The calming-tone thing wasn't working either, cause D was really hurt and couldn't hide it. "I'm the last one of your brother's sons. You should be embracing me."

This hit Aunt Sheryl. She took a step back, eyes downcast like she was finally going to be honest and it hurt a bit inside. "Look, D, to tell you the truth—"

"Please do."

"You're like a ghost to me. Yeah, all your brothers are dead. Your mother's sick. My brother done flipped out and left the damn country. Mommy's dead. Daddy's dead. Then you come to town like a fucking undertaker. I'm trying to get away from death, and you all wrapped up in it. You could at least wear a white shirt or white sneakers."

This made D laugh. A sad laugh, but a bit of mirth nonetheless. Walli, who'd been feeling as tight as a well-tuned snare drum, smiled. Even Aunt Sheryl loosened up a bit. The disagreement wasn't gone but at least the arguing was.

Over leftover roast beef, steamed veggies, and home fries, Sheryl finally filled in some of the gaps in the Big Danny/Dr. Funk relationship.

At Heaven's Gate, Big Danny hosted late-night jam sessions that transitioned into early-morning coke snorting and freebasing. Wisely, Big Danny didn't indulge past the sniffing stage, but he didn't judge when people started to smoke rocks. These coke-fueled sessions had the unintended consequence of getting him deeper into loan-sharking, since he'd often end up lending musicians money for blow. His pitch: *Owe me, or owe the Bloods or Crips.* He'd often take his cut out of musicians' salaries when they played Heaven's Gate or get them to gig just to be able to pay him back, arrangements that kept the club solvent for years.

One night Dr. Funk had a young woman with him who, excited by the scene and the coke, got out of pocket and started flirting with Rick James, who was hanging out. Earlier in his career, when Dr. Funk was rolling, he might have laughed it off. But at this particular moment

Rick's brand of punk-funk was ruling LA radio and the good doctor was feeling a touch insecure.

So Dr. Funk and Rick James got into a shouting match because the girl was standing too close to Rick. Whether Dr. Funk meant to hit her or not, no one knows, but when he swung at Rick he ended up connecting with the young woman—and if that wasn't bad enough, her head then hit the edge of a table. She was down and she was out.

Aunt Sheryl said she was murky on what happened next (D wasn't sure if that was true but kept quiet about it). All she knew for sure was that Rick James, Dr. Funk, and everyone else cleared out, and that the girl, whose name his aunt did not know, was taken to the hospital by Big Danny. Dr. Funk's name never ended up in a police report. After that, Big Danny and Dr. Funk stayed close, even as the musician's career began to ebb downward and his sanity seemed to fade.

Did his grandfather, covering for Dr. Funk back then, instigate a murder now? Could it even be, to some degree, justified? For the first time since R'Kaydia and Night and Serene Powers and half of LA had asked him to find Dr. Funk, D felt some hostility toward this woman-abusing funk-and-roll legend.

"You okay, D?"

"No," he told his aunt. "Not at all. I gotta get back to LA."

"What you gonna do now?"

"I think it's time I really did find Dr. Funk."

D was on the 5 highway, pushing seventy in Big Danny's Buick, making a mental checklist of people to question and requestion, when Al's name popped up on his phone. His old friend spoke like he was afraid to breathe.

"Bad news, D. Night has relapsed. Found him totally fucked up in his apartment. I hate to say this, but he must have gotten high at that pool party. I drove him out to this facility in Malibu. Amos wants to speak to you. You wanna get on the phone with him now?"

After a long pause: "You know I don't, Al. Any media on this yet?"

"Nothing's popped up on my Google Alert so far. The label is gonna flip the fuck out when the news breaks."

"You tellin', Al? I'm not." D heard his own voice—he sounded pitiful.

"These things tend to get out, D."

"You got Night's phone?"

"The facility doesn't play that."

"Text that fucking Sy Sarraf. He was at the pool today. I'm sure he laced Night. Tell him to meet me at the Nice Guy—I know the security guys there—and that I'm picking up for Night. Probably in an hour."

"What do you have in mind?" Al asked.

"An intervention."

CHAPTER FORTY-THREE

VIOLENT INTERVENTIONS

They were playing Fetty Wap's "Trap Queen," the tinny snap of its beat echoing through the men's room walls from the main room of the Nice Guy. A man in the next stall was taking a dump and singing along: "*Man, I swear I love her how she work the damn pole . . .*" Unfortunately, he sang without the aid of the Auto-Tune that gave Fetty's voice dimension.

D vaguely registered this off-key vocalizing as he flushed the toilet and pulled Sy Sarraf's head in and out of the bowl. Sy had happily received the text that D was picking up a "package" for Night. They'd gone into the men's room to do the transaction, but Night's new co-manager had a different deal in mind.

D had slipped the men's room attendant a fifty and said, "Silence is golden." Then he'd turned and shoved the slender drug dealer face-first into the nearest stall. The flushing had commenced right away. D didn't threaten or explain. He just submerged the Persian man's head repeatedly over a ten-minute period, allowing him to gasp a few vital breaths before starting over.

His point made, D lifted up Sy's head, turned him sideways, leaned in close, and growled like Christian Bale in *Batman*: "So glad you enjoy Night's music. Continue. But never, ever see him again."

D tossed a roll of toilet paper on Sy's wet John Varvatos jacket. As he exited the men's room, Fetty Wap's "Trap Queen" gave way to

Drake's "Started from the Bottom." But D didn't hear it. He was focused on the unpleasant phone call ahead of him.

"You were brought on board to help prevent just this kind of problem. But, in fact, you invited Night right into the kind of environment you were supposed to keep him out of. This is a fucking disaster, D."

Truthfully, D hadn't listened to any of the angry voice messages Amos Pilgrim had left for him. So Amos had sent him ten text messages with various levels of venom.

Now D sat with Al at Mel's Drive-In on Ventura Boulevard, not far from the studio and the apartment complex where they were living. It was a throwback drive-in hamburger spot that reveled in a connection to George Lucas's *American Graffiti*, that classic piece of California nostalgia. Al was picking at a salad (though he longed for a burger and fries) while D sat nursing a strawberry milkshake, savoring a bit of sweetness in his sour mood.

They'd been there a couple of hours as D downloaded all he'd heard at the pool party and out in Lancaster. Information? Yes, D now had plenty of that. But answers and understanding? No.

Al had listened quietly, making few comments and mostly serving as a blank slate on which D scrawled his discontent. Finally Al asked the question that had been nagging at him: "Can I get a taste of that milkshake?"

D pushed the glass across the table and Al gratefully gulped down the last of the pink concoction.

"Amazing," Al said after pushing the glass aside. "I'm supposed to avoid sugar and dairy, but that's like not breathing."

"I'm just spreading disorder wherever I go."

"Don't blame yourself, D. It's always the self-inflicted wounds that really hurt us. Anyway, have you looked at the basement studio behind Heaven's Gate?"

"Huh?"

"There's a basement studio underneath that shed in the back. It must have been a speakeasy back during Prohibition. It had an eight-track board and a sound booth. But it was mostly a private place to get high. If the story about Dr. Funk and that girl is true, then it probably happened down there."

"How come you didn't mention this before?"

"Until you related that story about the girl and the after-hours scene at Heaven's Gate, I'd completely forgotten about it. I bet you could chart the history of black music in LA by the noses that sniffed off that basement sink."

D was getting ready to head back to the apartment complex and get some rest when he spotted a dark blue BMW cruising by very slowly on Ventura. Another car splashed light on the driver and he saw her face, which was turned in his direction—strong, fierce, resolute. She was a warrior with an ancient soul and twenty-first-century hands. If his hunch was right, maybe he'd get a chance to see her in action tonight. Time to get some answers.

"Al," he said, "I think I'm gonna go check out that studio at Heaven's Gate."

"Now?"

"Why not? I've already had a crazy day. After that thing with Sarraf, my adrenaline is still pumping."

"What about Amos?

"Fuck it. He didn't want me around anyway."

D got in his car, headed down Ventura Boulevard, and then out of the Valley via Laurel Canyon. By this point he figured Serene had

232 8 TO FUNK AND DIE IN LA

bugged his car, so he took his time. No rush. It was late. The sun would crack the sky soon. The streets on the West Hollywood side were as empty as LA gets, so a ride that would normally take an hour only lasted thirty minutes.

He parked behind Heaven's Gate and walked right into the small structure in the back, a place where his grandfather used to store booze, a place D had played hide-and-seek one memorable teenage night with a brick house of a barmaid named Monique. Now the old chairs and tables stacked against the walls were covered in dust. There were boxes all around containing table linens, silverware, candles, ashtrays, and menus. It looked like the floor hadn't been swept in years.

D carefully inspected the place and soon spotted some footprints in the dust that vanished in front of a piece of raised floorboard. He walked over and gave the board a firm tug and it lifted right up, revealing a staircase that led down.

D descended and found himself surrounded by musical instruments and recording equipment, a refrigerator, a rack of clothes, scattered shoes, two hot plates, a VCR, a CD player, and an old white Apple computer. Over in a corner, on a mattress propped up on a pallet, Dr. Funk sat sipping apple juice and examining a small monitor by the bed.

"Thought you'd figure it out," Dr. Funk said. "It wasn't rocket science, but then again most people are earthbound, so anything celestial is scary—even if, as you see, my space isn't just earthbound but underground."

"How long have you been living down here?"

"A long time, I guess—if you measure things by numbers."

"My grandfather knew you were here?"

"Of course. He was my friend. He was gonna sell the place but held onto it for me. Those guys wanted to make this into some kind of museum. Like I was an exhibit. Big Danny kept all of them off me. He was a good man. It's why he got killed."

"What do you mean?"

"You been wanting my music, right? You want me to play you something?

"I would love that. It would be great. But first, you know . . . I don't understand. You know who killed my grandfather?"

"There's a lot of magic in this place. It's why I stay out here. It's why I'm still alive. It's why I still have blood in me. The vampires have tried to suck me dry. They have bitten me—even made me a little ill. But I got that type-A blood. Quality cells, my friend."

"Do you know who killed Big Danny?"

"Big Danny? My man, he killed himself. He drove himself off a cliff of anger. He tried to collect on every debt and not every debt can be settled. Once his wife died, he spent too much time looking back and not enough in the future. There are miracles everywhere. Dreams me and Dick Tracy had years ago are now everyday shit. But Big Danny kept collecting when he should have let all that go. I may look poor and pitiful to some. But I got peace of mind if nothing else. So tell me, you gonna sell this place?"

"Haven't decided. Maybe it should be a music school. You could stay here as long as you taught."

"I dunno . . . me and kids? Not sure that would be a great mix for me or them. I still get my royalties. I don't need a job. Anyway, these kids got computers. They make music on phones. That trap thing they do is all digital. But it would be nice if they knew E-flat, E-sharp, and E-minor. They have no idea how nice that would be. I'm not one to judge though. I've been judged too often to toss rocks through someone else's windows."

"My grandfather set aside some money for me if I took care of you. But you could have it."

"Big Danny was a special motherfucker. He could get along with a roach even if it climbed out of his shirt at Sunday dinner."

D and Dr. Funk immediately stopped talking when they heard the sound of someone walking on the floor above them. In the monitor, Serene Powers slowly approached the staircase.

"You know her?" Dr. Funk whispered.

"A bit. She's been looking for you. It's time to get this settled."

"Hello, gentlemen," she said as she descended.

"Serene."

Dr. Funk said, "She don't look calm to me."

"Serenity is fleeting, Maurice Stewart. But you already know that, don't you?"

"Serene, I let you follow me cause I need some answers. But I am not gonna let you hurt him."

"Maurice, do you remember Kelly Lee Minter?"

"Oh wow. Haven't heard that name in years. She your kin?"

"All women are my kin. All hurt women. All damaged women. All abused women."

"Serene thinks you did something to this woman. Something you deserve to be punished for."

"Kelly Lee," Dr Funk said. "I remember. So you come to see me like you the Punisher. Vengeance is yours, huh?"

"No," D said, "she's not gonna hurt you."

"Yes, she is," Dr. Funk said.

"Tell him, Maurice," Serene said. "Tell him what you did. What you did to Kelly Lee Minter and Nicole Neleh and Ashley Mui too. And maybe others."

"But," Dr. Funk said weakly, "only Kelly Lee died."

"*Only?* There's no number at which tragedy isn't tragedy."

"I didn't think she would die. We were doing what I did back then."

"A speedball, right?"

"I was floating on my own cloud," Dr. Funk said softly. "Way up there where only a royal few could breathe. I wanted company. A companion who would enjoy the rare air."

"So many companions, Dr. Funk," Serene said. "But this one, Kelly Lee—she got up so high she died." When the musician didn't reply, she turned to D. "And you know who covered it up? Your grandfather."

"I heard."

"Kelly Lee Minter. Seventeen going on thirty-five. He met Kelly Lee backstage at the Oakland Alameda County Coliseum at the height of his Dr. Funkosity. He spirited her away on his tour bus. Almost a child bride except he never married her."

Serene reached into her jacket pocket and tossed a photo at Dr. Funk's feet. D picked it up.

Dr. Funk didn't look at the photo. He just said, "Kelly Lee was a beautiful woman."

"Girl," Serene corrected.

"Teenager," Dr. Funk said defensively.

Serene moved toward him with a quickness D didn't anticipate and slapped Dr. Funk so hard he fell down. D, his professional pride damaged, lunged at Serene, reaching for her torso but only catching an arm. Serene turned her body and side-kicked D in his abdomen. As the air went out of him, he let go of her arm and went down on one knee.

Serene sprang around to D's head, but he was ready for it and blocked her leg with his left arm before punching her right in the stomach. This time Serene toppled down, caught her breath, and tensed for a counter-attack.

"Stop! Please stop!" Dr. Funk had scrambled to his feet, his face swollen and red. "D, there's no need to fight this woman over me. I know I need this punishment. I guess I've been waiting on her for a long time."

D stood up. "Did you kill my grandfather?"

"No." Serene stood up too and looked at him without flinching. "I'm not a murderer, D."

"So what are you going to do with Dr. Funk?"

"I'm not going to kill him."

"Then what?" It was Dr. Funk.

"I was hired to bring him to justice—to be punished by Kelly Lee's mother."

"Really?" Dr. Funk said.

"I am to bring you to her."

Serene pulled three more photographs from her jacket pocket and tossed them at Dr. Funk's feet. Each one revealed a comely brown-skinned teenager with large, luscious lips and big brown eyes. Dr. Funk gazed at them intently, his usually sleepy eyes becoming bright, alert, and sad.

Finally he said, "I wrote a song called 'Dirty Water.' I wrote it one morning in a hotel room somewhere in the Midwest. It was early. There were two women on the floor, one on top of the other. They looked ashy and drained, like clothes washed in dirty water. There was so much dirty water I thought the two women had drowned. Then I realized that it was me—I was the one who'd drowned. I was underwater. Deep. My lungs were like the gills of a fish. I'd drunk so much dirty water that I wasn't human anymore. When the two women awoke, they showered in clean water and went back to their lives. I was left in that dirty, dirty water. D, maybe this will get me clean."

Serene said, "It's your *last* chance, Maurice."

"No one owes me nothing. But I'm sure I owe people—a lot of people. D, see that locker? Watch over what's inside. I trusted your grandfather. I trust you."

Dr. Funk walked up to Serene, who took him by the arm and slowly ushered him toward the stairs. D trailed behind them. A white late-model Range Rover waited outside. As Dr. Funk slid into the front seat, Serene turned to D and said, "Sorry about your liver."

"Oh, it's like that."

"Um, yeah," she replied. "I have mad respect for you, D. Sorry we had to squabble in there."

"Me too."

"As for your grandfather, I think you need to look more closely at his list of debtors. I was following him and Red Dawg for a couple of months, and he was definitely collecting on his debts. My impression was—and it's only a guess—that he planned to invest it in something with a future."

"That's what you think, huh? You could have told me this before."

"I'm telling you now because I like you. I wasn't sure about that until now. By the way, that Korean girl you're fucking? I'd look into her family if I were you." Then she smiled, evil and mean, and walked away. As they drove off, Dr. Funk waved at him weakly from the passenger seat.

Back inside the basement studio, D opened Dr. Funk's locker and gazed upon forty or so years of unheard music history. A stack of iPod Minis, held together by a rubber band, were buried under some TDK cassettes. There were CDs with song titles scrawled upon them. There were DAT tapes—some with labels, some with block numbers written in red magic marker. Down at the bottom D unearthed several reel-to-reel tapes that had *Power Station* and *Record Plant* scribbled on them.

Maybe seventy different containers of music stacked in no discernible order filled the locker. The fan in him was overjoyed to have all this bounty at his disposal, but his practical music-biz pro side recognized the technological challenges of trying to listen to everything on these tapes.

Then there was figuring out who owned them or who might claim to own them once they entered the world. Scratch had been just one of Dr. Funk's many collaborators. Who else had he been working with over the last decade or so? This music was a logistical and legal nightmare. But his curiosity, plus his sense of responsibility to Dr. Funk and to music culture, inspired D to hatch a plan.

CHAPTER FORTY-FOUR

INCRIMINATING CONVERSATIONS

D was listening to the playback of a new Night song, "Watercolors," when Michelle's name flashed on his phone. He stepped out of the studio and into the hallway.

"Hello?" he said.

"We need to talk. Do you have a minute?"

"Of course. Please. What's wrong?"

"A lot, D."

An hour later they sat in a back corner of Caffé Primo on Sunset in West Hollywood. D thought she looked good but stressed. She spoke with her hands clasped together. She found it hard to meet his eyes.

"My father is a gentleman," she began. "He set the foundation for all our businesses. At a certain point, my mother stepped up and expanded everything. Now my brother—my brother was supposed to take everything to the next level. He was treated like a prince by my parents. But when push came to shove he was too spoiled to do what I do or what my sister does."

"Is that why your brother runs a convenience store in the hood instead of making real estate deals? Is he being punished?"

"He's been good at it since my father retired," she said defensively. "And with the Metro expanding toward LAX, it could become very profitable. You saw the coffee shop next door? We'll be selling gourmet goods at our place real soon."

"Sounds promising."

"But my brother has issues. He's made some bad friends. There are Korean thugs too."

"How close is he to these thugs?"

"Come over to this side of the table," she whispered.

D stepped around just as she started crying. "What are you trying to tell me about your brother?" She didn't answer, just wiped her eyes. "You don't have to say anything if you don't want to."

"He just has some bad friends and I know he feels like Dad was somehow disrespected by your grandfather."

"Why are you telling me this?"

"Because I was feeling bad. I know you need closure about your grandfather. A man named Young Joon Jung became a mentor to Lawrence. He acts like a regular businessman but he runs those doumi girls."

"Have you told anyone else about any of this?" he asked. He was holding Michelle's hand but he was also trying to figure out his next move.

D had just turned onto Ventura Boulevard from Coldwater Canyon when Gonzales returned his call. D pulled over and said, "Detective, what if I told you I knew for a fact that Jung-ho and Lawrence Pak owed my grandfather money."

"You found your grandfather's records, Mr. Hunter?"

"I just got some information from Red Dawg and others in the neighborhood. I believe it to be true."

"Red Dawg is a felon. Would any of these other people testify?"

"Not sure, detective."

"Is the amount enough that someone would contemplate murder?"

"I'm told it's a serious amount of money and that the debt lingered on for years."

"Look, Mr. Hunter, we always suspected that the Paks may have had a role in this. But without real details or outside confirmation, we can't go to the DA."

"Lawrence and his father gamble. Gambling and loan sharks are like peaches and cream, right?"

"I see you've been busy, Mr. Hunter. Don't get too busy. If you have hard information, share it with me. Otherwise, I might get the impression you're withholding evidence."

After the detective hung up, D was tempted to hand over the ledger book, explain the system to the police, and let them do their job. But that wasn't sitting right with him. He'd be putting a lot of people on blast who had run into hard times but weren't criminals. Plus, with Dr. Funk off with Serene, D finally had the time to be proactive in dealing with this.

He scrolled through his phone and then texted an old Brooklyn client: *Ride, I need your help.*

While he waited for a return text, D closed his eyes but could only muster bad thoughts.

CHAPTER FORTY-FIVE

A TAKEDOWN IN CHAPMAN SQUARE

The Toe Bang Cafe in Chapman Plaza was busy. Lawrence Pak was sitting with a woman at a back table when D walked in. He saw D before D saw him and mumbled, "Oh shit," under his breath. Marie Joo, his sometime girlfriend, thought Lawrence was impressed with her lastest observation about Drake, but he was actually reacting to the sight of D in a long black leather coat. Sure, it was a chilly night in LA, but that didn't warrant looking like a character from an old blaxploitation movie. Lawrence noticed that D wore gloves. *Not good*, he thought. *Not good at all.* So he excused himself and slid toward the kitchen, looking for the back door.

Instinctively, Lawrence knew that D knew. There was just something in the way he stood in the doorway and surveyed the room. He wasn't searching for a seat. No, he was looking for Lawrence. And, Lawrence admitted to himself, he should be.

Lawrence scampered past crates of beer, boxes of produce, a cook chopping up onions, and a waitress riffling through her pocketbook toward an open metal door. His car was parked a couple of blocks away and Lawrence, who'd been on his high school track team, figured he could be there in less than a minute. He'd apologize to Marie later. Then he'd make some calls about D.

Unfortunately for Lawrence, the next move wasn't his. When he came through the metal door, a baseball bat connected with his right shoulder and he went hurtling to the ground. The assailant's bat came down again, striking Lawrence on his right hip, as well as the two middle fingers on his right hand. The bat also snapped a bone in his pinkie. When Lawrence peered up he saw D, an already imposing figure, and an even bigger man holding a baseball bat like a twig. D reached down and placed a rag over Lawrence's face.

When Lawrence awoke, he found himself tied to a chair in a dingy basement. He saw a piano and some other musical instruments. D sat before him on a leather piano bench. In the background, with the baseball bat hanging leisurely from his left hand, was the big man who'd smashed him. His fingers and shoulder hurt like hell, and the industrial-strength wire holding him to the chair was squeezing all the blood from his extremities.

"You awake, Lawrence?"

"Yes."

"Okay," D said. "I'm gonna be more honest with you than you'll probably ever be with me, but here goes: I respect your mother, I really like your sister, and I understand your father. Your family is way cool by me. That said, I will make all of them weep and hate my guts forever if fucking you up royally gets me the answers I need."

"You fucking kidnapped me," Lawrence shot back. "You are the one in trouble."

D replied, "Maybe I should let my friend back there break every damn bone in your body."

Ride moved behind D and rubbed the tip of his bat against the concrete floor. It was a grinding, threatening sound that made Lawrence change his tone. "I know what you want to know, so don't hit me with that thing again, all right?"

"Depends on what you say and how much I believe you."

"Your father's death was not really my fault."

Ride walked up to Lawrence and pushed the tip of the bat against the captive's sore shoulder. He moaned and Ride let up. Ride didn't smile like he enjoyed this, but he didn't move away either.

"I never planned for him to die," Lawrence said quickly. "That wasn't my intention."

"So tell me what you intended and why," D said. "And take your time: I want to know everything."

And so he did: upon retiring, Lawrence's father gave him the retail store to run (after he failed at real estate), and Lawrence assumed management of all the businesses' debts. His father had always suspected that Big Danny and Sun Hee were having an affair (contrary to what he said to D), and he'd purposely dragged his feet in paying back any money he borrowed from Big Danny. Lawrence continued that policy, sure that Big Danny would never touch him since he was Sun Hee's son. But Red Dawg, since he was dealing with Lawrence and not his father, felt he could rough the son up.

But Lawrence wasn't going to take it from some punk-ass black wetback. So he sent an e-mail to Big Danny stating that he'd already paid most of the debt, but that Red Dawg must have pocketed the cash. This caused enough tension between Big Danny and Red Dawg that the older man began coming in himself to collect at Pak's store. "I thought Danny deserved a little payback for what he'd done to my family," Lawrence said. "He'd caused trouble between my parents, so I caused some in his business."

"But now Big Danny's dead and you're alive—at least for now," D said.

Lawrence sighed deeply. "My father grew tired of the drama. He told me to offer $8,500 to settle the debt once and for all. I was against it, but then I saw an opportunity."

"You hired someone to steal back the money from Big Danny."

"Yeah."

"But you're telling me the guy fucked up and killed him instead?"

"He came recommended by a Korean friend I play poker with. I mean thugs aren't on LinkedIn. A Chicano guy. Some gangbanger, I guess. He waited outside the day Big Danny came by. I gave a signal—handing him the money in a newspaper—and when Big Danny drove off, he followed him. The dumb spic must have been nervous."

D nodded to Ride, who pushed the bat into Lawrence's shoulder again. "No racial slurs, Lawrence," D said.

"Okay, my nigga," Lawrence deadpanned.

Ride smashed the bat into the merchant's right leg. Lawrence screamed and twisted in his seat.

When Lawrence stopped whimpering, D said, "I need two names: the shooter, and who recommended him."

"Paco Espinoza," he spat out. "Young Joon Jung."

Daylight was streaming through from a ground-level window behind him. Morning or afternoon? Lawrence couldn't tell. He tried not to focus on how sore his body was and the lack of blood in his arms and feet. Had D recorded or videotaped him? Maybe he was being live streamed? He guessed his admission was probably worthless as evidence. After all, he had been kidnapped and hit with a baseball bat. If that wasn't duress, what was? Yet in the court of public opinion, this could be bad. D could chop it up and put it on the Internet and ruin his life. But would he embarrass his mother and Michelle like that?

When D came back down the stairs, he was carrying a plate with two hard-boiled eggs, two pieces of toast, and a bottle of water. He put the plate on top of an electric piano and then walked over to Lawrence and untied him.

"What's happening?" Lawrence asked.

"There's a quick breakfast over there," D explained. "Once you've eaten, or not, I'll drive you to your store or home or to that girl's place. Wherever you want."

Lawrence wobbled when he stood up, as the blood began returning to his arms and legs. He was dizzy and leaned uneasily against the electric piano before wolfing down the eggs and guzzling water.

"Why are you doing this?"

"Your story checked out," D said. "But, if you go to the police about our conversation, you'll be making yourself an accessory to murder."

"So that's it?"

"No, that's not it. Not by a lot. But that's all the business between us."

It was early afternoon when Lawrence found himself in front of Heaven's Gate waiting for an Uber. When he glanced down at his phone, he saw several phone calls and text messages from his sister. From the tone of the texts, Lawrence knew his life had changed forever.

CHAPTER FORTY-SIX

D HAS A BUSY DAY

While Lawrence had been tied up in Dr. Funk's old basement, D had been a very busy man. He sat in his grandfather's green convertible near a city jail, smiling at how ridiculous this all was. He felt like a character in that old movie *Shaft*. The fact that he had a man tied up in the studio of a legendary musician who had himself been voluntarily "kidnapped" took this moment from mundane to insane.

From the second level of the parking structure, he could see past DTLA toward Pasadena, Claremont, and some other towns he had never been to. Maybe when all this was over he'd just take Big Danny's car and disappear into California, stopping wherever he ran out of gas to see what life was like without family ties or business connections. Sell the Buick and wander a bit. Isn't that what the American West always promised? Well, actually, that was for white men. *Go west, young man, and wander*. But D didn't want to wander. He just wanted to stop. He was pondering this when Walli entered the car.

"Yeah," Walli said, "Red Dawg was right. His name was Paco Espinoza."

D then made a call to Atlanta.

"How are you holding up?" It was Fly Ty Williams, mentor, father figure, and retired NYPD detective.

"Everything that's happened since my grandfather's shooting has been confusing. But I'm hoping you can help me. I need to get a picture of a dead felon. He was shanked to death at a LA County jail a couple of weeks ago—Paco Espinoza. Think you can do that for me?"

"I still got my links to a few databases," Fly Ty said. "Is this pressing?"

"Very. I got a man tied up somewhere. This will help me decide what to do about him."

"Sounds like you are making some bad decisions, D."

"Help me make the right one, Fly Ty. I need to see Paco's face."

D's next call was to Detective Gonzales. "I've heard some new rumors about my grandfather's murder."

The detective sighed into the phone. "What is it, Mr. Hunter?"

"I've been told he was shot by a man named Paco Espinoza, who might be in the LA County jail system right now."

"And who told you this?"

"A friend of the family heard something. I was told Espinoza knew that my grandfather had cash on him, and that it was a botched robbery. I hope this is helpful."

After a long pause, Gonzales said, "An actual name is always helpful. So, who is this family friend?"

"Just a guy from the hood that my grandfather helped in the past. He didn't want this guy to get away with killing his friend."

"Okay," the detective said skeptically, "I will look into this. You should come in sometime soon, Mr. Hunter. It would be good if we met face to face."

Two things done, D thought, but there was much more to do, all of it more difficult than a phone call. Despite Walli's protests, D dispatched him in an Uber back to Lancaster and then went to the Beverly Hot Springs in Koreatown for a dip in the hot pool and a firm massage from a beefy middle-aged woman. Back in the locker room, he found he had a text from Fly Ty containing a mug shot of

Paco Espinoza. He then forwarded the image to the number for a burner Walli had slipped to Red Dawg. By the time he'd showered and dressed, his incarcerated acquaintance had texted back a single word: *Yes.* D then drove down Western to the offices of Pak City Real Estate.

When D walked in, Alice was at the front desk filming herself on Snapchat.

"I need to see your mother and sister," he demanded. "It's an emergency."

A few minutes later he was in Sun Hee's office. Michelle looked from Espinoza's photo to her mother, who was staring harshly at D.

"This man killed my grandfather," D said. "He was hired by Young Joon Jung to rob him for your son. But apparently Paco got shook and shot him dead."

"Who told you all this?" Sun Hee asked.

"He did," D said, showing her a photo of Lawrence locked up in Dr. Funk's basement.

Sun Hee reached for her phone.

"He won't answer."

"Oh my god!" Michelle cried out.

"He's alive," D said, "and I haven't told the cops about him. But they do know about Espinoza." Michelle and Sun Hee traded glances. "By the way, Espinoza's dead."

"So what do you want from us?" Sun Hee asked.

"I could turn Lawrence over to the cops and he would deny having anything to do with the murder. But that would make the police do some looking into Lawrence, your husband, and your family's relationship to my grandfather. Maybe they'll find nothing and say it's a dead end. But maybe they'd think the gambling and loan-sharking connection gave son and father motive. The police have always suspected that this is all connected to loan-sharking."

"So you're giving us the choice of how to deal with Lawrence," Sun Hee surmised.

"Yes," D said. "Because of Michelle."

Michelle turned to D and started to cry quietly. Her mother barked at her in Korean and Michelle barked right back. The two of them went back and forth as D waited for them to work it out.

"I thank you, D," Sun Hee eventually said. "We owe you a great debt for letting me handle my son. But as I told you before, my daughter and you have no future."

"That's *my* choice, Ma," Michelle said. "This is *my* life."

"She's right, Michelle," D cut in. "I just feel like it would be difficult. Too much family history."

"You don't love me?" Michelle asked.

"That's not the issue now," he said. "Right now I need to deal with Young Joon Jung. He can implicate your brother in this murder."

"Whatever you need to do," Sun Hee said.

"I will call you in a bit."

D didn't hug Michelle or even say goodbye to her. He just walked out of the office and into the mall, his eyes tearing up but his mind on his next move.

D would have preferred to actually go to R'Kaydia's office but he called her since time was of the essence.

"How are you, D?"

"I have a proposal. I have possession of some things you might want and you have a contact number I need."

"Go on."

"I have about thirty years of demos, masters, and unpublished songs by Dr. Funk—enough to make several hologram albums.

"Dr. Funk gave these to you?"

"Yes. I saw him a few days ago. He didn't sign any paperwork but I have a truckful of stuff that wasn't recorded under any of his previous recording agreements. You interested?"

"What do you want, D?"

"A number for Serene Powers."

"Who?"

"Serene Powers. The Amazon you had searching for Dr. Funk before me."

"You figured that out, huh? Good on your, Mr. Bodyguard. I know you don't think she's cute, so why do you want to contact her?"

"None of your business. But no contact info, no Dr. Funk music."

"I will have someone call you. That's how it works. I expect those tapes this week."

The next day D was driving south on Crenshaw when an unknown number popped up on his Samsung. An older woman's serious, dignified voice said, "Hello Mr. Hunter. Serene Powers has mentioned you. A pleasure to speak with you."

"And who am I speaking to?"

"My name isn't necessary, but your purpose is. What do you want?"

D had reached out to Fly Ty again the night before, preparing for this pitch. Now he delivered it with gusto: "Young Joon Jung is a bad man. By day he owns bars and clubs in Koreatown and Downtown LA. He also runs a prostitution ring. He employs women from Asia, Mexico, and Central America to work as nannies in LA, but then they become playthings for horny old dudes at massage parlors and brothels. I have people who can identify where he works and where he stays. The LAPD apparently can't touch him. But Serene could."

"Yes," the woman said. "I see we already have a file on him. As you know, Serene is dealing with a situation right now."

"I know. Will I see Dr. Funk again?"

"I'm sure you will, Mr. Hunter. As for Young Joon Jung—if you can be patient, Serene will handle this when she returns to LA next week."

"How can I trust you?"

"You can't. But Serene likes you. Says you take a good punch."

"I guess that's a positive sign."

"For Serene that's an extreme compliment. D, I am going to text you a number. Contact me in a couple of days and I will update you about Serene's plans. But believe me, Young Joon Jung will not be happy. Good day to you."

Leaving this in Serene's hands felt like D's only play. He'd gone pretty far out on a limb in grabbing Lawrence Pak. But targeting a major Korean mogul with only Ride as backup was way too ambitious. Serene clearly had connections and a network of some kind to play female avenger. He could wait awhile for Mr. Young Joon Jung. Besides, kicking ass with Serene Powers would be fun.

CHAPTER FORTY-SEVEN
A BRIEF MUSICAL MEETING

"**Y**ou hungry?"

"No," Night said. "The food there was pretty good." He stared out the window at a couple of Lululemon-clad women exiting a yoga class. "Ahhh, man. It's good to be alive."

"Were you worried you weren't gonna be?" D asked.

"I thought about it when I was in rehab. There's so much great shit to do. What if I don't do my share? You know, I feel like I'm just a damn footnote in this music game. What if I could have been a whole chapter, maybe a big old book?"

"Most people are footnotes."

"Back when I was hustling in New York I used to sleep with old women to pay the bills."

"I remember."

"That whole time I dreamed of being in the position I'm in now. But what do I do? I fucked it up. I fucked it up a couple of times."

"It ain't over, Night. Your man Amos tried to fire me but I work for you, not him. You just gotta focus. You gotta bring it home this time. By the way, while you were away I sequenced the LP."

"Really?" Night said, surprised. "You are taking this manager shit serious."

"Maybe too serious." They both laughed. "I wanted to see how certain things fit together. I want you to hear it. Even if you hate it, I think it might inspire you as we move forward."

"Okay, manager—or is it producer?"

"I have another surprise for you. I got stems for some unfinished Dr. Funk tracks."

"Oh shit. They at the studio?"

"Word."

"Well, word the fuck up. Studio, please."

On first listen Night didn't move. He just took it all in, letting the music wash over him. On the second and third plays he paced around the control room, his fingers stabbing at imaginary keyboards and plucking an air bass. D and engineer Allen Hughes just sat back, excited by Night's excitement. After combing through hours of Dr. Funk material, D had selected three tracks from the mid-eighties for Night to study—electroboogie productions that had both live and programmed drums. Night fixated on the first track, which had the unadventurous name of "Groove #13." After the fourth play Night sat on the sofa next to D and said, "He told me it would all work out."

"Who?"

"Dr. Funk. He came by the rehab facility."

"What?"

"Yeah. Everyone there knew him. He'd been in a few times himself. He came to the front desk and asked for me. Told me he'd left some music where I could find it."

"Meaning with me?"

"I wasn't sure, but when you said you had some of his music, I knew. He said it would get to me. He also said some extra-fly shit. He said, *I made it legendary. You make it contemporary and we'll both go to heaven hand in hand.* Ain't that some shit? That's a lyric for sure."

"Was there a woman with him?"

"Serene?"

"That's her."

"Yeah, she had a serious vibe. But really sweet too. Kinda sexy in a Serena-and-Venus way. She told me I should write about tragic love. Dr. Funk cosigned it. Something to think about . . . Maybe a concept album about doomed love. I like that."

"Did she say where they were going?"

"He just said he'd check in with me once they got off the road. I had the impression they were headed toward the Bay. Crazy, huh? You think they're fucking?"

"Nope. But then again, with Dr. Funk crazy is the norm. Okay, check out my sequencing in case you wanna fire me."

"Oh yeah, D," Night said with a smile. "You as good as gone."

CHAPTER FORTY-EIGHT
BITTER LIKE ALE

Sam, the minivan driver, sat in the parking garage at LAX waiting on a text from Mr. Chung, who was arriving on Korean Airlines from Seoul. Sam was a ruddy-faced, middle-aged man who took life as it came, which for him was mostly a dark and bitter ale. He wasn't tough enough to be a baller or big enough to be a brawler. So Sam did what he could and, when the opportunity arose, took whatever fell from the tree.

Sam glanced in the rearview mirror at "Victoria," or whatever they were calling her. He looked at her long, pale, slender legs and the short aqua dress that clung to her body, hoping this young woman wouldn't be too worn by the time she was passed down to him. She was maybe seventeen, but Sam didn't want to linger on her age. He didn't want to feel the slightest pinprick of conscience. Tonight, if she met his approval, she'd be Mr. Chung's companion.

A fit, stern-faced black woman in a dark-blue tracksuit opened the minivan's passenger-side door.

"What are you doing?" Sam shouted.

"I'm here to ask you a question," Serene Powers said. "Where will Young Joon Jung be tonight?"

"Get out of my car!" Sam yelled.

Serene replied by grabbing Sam's right hand and bending back his wrist. Sam screamed. Victoria just looked on. She'd already seen enough bad things on her journey to LA to know silence was usually a virtue.

"Again. Where will Young Joon Jung be tonight? Wilshire Acupuncture? The Sixth Street Tavern?"

Sam's body contorted in so much pain that he literally couldn't speak. Serene let go of his wrist.

"Wilshire . . . He's at Wilshire every Tuesday. Please, no more," he howled.

"Cool," Serene said. "I was just checking. If I were you, I wouldn't hang around here any longer tonight. But driving is gonna be a problem for you. Normally I'd say Uber back home, but—" she reached into Sam's blazer and took his phone, "you're gonna have to cab it. Tell your next employer to get you a new one."

The driver's door then opened and Ride reached in with his huge hands and plucked Sam out from his seat and tossed him to the ground. Upon seeing Ride, Victoria looked like she wanted to scream, but she thought better of it when the side door opened and another large man wearing all black entered and sat down next to her.

"Hello, my name is D Hunter," he said. "We won't hurt you. What's your name?"

"Victoria," she said.

Serene cut in and asked the same question in Korean.

Victoria told her that she was actually Mina Bo-Young.

"Okay," Serene continued in Korean, "we are going to help you and the other girls get home. But you have to help us."

Serene, who'd had considerable practice dealing with scared teenagers, laid out her plan as Ride guided them away from LAX en route to Koreatown. Men were busy exploiting woman all over the world, Serene thought as she spied two men hassling a young woman in front of an airport hotel. She couldn't save everybody. She could whip men's asses twenty-four hours a day and not make a dent in their bullshit.

So she focused on high-value targets like Young, the king pimp of K-Town.

"Young likes to personally break in new girls," she explained to D and Ride, "and we know two other women just came in from Thailand. I just wanted to make sure we were going to the right spot."

"Are you gonna kill this guy, D?" Ride asked.

"If I have to."

"No you won't," Serene corrected him. "I need him alive to gather information on his business. I'll turn him into the police when I'm ready. Are we clear on this?"

"Yes," D said.

"You one bad bitch, huh?" It was Ride.

"Yes I am, but you already know. Don't doubt me."

"I never met a woman like you," Ride said, sounding lovestruck.

"No one has," D seconded.

Serene was not flattered. "Gents, your presence is useful, but I will do what I have to do. You feel me?"

She turned on SiriusXM Radio and found an oldies R&B station. While they rolled across Los Angeles toward Koreatown they grooved to One Way's "Cutie Pie," the Bar-Kays' "Holy Ghost," Lakeside's "Fantastic Voyage," and other vintage recordings. Mina thought her three black rescuers were so alien they might as well be from Mars, though the way they sang along to the songs made them seem a bit less scary.

War's "Slippin' into Darkness" was playing as they parked down the block from Wilshire Acupuncture. Ride pulled Big Danny's shotgun from beside his seat. D had the family Beretta in his waistband. Serene tucked a Glock into her pants. "I normally work alone," she said. "I brought you two along because of what happened to D's grandfather, but know that I'm in charge. Follow my plan. Follow my lead. Everyone in this minivan clear?"

Both men said yes and then exited the car, heading in different directions. Serene reached out and took Mina's hand. "You just need to be brave for a little while tonight and you'll be free of all these nasty men. Okay?"

Serene told Mina to press the bell by the front door, then walked up behind her and did the same. She glanced up at the security camera and smiled, hoping she looked like a potential customer coming to loosen some kinks. The door buzzed open and a matronly looking Korean woman in hospital whites waved them both in.

"I'm here for an acupuncture treatment," Serene said. "I have a sore shoulder." As the Korean woman sized her up, Mina disappeared through a beaded doorway.

"Victoria," the woman called over her shoulder, "where is Mr. Chung?" When Mina didn't answer the woman followed her through the beaded doorway, giving Serene the opportunity to open the door again and let Ride in. Hearing the door slam, the Korean woman rushed back over to the small desk, but Serene got there first. She grabbed the woman's left arm and pulled it roughly. This woman was no punk; she was ready to tussle but Serene made that moot with a short, quick left hand. The woman was down and out.

"Damn!" Ride said.

Mina emerged from the back with a set of keys, which she handed to Serene. "This way," she said, then led them through the beaded doorway and down a hallway of closed doors. Mina nodded at the last door on the left. Serene reared back and kicked it in. Young Joon Jung, his gut protruding and his burgundy bathrobe open, was checking messages on his cell phone as a young Asian woman sucked his dick and another young woman looked on.

Young had a very bad next minute. Startled, the young woman bit down on his dick. Ride then walked over and punched him in the chest before Serene slipped a hood over his head. As they dragged Young into the hallway, a white man in shorts walked out of an adjoining room with needles protruding from both shoulders and his back—evidently he didn't know about the clinic's side business. "What's going on?" he asked, but no one answered.

Mina had rounded up three girls from the various rooms—Korean, Thai, and Vietnamese, all under twenty—who were talking nervously in broken English. When two new Thai girls emerged from the room, Mina came over and tried to calm them down. The idea of freedom had changed her from a suspicious, quiet girl into a leader.

Serene heard a grunt behind her. She turned to see D knocking a burly but out-of-shape security guard to the ground with a fist upside his head.

"We have Young," she said to D, who walked over to the hooded man and smacked him in the center of his face, breaking his nose and loosening his top front teeth.

"Is the back room ready?" Serene asked.

"Follow me," D said, grabbing Young by his bathrobe and pulling him through a door at the end of the hall. Inside that room were security monitors, computers, and S&M paraphernalia—most of it smashed to bits. He picked up a backpack from the floor. "I got the drives."

Serene pulled out her phone and sent a text. Ride, Mina, and the five girls now gathered together in a corner of the room. Serene glanced at her watch and replied, "Let's move everyone into the alley." The scared girls, the hooded Young, and the three rescuers walked through the back door that D had broken and stepped into the alley. The girls were growing hysterical. Who were all these black people?

A dark van came flying down the alley. A white woman—late thirties, with a military bearing—hopped out, nodded at Serene, and opened the van's back door. Serene and Ride ushered them into the vehicle. D stood with one arm around Young's neck. This was one of the three men who helped kill his grandfather, but the only one he'd had the opportunity to truly hurt.

"Give him to me," Serene demanded.

"Why? So he can pay someone off and go free?"

"I am set up to handle this, D. You'll never get him on that murder charge. With the drives and the girls I can get him punished for human trafficking. Seriously punished. All you are about to do is get yourself a manslaughter beef."

The white woman came up behind Serene, whispered in her ear, and waited to see D's play. She smiled at Ride with all the warmth of an ice cream truck freezer.

"You taking him to the same place you took Dr. Funk?" D asked with a heavy dose of sarcasm.

"No. Not anywhere close. Dr. Funk will be back in Los Angeles very soon. I'm sure he'll fill you in then. But this man here—before he sees the inside of a police station he'll see the dark side of hell. That I promise."

Reluctantly, D handed Young over and then watched as the white woman strapped him into the passenger seat of the van.

"You'll hear from me, D," Serene said.

"Will I?"

"Yes. You have heart. I don't know many men who do." She leaned over and hugged him.

Ride said, "What about me?"

"You want a hug?" she asked.

"Hell yeah."

Serene walked over and kicked him in the thigh, sending the big man to the ground. "Ride," she said, "don't you ever put your hands on a woman again."

"Fuck you," Ride said.

She said nothing and jumped into the back of the van, which then disappeared down the alley.

Ride struggled to get to his feet, bracing himself against D. "Let's get the fuck outta here before those fools back there wake up."

"Yup," D said, guiding the big man away from the back door and toward a much-needed meal.

"How about treating me to dinner? You know any good Korean barbecue places?"

"Shut up," D said. "We're having Mexican."

CHAPTER FORTY-NINE

HOPING FOR JUSTICE

"So," Detective Gonzales said, sitting in a DTLA Starbucks, his cappuccino steaming before him like a gift waiting to be opened. "I looked into the Espinoza situation and, yes, he was stabbed to death in a nearby correctional facility, assailants unknown."

"Was he a professional hit man?"

"He had multiple assault charges. A conviction for battery. In fact, he was awaiting sentencing for a fight at a K-Town massage parlor and was found with $2,000 cash in his possession. It doesn't sound like he was a real shooter—just a thief who ran afoul of the wrong people."

"Any theories why he was killed?"

"Espinoza had some affiliation with Calle 18. It's possible they heard about his windfall and someone demanded tribute. He was living in Pico-Union, which was their turf." The detective took a sip of his coffee, giving D a chance to mull over this inconclusive information.

"So is my grandfather's case now cold?"

"If you can't produce his records and your friend Red Dawg isn't helpful, then it's hard to know how to proceed. This Espinoza guy is interesting but dead. We never found a gun that matched the murder weapon. It's hard to connect the dots now. If Espinoza was hired to rob or kill your grandfather, then that business angle is our best bet for finding suspects."

D sat back in his chair, having decided that he wouldn't hand over his grandfather's records since he was confident they'd found the perpetrator in Young Joon Jung. Moreover, his tangled connections with the Pak family would make any further investigation by LAPD deeply embarrassing. What would Aunt Sheryl think of all this? It was a secret that needed to be kept from his family, as well as Detective Gonzales.

"Okay, detective," he said, "I will speak with my family. If my grandfather's list turns up, I will get it to you immediately."

"Sorry about how things have worked out so far. But know that I'm keeping the case open for now. Don't worry."

D walked out of the Starbucks and onto the street, wishing he could have had more confidence in the justice system. But there was nothing in recent American history that guaranteed justice for his grandfather, an old black man who had lived on both sides of the law. So he'd gotten the best justice he could. He hoped it was good enough.

As he went to pick up the Electra 225 from a municipal parking garage, D checked his smartphone. There was a text message from a number he didn't recognize, containing a link to an English translation of an article from the *Korea Times*. The headline read, "K-Town Businessman Indicted for Human Trafficking."

He scrolled through the story:

Prominent Koreatown businessman Young Joon Jung was arrested for human trafficking by officers from Immigration and Customs Enforcement. In total, twenty-seven people were arrested at approximately fifty brothels in Operation Gilded Cage. One hundred and fifty illegal aliens have been detained and are being interviewed to ascertain whether they are victims of human trafficking. Young Joon Jung, who owns a variety of businesses in Los Angeles, is a member of the Koreatown Chamber of Commerce and has been a fixture in the neighborhood for two decades.

D texted back, *Thank you, Serene,* and went to find his big green ride.

CHAPTER FIFTY

FLOATING THE FUNK IN CUPERTINO

Dr. Funk floated down onto the outdoor stage with a bit of digital flutter. But, by the time his platform-shoed feet landed atop the piano Night was playing, the hologram was as solid as technology would allow. In fact, his purple-and-red jumpsuit was so vivid that Night, his band, and the whole backyard seemed to fall under its shadow.

D and Al stood stage right, hoping Night would remember all the cues. At rehearsal earlier that afternoon, the floating Dr. Funk had spooked him, causing Night to come in late on the song and step on the vocals of his digitized duet partner.

But on this bright Northern California afternoon, before a crowd of Silicon Valley bigwigs, most of whom knew Dr. Funk's music primarily via hip hop samples, Night was in a groove. *Get in where you fit in*, D thought as he gazed at the young white and Asian folks gyrating in an amalgamation of several eras of hip hop dance by their picnic tables.

Dancing down near the front of the stage was R'Kaydia and her Facebook fanboy. She was dropping it like it was hot for the social media geek, and he was ecstatic at her pulsating pulchritude.

"So," Al said, "this all worked out?"

"Yeah. It could be better, though," D replied.

"Speak."

D turned away from the stage and said, "We should get a bigger

piece of this hologram deal. I mean, without us they'd have the technology but wouldn't have a clue how to stage it. Feel me?"

"But we are getting a piece through Amos," Al said.

"What if we said, *Fuck Amos Pilgrim,* and did a deal direct with
R'Kaydia and Facebook? Or just went right to the Facebook guy ourselves?"

Al thought it over. "We'd have to have our own company, and you'd
have to commit to being a full-time manager."

"And you'd have to stop talking about retiring."

As Dr. Funk floated back into the sky and Night waved goodbye
to the hologram to Silicon Valley cheers, D and Al smiled and shook
hands.

"When do we make our move?" Al wondered.

"Very, very soon," D said smoothly.

CHAPTER FIFTY-ONE

AUNT SHERYL SHAKES HER HEAD

Walli was tending to hamburgers on the grill. He had on a brand-new blue-and-gold Los Angeles Rams #29 Eric Dickerson jersey that D had purchased for him, and wore Bose headphones attached to the iPhone dangling out of his back pocket. As he flipped burgers, Walli rhymed along to Kendrick Lamar's "King Kunta." He was reciting the words but he was thinking of Angelique, a cute brown-skinned girl with Nicki Minaj curves and straight A's in English he'd met in Lancaster. They were conversing on Snapchat and, happily, he didn't have to hide her presence in his life.

So he wasn't paying attention as D explained the fate of Big Danny's killers to Aunt Sheryl. She nodded when D said the triggerman Espinoza was dead, apparently at Red Dawg's instigation (if not his hands). Young Joon Jung, who had recommended him, was in federal custody and facing thirty years in prison and liquidation of all his assets. But Lawrence Pak was somewhere in South Korea, not in police custody, not facing any obvious penalties, and very much alive.

"So," Aunt Sheryl said, "because you fucked this Korean chick and you like her mama, you gave this man who arranged for your grandfather's death a pass? Is that what I'm hearing?"

"Hear me out, okay? I believe that Granddaddy and that woman had a serious relationship. Whether or not they were lovers, I know they were close—close enough that her husband and son resented him even as they took his money. As I've learned, Granddaddy had a lot of different relationships and they had all kinds of levels—some of them helpful to people and some of them destructive. Lawrence never intended for this to happen. What he did was vindictive. It was spiteful. But I don't believe it was murder. The fact is, he doesn't speak Korean well. He's never spent any time there. It's like he's in exile. Plus, do you have any confidence, given the facts and evidence we have, that the criminal justice system would do anything to him at this point?"

"So you're the judge and jury, huh?"

"This was the best result I could manage. I'm a damn bodyguard. Maybe I'm a manager. For whatever reason I end up in these weird investigations. I'm just making it up as I go along. I don't know what justice really is in America. I'm just trying to do what I can, how I can."

"You could give the police the ledger." Sheryl lit up a Newport and waited for D's response.

"I burned it," he said after a pause. "It's the record of a lot of deeds, a few of them dirty. Let the past stay in the past."

"I don't feel good about this, D." She shook her head and glanced over at Walli, who was still rhyming and flipping the burgers. "I think you should go."

"What?"

"You should go." Her anger was rising. "I can't eat with you right now. I need some time, D. Please leave."

On his way out, D placed an envelope in his aunt's lap. It was her share of the money released by Big Danny's executor for aiding Dr. Funk. They were supposed to be celebrating that money, most of which was being set aside for Walli's college. But Aunt Sheryl didn't want to share any food with her nephew on this hot Lancaster afternoon.

Walli noticed D heading inside. "D," he called out, "they're almost done."

"He has to go," his mother responded. "Some music business stuff back in LA. But bring me my burger. I'm hungry."

CHAPTER FIFTY-TWO

SUNDAY AFTERNOON
AT THE ACE HOTEL

On Sunday afternoons, the Ace Hotel's rooftop bar was usually the home base for young white folks sporting hipster beards or print dresses and gold Birkenstocks. And that demo was still in attendance, but there were also middle-aged Chicano men in Locs, with carefully manicured mustaches and black straw stingy brims, their women with severe black eyeliner, beehive hairdos, and generous waistlines. Couples danced to DJ Ruben's mix of R&B 45s from the 1960s, an intoxicating blend that had Al Brown impressed.

"Shit," he said while downing his second margarita, "that guy is spinning stuff I've never even heard. I know most of these artists but not all these records. That last track was 'Hello Stranger' by Barbara Lewis. I met this nurse at a bar on 1-2-5 Street one night. Name of Louise. That was our song."

"Listen to this man," Night agreed. "He's flashing way back. We better get some Viagra, cause he's about to jump on one of these chicas right now."

"Why not?" Al said

"Oh shit, D," Night said. "This music is getting Al open."

"Hey," D said, "it's a lovely day. The music is good. The drinks are good. And the food is gonna be good too. After we leave here, let's hit this dumpling spot I heard about in Glendale called Din Tai Fung."

"So," Night said, "sounds like you're getting used to being in LA, Mr. Brooklyn?"

"You gotta find your spots out here," D replied. "They don't come to you. I actually wouldn't know about this scene without Red Dawg. Let's toast him." They all raised their glasses and clinked. "He gets out in a couple of weeks. Be good to see him."

"That's surprising," Al said.

"We all do what we know how to do," D said.

Night checked his phone and his eyes went wide.

"She must be hot," Al teased. "D, he just met this singer from New York named Eva. Great voice. Great body."

This was news to D. That girl got around. At some point he'd pull Night's coat about her.

"It isn't about her," Night said. "We need to pay the check and go downstairs."

"What's up?" D asked.

"A surprise."

Night and Al went down first as D handled the check and then gave DJ Ruben a hug. When he got outside he didn't see his friends, but there was an ugly old SUV double-parked out front. The passenger-side door opened and Dr. Funk stuck his head out. "You coming with us? Your friends are in the back." D hopped inside and the vehicle pulled away.

"How are you?"

"It's been a hell of a couple of months, young man," Dr. Funk said. "That Serene took me up to the Bay. She put me in front of Kelly Lee's mother. It was rough—a lot of crying and a lot of honesty. She had painful memories and I did too. It was stuff I hadn't expressed to any-one, including myself. A lot went on between us. I don't even have the words. I have been calling people who I hurt, people I damaged when I was living like I was the only person who mattered."

"Did Serene make you do all this?"

"When that Serene strongly suggests something, it's wise to pay attention . . . So where were you guys heading?"

"Out to a restaurant in Glendale."

"Let's go. We got a lot to catch up about."

CHAPTER FIFTY-THREE

LAST DANCE IN K-TOWN

Former A Tribe Called Quest member Ali Shaheed Muhammad was mixing P-Funk's "(Not Just) Knee Deep" into the Dr. Funk track "Hard and Fast" in the DJ booth in the Line Hotel's vast lobby. He glanced down at D and smiled. He didn't usually play requests, but made an exception for his old New York homey. Ali played there Thursday nights, drawing the kind of rainbow crowd that made club-crawling around Koreatown fun. D had just eaten alone at the Pot and now, with a ginger ale in hand, stood by the DJ booth like he used to when he did club security.

But his life was different now. He was managing Night full-time and had become the go-to person for folks looking to license, sample, or purchase anything to do with Dr. Funk. He was even in the market for a place in LA, cause he figured he'd be out here a lot.

D was standing there with his eyes closed, just vibing to the music, when someone touched his arm.

"Perfect timing," he said. "I need a place on the LA side of the hill."

Michelle shook her head and smiled. "You'll need a new broker, D."

"Why? You've done a good job for my family."

"I guess. But in retrospect, I owed your family," she said softly.

"No you didn't, Michelle. What happened wasn't your fault and had nothing to do with you."

"If I hadn't met you, it would have all been different. But now—"

She stopped herself, then took a deep breath. "You know my brother is gone."

He knew but decided to act innocent. "I saw the store was closed up."

"We're gonna lease it to a Honduran family. Lawrence ended up in Korea. My mother told him not to come back. She's brokenhearted about everything."

"No happy endings for anyone, I guess."

They both fell silent for a minute. Finally, she said, "I'm here with someone."

"You and the Chaos, plus-one, huh?"

"Something like that. Look, I'll e-mail you some real estate recommendations. But that's all." Michelle reached up, pulled D close, and kissed him deeply. "Okay," she said when she let him go, then disappeared into the crowd.

D walked out to the patio bordering Wilshire Boulevard. A chef was grilling pieces of chicken and pork and bouncing to Ali Shaheed's selections. To his right, a Mexican kid with spiky hair and wearing a J Dilla as Schroeder T-shirt was kicking game to a black girl with a blond Mohawk in a purple-and-white blouse. D's head turned when he heard the honking of car horns.

Out in the middle of Wilshire was a shirtless, fit, gray-bearded but bald middle-aged black man in ill-fitting jeans and messed-up Nikes, who was challenging cars to run him over. He was defiant in his craziness, tossing insults and middle fingers at automobiles that, with one angry pedal press, could kill him dead.

His exact age was hard to determine. Black might not crack, but it can definitely break. It was only a matter of time before someone called the LAPD, leaving this poor black man's uncertain fate in even greater peril.

The homeless man turned toward D and their eyes locked. Though dirty and dizzy, he looked familiar. This was a face from the past, a face buried beneath memories and tears, hugs and fears. It was the face of all his dead brothers and his absent father and his slain grandfather and all the dead black men of this decade and this century, and all who had fallen for centuries before.

Was the man beyond help? Would walking out into Wilshire Boulevard and snatching this man bring him back to the world, or would D just be opening the door to another unsolvable tragedy? D stepped off the patio, considered the passing cars, and then headed out into Wilshire Boulevard toward a present intimately haunted by the past.